THE GIRLS IN PINE BROOKE

A.J. RIVERS

The Girls in Pine Brooke
Copyright © 2024 by A.J. Rivers

All rights reserved. Without limiting the rights under copyright reserved above, no part of this publication may be reproduced, stored in or introduced into retrieval system, or transmitted, in any form, or by any means (electronic, mechanical, photocopying, recording, or otherwise) without the prior written permission of both the copyright owner and the above publisher of this book.

This is a work of fiction. Names, characters, places, brands, media, and incidents are either the products of the author's imagination or are used fictitiously. The author acknowledges the trademarked status and trademark owners of various products referenced in this work of fiction, which have been used without permission. The publication/use of these trademarks is not authorized, associated with, or sponsored by the trademark owners.

PROLOGUE

THE GIRL'S HEART STUTTERED IN HER CHEST BEFORE RESUMING ITS fast pace. A staccato beat thundered against her ribcage. She gasped for air as her eyes adjusted to the new darkness. The moon slid behind a clump of clouds. She didn't know where she was without light. Or with. The wooded area had a familiar feel to it; like if she had run away during the day, she might have been able to find something she recognized. But in the dark, everything was different, scary, and unknown. She leaned against a tree to catch her breath.

A burning sensation radiated up her throat with every breath.

"Now, why would you make this any harder than it needs to be?"

A shudder rippled through her. She started moving. The man's voice rubbed against her skin like sandpaper. It was closer than it should have been. She felt like she had been running for hours, going in circles. All the trees looked the same in the darkness, but she kept moving. She had to. At this point, she couldn't go back. She didn't know what was going to happen, but she knew it wasn't good.

The man had taken her days ago. Maybe weeks. Time slipped by so quickly. It slipped through her fingers like water; she could never hold on to it, never keep track of it. The days blended together so seamlessly that she couldn't tell where one ended and the other began.

"Come on now," his voice was closer now. The girl moved through the trees, searching for any ounce of light that she could find. Or an opening. "I'm going to find you eventually. There's no point in trying to get away."

Her foot snagged on a fallen branch, and she stumbled, a yelp escaping from her mouth while she tried to fix her footing. Her hand clamped over her mouth.

A soft chuckle came from behind her. She ran, stumbling over branches and rocks. She had to get away.

"I just have to make one more stop, and I'll take you home," the man had said when he shoved her into the passenger side of his car. He had said he was taking her home, and she had wanted to believe him. She wanted to go home to her mother and father. She pictured their faces as the car bumped along on the road. She pictured how happy they would be that she had finally come back home.

But something soured in her stomach. No matter how she tried to relax or how she tried to hope—to believe—that she was going home, her body wouldn't let her. Her shoulders stayed tense. Her muscles stayed alert. Her mind calculating. There was something not right about her ride home. Just like deep down she knew there was something not right about him, when he offered to take her home. She knew him. Or rather, she knew of him. He was a lovely man. Everyone said so. He had seemed so kind when he stopped her from walking. So genuinely concerned about her safety.

"I wouldn't want a daughter of mine walking home so late at night. There are too many creeps out there today. It's not like when I was a kid. Back then, we knew who the creeps were and how to avoid them. But now... it could be anyone."

How could she have known he was talking about himself? But something in her knew. Her bones screamed *run*. Her hand had found the lock, and she was ready to open the door, but she couldn't. She couldn't do it. Though her body told her one thing, her mind told her another. *Stop being paranoid. He's just a nice man. Don't be rude.* He had kindly offered to drive her home even though she lived one town over. It would be rude to think he was out to hurt her.

She should have listened, though. She should have listened to her body, opened the door, jumped out of the moving car, and ran for her life. But she hadn't. When he then shoved her into the trunk and told her he was taking her home, her body spoke up again. Her body told her to run—try to escape. And that time, she listened. As soon as he popped the trunk, she took the flashlight in her hand and swung it. He yelped and stumbled back. Taking the opening, she crawled out of the car and ran.

She knew he wasn't taking her home. The wooded area she was now stumbling through was nowhere near her house. Nowhere near her parents. He had lied. He was probably bringing her out to kill her. If he were, he'd have to work for it. She stumbled on another rock and lost her footing. Her knees crashed to the ground, and she winced. Pain radiated up her leg into her hip. She bit back a scream as she used a tree trunk to leverage herself back onto her feet. She ran past trees; branches clipped her arms and her neck. She kept moving.

"Now, girl, you know you're going to get lost out here in the dark like this. Come back to the car so I can take you home."

A shiver tore through her. She kept running, wincing every time she stepped down on her ankle. The pain just on the edge of being unbearable. She couldn't pay attention to it. She had to keep running. She needed to find an opening. A space in the woods where the trees opened up.

Her shoulder slammed into another tree, but she didn't let it stop her.

"Come on. I can't leave you out here all night. You know your parents must be worried about you. Let me take you home."

How was that possible? His voice seemed closer than it had before—too close. Either she was getting closer to him by going in circles, or even in the darkness, he could still find her. She moved faster and ran harder. She felt it before she saw it.

The large rock underneath her feet, her body leaning into a fall, too quick to stop, yet it still felt like it happened in slow motion—a fall taking hours instead of seconds. It wasn't until she fell that she finally realized where she was—the woods she used to camp in when she was younger with her uncle and cousins. It looked so different then, in the daylight.

The first rock she fell against dug into her back. A scream bubbled up her throat. She couldn't stop it from coming out of her mouth. He was going to hear it and know where she was. But she couldn't stop it.

The second rock, followed by the third, which was more of a boulder jutting out from the hill, slammed into her neck.

It was the last thing she heard.

CHAPTER ONE

Riley Quinn

"It's not even that serious." I lifted my hand to examine the damage. It was a little bruised already, my lightly tanned skin darkening along the edges of my fingers and along my wrist. But it wasn't broken. I wiggled my fingers in my partner Zelina's face. She rolled her eyes.

"It needs to be checked. You could have sprained a ligament or something."

It was my turn to roll my eyes. It was fine. I was fine. I stared at the back seat while she drove. A tall man with hazel eyes and too many tattoos sat slumped, his hands cuffed behind his back. He held my gaze for a long moment before looking away.

Oscar Scott was a low-level drug dealer, mostly dealing in weed and crack.

"You okay back there?"

His lips curled into a small smile. "How's the hand?"

I should hit him, wipe the grin off his stupid face. I didn't have cause for it any longer, but I still wanted to. The arrest should have gone smoothly—it was routine, after all. But Oscar decided he wanted to fight back.

I went to cuff him, and he grabbed my wrist and twisted my arm, dragging me to the ground before I could catch my breath.

When I looked up, Oscar was bent over me with Zelina at his back, gun pressed to the back of his head. His finger twitched around my wrist.

"You move, I pull the trigger," said Zelina, a smile on the edge of her lips. He was more amenable to being arrested after that. He was a wiry twenty-something who had been in and out of jail since his early teens. He was stronger than he looked.

I shook my head as the scene flashed in my mind. I could have kicked myself for being taken down by someone like him. I knew better. I was just glad that no one was around to see it. I'd never hear the end of it from the other guys at the station. Bad enough, I'd have to hear it from Zelina from now on.

We drove him to the precinct and got him checked. Zelina took the drugs we found on him and logged them into evidence. I walked over to my desk. Pain, pulsing and hot, reverberated up my forearm. Every time I moved, the pain curled into my bones. My fingers grew weak. I sat at my desk and held my wrist in my other hand.

The pain wasn't so bad if I just kept it still. If I didn't move, everything was fine.

"Go to the clinic, Detective Quinn." Zelina's voice was stern and loud.

"It's fine, Detective Carter," I fired back. But I winced as I dropped my hand in my lap.

"If you don't go right now, I'm calling your mother."

I bristled at the comment. I was an adult! How dare she threaten me with my mother. I stood up and grabbed my keys out of my desk drawer with my left hand. Not because I was afraid of my mother, though. I just didn't want her to worry. And she would worry. She was always fussing and worrying over me and my job. She knew I could take care of myself, but she was my *mother*.

"No matter how old you get, you never stop being her baby," said my aunt after my mother had intruded on my life for the millionth time. "You might as well get used to it."

I was still trying to get used to it. I had been back in Pine Brooke for a few years now. I moved back home from Los Angeles to get away from the city. The bright lights and loud noises. The people—too many people. It seemed like the place to be when I was younger. When I was in my teens, I dreamed of nothing else… getting out of Pine Brooke and making my mark on the world. But the world had made its mark on me. A gaping, festering wound that refused to heal and reopened every year as a reminder. In LA, I had my own life away from the prying eyes of my family and, more importantly, my mother. But I was back in Pine Brooke, and she was there. They were all there, and nothing traveled faster than gossip in a small town.

"I'm going. I'm going." The clinic was close enough to the station that I could walk. The sun had set an hour ago, and the sky was no longer bright blue but light purple. I walked down one street, crossed to the next, and rounded the corner. The clinic was a large white building on the next corner. Memories flashed by of having gone to this same clinic ever since I was a child.

After Doctor Malcolm had his stroke, he brought in another doctor to take his place. He could still get around and was as sharp as a tack, but felt like he couldn't—or rather shouldn't—continue practicing medicine.

"I can't believe you're just going to walk away," had said my mother, April Quinn. She was the kind of woman who liked everything to stay the same. She hated change, and his leaving was a sign of change. He wasn't leaving town, but he would no longer be her doctor, and that didn't sit right with her. The town threw a party for the doctor when he announced his retirement. Some folks were happy for him, while others spent the night trying to talk him into staying on at the clinic. It didn't work.

"I understand how you all feel; believe me, I do." He stroked his thick black beard peppered with gray. Doctor Malcolm was a handsome older man with deep cinnamon-colored skin and honey-colored eyes. He was the most personable doctor I had ever met, and I was sad to see him go, but I, unlike some others, respected his choice. "And I appreciate the love and the concern for my health. I really do. And while I do hate to retire, I feel like it is a must. People who have had strokes often have another, or something else could go wrong, and I… I just don't want to take that chance. I don't want my health to impair my judgment in a way that might hurt one of you. I wouldn't be able to live with myself. That being said, I have enlisted another doctor who will be here soon to take over the clinic."

That was a few months ago. Doctor Elwood came into town quietly and efficiently. I hadn't heard a peep out of him since. No one had, really, unless they had cause to go to the clinic. He might have been a good doctor, but he wasn't as friendly as Doctor Malcolm.

I opened the door and stepped into the cool lobby of the clinic. Our clinic was an old two-story home that had been converted sometime in the late 1800s. The family had moved or died and the town needed a hospital, so the house was commandeered. It was never reverted back.

The lobby or foyer had gotten a facelift since I was a child. It was no longer cocooned in dark woods and all different types of browns. The flooring had been changed to light gray wood, and the walls had been lightened. It was bright and airy and much better than before.

"Can I help you?" asked a rough voice to my left.

I blinked. "Um… yeah. Can you take a look at my wrist? I think it was sprained."

"Sure, come on back." His tone was flat, and there was no trace of concern or empathy.

I followed him through the doorway and down a hall to an exam room. The clinic was large enough for more than one doctor to see patients but there had ever only been one at a time. The town was relatively small, so we didn't need more than one doctor. Would have been nice though to have more variety.

I leaned against the exam table still holding my arm. Doctor Elwood walked over to a large cabinet and started grabbing things from it. He returned to the exam table and set them down. Then he took my hand in his. His hands were soft and silky.

He wasn't a bad-looking man. Actually, I could understand why so many of the women in town had feigned so many injuries the past few months. His eyes were the brightest green, like emeralds glinting in the light. You could tell he took care of himself. He might not have been hitting the gym every morning, but he was fit with broad shoulders, and a muscular upper body that I could see through his pale blue shirt.

His chiseled features were something to marvel at. I cast my eyes to my hand before he caught me staring at him. The doctor stayed silent while he moved my hand. I winced with every movement.

I inhaled sharply, and only then did he look me in the eyes.

"How did you do this to yourself?" His tone flat, like he didn't really care.

"Arresting a drug dealer. He was stronger than he looked."

"People often are." He sighed as he took some bandages and started wrapping my wrist. "It's just a sprain. Nothing is broken but you should take it easy for a couple of days. Ice it when you get home and if the pain gets to be too much take some Tylenol." He finished wrapping my hand. "Are you right-handed?"

"Yup."

"That's going to suck," he said as he let go of my hand and started gathering his supplies to put back in the cabinet.

"Anyone ever tell you, you have a lovely bedside manner? I imagine it doesn't come up a lot."

He closed the cabinet and leaned against it, arms folded across his chest. "You know what, I've actually been told I was perfectly pleasant."

"By anyone other than your mother?"

A smile pulled at the corner of his mouth. "A lot of my patients."

"Their bar must be pretty low. If you can't be nice to your patients or put some concern in your tone maybe you ought to find another profession." I headed toward the door.

"Maybe you should find another doctor… if only there was another clinic around here… hmm."

I opened the door and walked out of the room. He was more of an asshole than I thought he'd be. He was no Doctor Malcolm. His bedside manner, or rather lack thereof, left a lot to be desired. I wouldn't go back unless I had to. I hoped I never did.

By the time I got back to the station, my blood was hot for no reason. It was a short exchange that meant nothing. But it made me wonder how he treated the other patients, or if it was just me. I hadn't heard anyone complaining about him.

"It's just a sprain," I announced, holding up my hand.

Zelina wiggled her eyebrows. "You see the hot doctor?"

"He's not very personable." I sat down at my desk, ready to finish my paperwork.

She shrugged. "Well, you know he's a widower, right?"

I blinked. "Oh."

"Yeah, his wife died in some horrible accident a few years ago. That's what I hear anyway. He moved here to start fresh. It's really sad."

"Well, now I feel bad," I said.

"You should. Everyone else says he's pretty pleasant."

"Yeah, well, I'm not everyone else."

Zelina chuckled, and I rolled my eyes. She had done most of the paperwork. I added a few details and then filed it away. I was going to stop by the coffee shop on my way home, but I didn't feel like it. I glanced at the clock on my dashboard. My mother was probably still there. She owned the coffee shop. My little sister worked there while she was home during the summer, and my father, who was the head baker, did too. They were all probably still there, shutting down the kitchen. I drove by on my way and saw their cars, but I didn't stop. I wasn't in the mood to talk or to be questioned. I knew my mother was going to question why my arm was wrapped up, but I didn't feel like answering any questions.

Ever Lake was on the far side of town from the shore, but it was a few feet away from my front porch. I picked living here because it was far away enough from the center of town while still being part of the town. It was quiet and peaceful. It was a great place to come home to after a long day of work, even if I came home to an empty house. It was still nice.

It was an old cabin by the lake that had been renovated twice before I moved in and once after. It was in pretty good shape, but I still needed to change a few things. I modernized it a bit. I changed the floors from the ghastly orange and pink tiles to a nice dark wood. I modernized the kitchen a bit and put a tub in the main bedroom ensuite.

I opened the door and sighed. My shoulders instantly dropped as I closed the door behind me and locked it. Something about walking through the door always relaxed me.

"Hi, Luna!" My black labrador jumped on me as soon as I walked in. It could have been because she was happy to see me, but it could also have meant she was hungry or wanted to go outside. I scratched behind her ear and she wagged her tail. "Let's get you outside, and I'll fix you something to eat."

I unlocked the door and opened it, and stepped aside so she could walk out. Luna barreled out the door in a full run. She ran toward the lake, stopped, and then ran back. Seeing a bird, she followed it, and I watched her from the doorway for a long moment before heading into the kitchen to wash my hands.

I have always refused to buy dog food. Luna was a gift from a friend a few years ago during a time when I really needed her. She was the cutest puppy. So full of life and curious about the world around her. Having her forced me to go outside, and go for walks. To focus on something other than my own grief and sadness.

I wanted to take care of her, spoil her. But dog food was expensive, so I just started making it myself. I took a container out of the fridge and grabbed a spoon. I scooped her food into her dish—ground turkey and chicken, brown rice, peas, and carrots—and refilled her water bowl. There was no need to call her in. She'd come back when she was ready to eat.

Before I could turn the light off in the kitchen, Luna stuck her nose through the doorway. She eyed her dish and slowly padded over. I closed the door behind her. While she ate, I jumped in the shower and put on my pajamas.

I spent the rest of the night with Luna. I made myself a turkey sandwich with salt and vinegar chips and a glass of red wine and watched TV until my eyes were heavy. Luna crawled in bed next to me as usual, and we both fell asleep.

CHAPTER TWO

Logan Elwood

"So let me make sure I got this right." I slid the stool back, so I was still in front of the exam table but far away enough to get a good look at the patient, my arms folded across my chest. I thought moving to a small town was a chance to relax. I still expected to work, but not this much. It was getting to be ridiculous. It amazed me how the people who lived here lasted as long as they had. I was getting new patients with a variety of ailments damn near every day.

"I'm looking at your chart, Mr. Erickson, and this isn't the first time you've been here for the clap. Not even the first time this year. How does that happen?"

THE GIRLS IN PINE BROOKE

The twenty-year-old young man in front of me was in excellent shape. He looked like the kind of guy that made girls younger than him and older than me swoon. Dimples, piercing blue eyes, and short black hair. Muscled and in shape but he wasn't very smart. I swallowed that comment and waited for his response.

He looked around the room as a grin sprouted on his lips. "I didn't think I'd have to explain that to you. Aren't you a doctor?" He chuckled.

I swallowed a mean comment and pushed back an eye roll for later. "Yes, I know how it works. I'm just confused on why you *keep* getting it. Four times this year."

"I get around," he said with a shrug.

"Stay home. Stop passing yourself around." My neck was hot. Nothing made me angrier than stupidity. "It might not seem like a big deal, but it is. You keep getting the same sexual disease over and over again, it could lead to others. Some more dangerous and longer lasting than this one. It could do severe damage to your body."

He rolled his eyes. I wanted to smack some sense into him. I was tempted to take his phone and show him some pictures of genital herpes and what AIDS does to the body.

Instead, I signed a script for antibiotics and kicked him out of the clinic. I had his cellphone number. When I was a little calmer, I'd start texting him pictures of sexually transmitted diseases. A picture a day for a week might do it, starting with herpes and maybe ending with syphilis.

"What the hell is going on in this town?" I asked the empty room. I shook my head as I closed the door behind him. It was certainly stranger than I imagined.

The people were nice, though. Strange as all hell but nice. Some nicer than others. Some more intrusive than others.

Mrs. Caputo, who told me she was new to the town even though she had been here for fifteen years, asked me a million questions when she came to see me. She asked me more questions than I asked her about her condition.

"You're a breath of fresh air. We've needed some fresh meat around her for a long time but most people don't want to live in small towns anymore. They think life here is too slow I guess."

"Or they're thinking about *Deliverance*," I said as I glanced at her chart.

She snorted at that. A smile tugged at my lips. She was funny and had a good sense of humor. Intrusive questions every time I saw her, but she was nice and baked me cookies.

I learned from her that unless you were born in this town or the town next to it, you were new. And you would probably always be seen as a new person. She had been there for years, and everyone still saw her as a new resident. It was weird, but I figured it was how small towns worked. Or how this one worked anyway.

Pine Brooke was the first small town I had ever lived in. It was an adjustment, but at times, it felt like I was still in the city, especially since I kept getting the strangest people in the clinic.

"Hello, doctor."

I stilled near my desk. I knew the voice and I knew what was coming. "Good evening Mrs. Raydor. How are you?"

She shrugged. "I'm okay, I guess. However, I was having some chest palpitations earlier. I didn't want to bother you, but then I was going to bed, and it happened again. It caught me off guard, so I decided to come on down. Are you busy? I can come back tomorrow."

I had come to notice that Mrs. Raydor didn't like feeling like a burden. She was very nice and polite and often neglected herself to make those around her more comfortable.

"I have nowhere else to be, Mrs. Raydor. Describe how you are feeling?" I glanced back down the hallway. "Come on, let's get you into an exam room." I led her down the hallway to the exam room opposite my last patient. I needed to disinfect it first. "Okay now, tell me what's going on."

She sat on the cushioned table in front of me while I sat on the stool and wheeled myself in front of her. Mrs. Raydor was in her early sixties and pretty fit for an older woman. She liked walking around town and rarely used her car unless she had to. She also swam in the community pool a few times a week.

"Well, they are just palpitations, I guess. Like my heart skips a beat, it catches me off guard because it happens so suddenly."

"Are you experiencing any pain anywhere else?"

She shrugged. "Well... I don't think it is anything serious, but I've had a cramp in my leg the past couple of days. I've been trying to drink more water and improve my circulation."

"Is it just the one leg?"

She nodded. "My right one."

"Okay, swing your legs up here, and I'll take a look."

Mrs. Raydor scooted back and swung her legs up on the table. "I hate to be a bother. I know this is just all in my mind and not a big deal," she said quietly. "I hate that I'm ruining your evening. I know you have that lovely girl to get back home to."

I smiled. "It's not a bother Mrs. Raydor. Literally my job, actually. And my daughter could use a break from me. She loves our nanny. And I don't want to send you home thinking it's nothing and it could be something. Like I told you, it's better to come in and get checked out and learn that it's nothing than to stay home, assuming it will go away, and it turns out to be something big. Or something that could have been avoided. You're never a bother, so don't worry." I pushed up her pants leg to examine her right leg. Her calf was warm and hard to the touch. I examined her left leg for comparison. Her right leg was slightly bigger and a light shade of red.

"Okay. The pain... what does it feel like?" I started at her ankle and moved up to her knee, pressing on her leg. She winced when I touched her calf.

"It feels like a charley horse that won't go away."

I sighed. "Okay. And with your chest, just the palpitations?"

"There was some pain yesterday but not today."

"Describe it?"

"Sharp. It only lasted a second, and then it was gone. Just like that."

I nodded slowly. I had an idea what the problem was. "Okay." I glanced at the door. I had sent my nurse home early as it was a pretty slow day, and I didn't think I was going to need her tonight. I had been on my way home before she walked through the door.

"Okay, I think I know what's wrong, but in order to be sure, I need to run some tests. I think that it's best I take you to the hospital in Woodvine to get the test run."

"Is that necessary?" She sat up. "I don't want to be a bother. I could just come back in the morning when your nurse is here if that would make it easier."

It would have made it easier, but I had a bad feeling about letting her go home. "I understand that. But there could be a blood clot in your leg. There is some discoloration and slight swelling. If there is, we need to dissolve it before it travels to your heart or your lungs. If it does, it becomes dangerous and often deadly. I don't want to let you go home and go to sleep and then that's the last time I see you. The equipment I need is at the hospital, and there is someone there who can read the scans and make sure everything is okay."

Her mouth twisted in uncertainty for a moment, and then she nodded. "I guess so. If you feel like it should be done."

"I do. I really do."

The hospital in Woodvine was the closest largest hospital to Pine Brooke. It wasn't as big as the one I worked at before I moved here, but it had all the equipment we needed. It took an hour before we could get in. Mrs. Raydor's nervousness grew as time went on. To me, it seemed like it was more out of fear than wanting to be a bother. What if they found something bad? The worry was etched into her face, sculpted into the lines cradling her eyes. I held her hand. Stroking her thumb with mine and squeezing every once in a while. Her nervousness leaked into me.

If it was a blood clot, we'd have to see if we could dissolve it. If we couldn't, it would have to be removed surgically. I said a short prayer that it was only the one clot and that no more had worked their way through her body.

The last prayer went unanswered, but I was thankful we got her to the hospital in time. If I had let her go home like she wanted, she would have died. After an EKG and an ultrasound, we found three clots. The tech had the idea to look for more, so we did. There was one in her leg, one in her lung, and another in her neck. One too close to her heart and the other too close to her brain. We could have dissolved them with blood thinners. But I wasn't sure whether it would work or not. The one in her neck was concerning. If it moved before the thinners started working, she could die.

After consulting a surgeon, we decided to operate. I waited around for them to finish before I went home. I wanted to make sure the surgery went well and that she came out of anesthesia okay.

"You stayed?" She asked groggily.

"Of course. I wanted to make sure everything was okay. They were able to get the clot in your neck and your lungs. Everything is okay, but you are going to have to stay for a little while. The clot in your leg disappeared. It might have dissolved on its own, but they aren't sure, so you need to be monitored."

"Okay," she said sleepily. Her eyes closed before I could say anything else. The surgeon would have to come in to explain everything to her. I doubted she'd remember any of our conversation. I squeezed her hand before I left.

I glanced at my watch as I walked back to my car. Dani should have been asleep by then. She liked waiting up for me, but it was almost midnight.

I lived close to the clinic. So close I could walk home from work if I wanted to. Close to the lake, too. It was practically in our backyard. Dani loved the place as soon as we walked in. She liked that it was close to the lake, and had a library and a reading nook that overlooked the water. She also liked the fact that it was close enough to the school, so she didn't have to take the bus.

I wasn't sure about her walking, but her nanny, Bonnie, seemed to think it was a good idea. She said it would teach her some independence while keeping her in earshot if anything went wrong.

You could stand on our front porch and watch the entrance to the school, which she did every morning.

I pulled into the driveway and sighed as I took the key out of the ignition. The porch light was on, but the lights inside the house were out. "Probably sleeping."

I crawled out of the car and slunk up to the door. Inside the house was quiet. No TV. No talking. Nothing. I let it envelop me in its silence. Something I had wanted to hear all day.

It wasn't that I hated my job, I loved it. I loved helping people. It wasn't that I hated being around people—once upon a time, I loved it.

My wife had kept the house filled with people. Family, friends. There was always someone coming over for dinner or someone staying in the guestroom for a couple of nights. She was the most hospitable person I had ever known.

"She likes the house," she told me once; about her sister Jamie who was spending the weekend for the thousandth time that year. Of course, she loved the house. She wasn't paying any of the bills or taking on any of the responsibility. If I had that arrangement, I would have loved it too.

"Then she needs to buy her own house. She's here every weekend."

"No she's not. Don't be mean."

I didn't think I was being mean, just honest. Jamie loved her sister a little too much. She was always around. I thought things might settle once we got married and moved in together, but nothing changed. Jamie still liked coming over on weekends and monopolizing her time. When she was around, I felt like an intruder in my home. Intruding on their private time together. Their *sister* time. No matter how much Jamie annoyed her, she never turned her away. She never turned anyone away.

If you needed a place to stay, our house was your safest bet.

But Marie's gone now. My house, which was never quiet before, was nothing but quiet. People didn't visit like they used to, and the old house was full of memories, so I had to move. Some old friends kept vowing to come and visit the new place, but we all knew they wouldn't. They were mainly her friends, and now that she's gone, so are they.

I dropped my keys onto the console and kicked off my shoes. The tension in my shoulders eased as soon as my feet felt the cool hardwood of the foyer. After grabbing a beer out of the fridge, I went upstairs to my bedroom. Bonnie waited in the hallway with a bat.

"Good night to you, too." I held up my hands.

"I thought that was you, but I wasn't sure."

I waved. "Just me." I pointed at Dani's door. "She asleep?"

"Hours ago. Even caught her snoring for a little while. She tried to wait up for you."

I shook my head. "Yeah. I had to take a patient to the hospital in Woodvine and stayed with her through surgery."

"Figured you got caught up. Well, I'll take my bat back to bed."

"Thank you for standing guard."

She chuckled as she closed her door. Her bedroom and Dani's were on the left side of the hallway, along with an extra bedroom and a bathroom.

My bedroom was on the other side. Just two doors, my bedroom, and a closet that was turned into a laundry room. I walked into my room and closed the door behind me. The only thing I wanted to do was down my beer and get some sleep.

CHAPTER THREE

Riley Quinn

M ORNINGS WERE MY FAVORITE TIME OF DAY. WHEN THE WORLD hadn't fully woken up yet, and the stillness was palpable. The lake was quietest in the morning, and I made my morning coffee and followed Luna outside on the porch. She chased a hummingbird that proved to be too fast for her while I sat in the old rocking chair and stared at the water.

The rising sun, a gentle brush of hazy orange and purple, bluing at the edges, painted the sky. I was usually showered and dressed by six, even though I didn't have to get to the station until eight. Rising early gifted me a precious hour or so to bask in solitude. A serene morning, like a soothing balm, set the pace for the day. If my mornings were chaotic, it tainted my mood for the rest of the day.

"Begin as you mean to go on," my mother would say.

I sipped my coffee and watched Luna pad near the lake's edge. She never got in the water, not fully. Just as far as to cover her paws, and then she ran back. She seemed afraid of it or unsure of its depths. She didn't trust the water, but she liked seeing the turtles that played in the water with the fish. She skimmed the water looking for something.

Luna always made me giggle. Her curiosity and her clumsiness. She stumbled into the water a little and then scrambled to get out. A giggle bubbled up. She looked horrified as she ran away from the lake, bouncing along the edge with the rocks until her paws touched the grass of my yard again. She lay down as if she were exhausted.

I laughed. My phone vibrated next to me. I glanced at the screen, half expecting to see my mother's face, but surprisingly, it wasn't her.

Alison Moore's number flashed on the screen. My heart stammered for a moment. I hadn't seen or talked to her in months—almost a year. She was one of my best friends when I lived in LA. We spoke every day, sometimes more than once a day. She knew everything about me, and I, her.

Our small friend group went everywhere together. We did everything together. But in the years since I left, our conversations had dwindled. Our interactions became practically nonexistent. Sometimes I missed them. Actually, I always missed them. I'd never admit it to them or anyone else. If anyone asked, I'd say I wanted a new start and decided to let go of everything in my past including old friends.

Part of that was true, but not the whole truth. Letting them go was difficult, but I had to. I needed to move on, and I couldn't look into their faces every day. It was better that way. I got a fresh start, and they didn't have to pretend they didn't blame me for what happened. I knew they did. They had to. I did. I watched the screen dim and then turn black. It lit up again a second later. She had left a voicemail. I'd check it later. I knew what it said. The same as the others.

Hey girlie, just calling to check in. Call me back when you get the time. I miss you. We need to meet up and soon. I miss all of us together like we used to be. Love you. Bye.

It was always the same. But there was no 'all of us'. Not anymore. We could never be like we used to be, and I seemed to have been the only one who could accept that. We all just needed to move on.

I sighed as I brought the coffee cup to my lips. Today was going to be a long day. I already felt it in my bones. I was usually right about these kinds of things. This town had changed drastically since I moved away. It was a quiet, peaceful town. Nothing ever happened. The biggest, most shocking thing that happened when I was a teenager was when

Mr. Wilkinson came home from work early and found his wife in bed with their neighbor's wife. It caused a big uproar in the town. There had been whispers, but nothing loud enough to get back to either of their husbands.

He shot them both with his sawed-off shotgun. His wife died instantly, but Mrs. Gilling survived her wounds and testified against him in court. It was the one trial I remembered everyone following. They talked about it all over town, even at school. He went to prison, and she divorced her husband and moved away.

Mr. Gilling died a year or two before I moved back. He had moved on, got married, and had two children. Mr. Wilkinson died in prison. No one talked about them any longer but we all still remember what happened. The most shocking thing to hit the town in my lifetime.

But now, a lot of the crime from the bigger cities had trickled down to us. Still not as dangerous, but more so than it used to be. When I moved back, I half expected a more relaxing job. I didn't remember the cops having to do a lot of work when I was a teenager. Mostly, we just saw them sitting around or driving around town. I definitely thought there would be more sitting and riding around in the car with my partner. Boy, was I wrong. Drugs had become an epidemic in the towns around us, and now, it was starting to leech into Pine Brooke.

My phone buzzed next to me while playing the song "Bad Boys." A grin bloomed on my lips. The ringtone always made me smile. I knew it was Zelina without even looking at the screen.

"Yes?"

"We have a case."

"More drugs?" I stared at the lake. Luna had regained her courage padding toward the edge of the lake again chasing a bird.

"Nope. They found a body in the woods."

My heart paused in my chest for a moment. Now that was a first. Sure we had the occasional murder—but they were usually in the home. "Okay. I'm on my way." I hung up the phone and whistled for Luna. I kept her in a crate some days while I was at work to get her used to it. She didn't like it and neither did I, but I didn't want her running around the lake while there was no one there to watch her. It was dangerous.

I put her in her crate with her toys and her water bowl. My sister knew to come around lunch time to feed her and let her outside for a walk. After finishing my coffee I placed the cup in the sink and then grabbed my keys and phone and badge before heading out the door.

Images flooded my mind. I wondered who the body belonged to. If it was someone Zelina recognized she would have said that first. She was one of the most direct people I had ever met. She sugarcoated nothing. Part of me believed she didn't know how to lie. She either didn't know how or just didn't want to.

I drove to the town and made my way to the scene. There were few wooded areas in and around town. The scene could have been in one of two places. I was glad when I saw the coroner's van and the other police cars that I had chosen right on the first guess.

I jumped out of my car just as Zelina started walking over.

"I don't even know what to say." She glanced back at the scene and shook her head.

"That bad?"

"It's not great. And to me, it's a little confusing. I'm waiting for Keith to take a look. See if he could try to make sense of it."

"Well, walk me through it." I slipped on a pair of gloves while I followed her lead.

"Some kids were walking through the woods this morning. They said they were just going for a walk, but the lingering weed smell says differently."

I blew out a silent laugh. "Got it."

"They found her. At first, they thought she had fallen down the hill. I mean, it's kind of a hill, but… there's a slope but also a kind of cliff thing happening. Anyway, they thought she had fallen, so they carefully got down to help her, and she was cold, and then they saw her neck, and they knew she was dead."

"Okay." I wiggled my fingers in the gloves. "Sounds like some kind of accident or something. Why is this a police matter?"

Zelina nodded slowly. "That's what I said to the patrol officer. You don't call a detective for someone getting lost in the woods. But then he told me to look at the body. Officer Hayes doesn't get worked up easily, so I… looked at the body." She shrugged. "He might be on to something."

The part hill, part cliff, was something I remembered from my teenage years. The hill came out of nowhere, and if you weren't paying attention, you were on it before you even realized. The hill went up and came down slightly to a cliff filled with jagged rocks. From the cliff it was a straight drop to the ground below. I always thought of it as a mountain, which didn't grow tall enough to be one, so it settled on being a hill. But it was still pretty angry about having to settle, as we all often are, so it grew jagged rocks that might kill all who decide to walk up it.

My mother told me I was crazy about my theory, but when you look at it, it checks out. I called it LAH, Little Angry Hill. Zelina thought it was funny.

The girl was at the bottom of LAH. If the kids went down to help her, they must have been high. I could tell she was dead before I got close to her. Her arms and legs were at odd angles around her, but her neck... her neck was broken, and the bone jutted out from beneath her skin.

"Horrible way to die," I whispered.

Keith looked up. "True. The fall... you feel yourself falling, and you know you can't stop it. The fear is unimaginable. But the neck break was pretty instantaneous. She was dead before she got down here."

"Well that's something," said Zelina, raising a napkin to her nose. The girl had been out there for a while and was pretty ripe.

"They didn't smell her before they got to her?" I looked at Zelina, eyebrow slightly raised, my lips fighting a smile. "The smell is pretty dank."

"So is their weed." She chuckled. "Hell, I couldn't smell her when they were around."

"Oh, that's too loud."

Keith laughed. "I wish you hadn't sent them away."

I looked at Zelina and nodded. She rolled her eyes. I watched as he checked the body. Keith was our new coroner. He was nicer than the old one, less cantankerous. He knew how to take and make a joke, and he didn't look like he did things to the body before and *after* he cut them up. A vast improvement from the last one.

"Okay. I'm looking at the body, and right now, this is just looking like an accident. She was probably out here in the dark and got turned around. It happens a lot more than it should. You would think people around here knew better than to come out here at night," I said.

Keith nodded. "Give me a moment. Based on decomposition, she's been out here two days. I can't be precise because of all the insects and critters that have fed on her. And it's been extremely hot the last few days. That being said, because there are still parts of her left that weren't chewed on and her face is intact, I would say she's been out here a day, maybe two, but no more than that."

"Okay..." I inched toward the body. The smell was suffocating for her to still be relatively fresh. I covered my nose with my gloved hand. I wanted to get a closer look at the body. There was something about her. I took a picture of her face. It was still intact even though there was some blood on it. "What is that on her wrist?"

Keith rolled up her sleeves. There was blood on her arms and hands, but there was something else. A deep red indentation that was there before she died.

"Yeah, I see what you're talking about." Keith pushed up her other sleeve and we all saw the same red mark around her wrist. I pushed up her pants and saw the same red marks around her ankles. "She was tied up—or rather—cuffed." He moved her wrist to right in front of his face. "Looks like there are some silver flecks in the wound. I'll swab it and see if I can figure out what it is."

"Thanks. Okay, so someone was holding her captive out here?" I looked around the area. It was pretty remote. No one could have heard her scream unless they were walking by. I took a deep breath. "Does she look familiar to you?" I looked back at Zelina who just shook her head.

"I thought I might recognize the person when I got here but I've stared at her for a while and nothing. But I was thinking she might not be from around here. Maybe one of the other towns around here, and then that could be why she didn't know about your Little Angry Hill."

Keith snorted a laugh. "I could get a DNA sample, put it in the system, and fingerprints." He stared at her for a long moment. "I doubt she has a record, but it's worth a shot. She looks no older than sixteen. If that."

"Sixteen-year-olds have records," said Zelina. "I did."

Keith blinked as he stared at her.

"Oh yeah, she was a rebel," I said a laugh on the edge of my voice. "Knocking over liquor stores and boosting cars."

"You do not sound right saying any of those words," she said, grinning. "I didn't *boost* cars. And I don't drink liquor. It was mostly shoplifting and then a robbery or two. A fight or—"

"Several," I finished.

"It wasn't several. A few."

"A few is three or more."

Zelina rolled her eyes. "It was three or more."

"Several is more than seven, I believe."

Zelina gaped at me. "I don't think that's true. I'm Googling your facts when we get back to the station."

I laughed. I didn't know if I was right or not. If I wasn't, she would definitely bring it up later. "We should walk the hill. See where she came from."

Zelina took one side and I the other. We scanned the area along with patrol officers looking for anything that seemed out of place. Anything that didn't belong in the woods. There were beer bottles, a few wine bottles, condom wrappers, and used condoms.

"I didn't know people partied in the woods like this," said Zelina.

I looked at her and laughed.

"No, I'm serious. I didn't know this was how y'all got down in a small town. I am shocked!" Zelina moved to Pine Brooke because of her grandmother when she was a teenager. Her father died, and her mother had five kids to feed and take care of on her own. She couldn't do it, so she sent Zelina and Denzel to live with their grandmother. While her brother graduated and left for college, never returning except on holidays, Zelina went to college and then came back. She was there to take care of her grandmother Flora when she got sick, and she was there to pick up the pieces when she died from a heart attack in the middle of the night.

She decided to stay even though there were times she missed being in a big city like New York. That was part of why we got along so well. Both of us had found ourselves here after the big city.

"These woods have always been the hangout spot for the young people in town," I said, my eyes scanning the ground as I walked.

"Was it when I got here? I don't remember that." Zelina didn't have many friends before college on account that she was still trying to find herself and struggling with the death of her father. She was quiet. So quiet I didn't notice her in high school, and we shared some of the same classes. I knew the name, but I couldn't remember what she looked like until I moved back, and there she was.

"Some of the kids used to party here. Far enough away, you could turn the music up loud and just have fun."

She snickered. "I love how you say 'the kids' like you weren't part of it."

"Excuse me? I was an angel growing up. Didn't party or get into trouble. Never hung out here drinking in the woods." I heard the smile on the edge of my voice.

A cackle split the silence of the woods. When Zelina thought something was exceptionally funny, she cackled. Loud and uncontrollable. "You forget I talk to your mother, and she has a completely different story of your childhood. And pictures to prove it."

"I have got to burn those pictures. She keeps showing them to people."

Zelina stopped, shifting immediately back into work mode. "Someone was running through here."

I nodded. I spotted the broken branches and twigs along the path we were walking.

"Yeah, I see footprints. They look pretty fresh, but they could have been from the boys or someone else."

"True. We need molds of all of them just in case." Zelina gestured to one of the crime scene guys to come over. She pointed to the footprints.

Zelina was great at tracking. Her grandmother and grandfather had taught her. They were both hunters and took her with them once she moved in. Her brother wasn't a fan. I watched her as she moved through the trees carefully and stooped low to the ground. We moved through the trees, zigging and zagging. Practically going in circles.

I waited for her to say something before I jumped to conclusions.

"From what I can see, two people were going in circles. One in bare feet, the other in boots. The girl wasn't wearing any shoes, so those prints are likely hers. The boots were probably someone chasing her. She was going in circles."

"Must have gotten turned around in the darkness. It's easy to do out here."

"Yeah, especially if you don't know the area." I looked around. The crime scene guys were still looking through the trees. I hoped someone found a strip of her clothing or the clothing of the person who was chasing her.

"Let's move closer to the top of the hill," said Zelina. She kept her head down, eyes glued to the ground. We neared the hill. "The shoe prints stop here, but hers keep going."

"So whoever was chasing her stopped here while she went over the edge. So either they knew where she was going and stopped short and watched her go over or…"

"Maybe they watched her fall and stopped short before they went over," said Zelina.

"Both possible. My question is, did they bring her here or did she run here from somewhere else? Like she saw a chance to break out of wherever she was being held and took it? Or did he bring her here and she got away from him?"

"Those are good questions to ask." We neared the edge of the cliff and looked down at her body and Keith gesturing to the crime scene guys around him.

"I wonder what she was thinking as she went down," I said, my voice barely above a whisper.

"Scary thought," said Zelina. "I'm guessing it depends on what happened to her before she fell, what he did to her. She might have been happy to fall."

That was a sobering thought. To think that someone would have been happier to fall to their death than to keep going. *What happened to her? And who was she?*

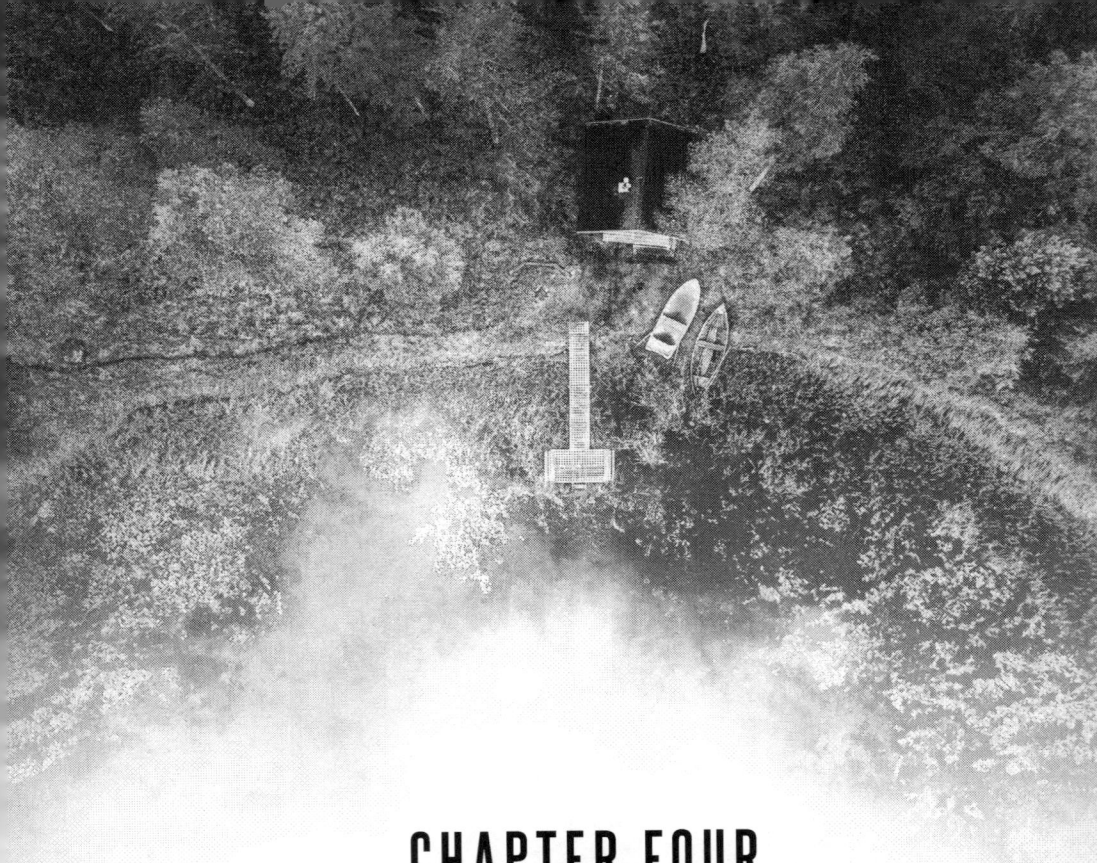

CHAPTER FOUR

Logan Elwood

"**A**ND WHERE WERE YOU LAST NIGHT?" Danielle stood in the doorway to the kitchen with her arms crossed and her lips pushed into a pout.

"I was working."

She set her hands on her hips. "Mm-hmm."

I had to laugh. She sounded just like her nanny. "I had an emergency. I had to stay late with a patient to make sure she was okay, and her surgery was successful."

Her arms fell to her sides. "Is she okay?"

"She was when I left her last night, but I'm going to check on her now and make sure everything is still okay."

Dani rocked back on her heels. "I guess that's okay. Since she needed you. I had math homework to do and could have used your services yesterday."

A smile pulled at my lips. "I'm sorry I couldn't help you with your math homework."

"It's okay. Miss Bonnie's pretty good at math. She was a good substitute."

"I'm glad to hear it." Danielle was only seven, but she was smart. Smarter than me. She was an avid reader, reading far above her grade level. I was always amazed by how her mind worked. When I was seven, I thought about nothing but playing outside and running around.

As she stood there, striking her best guilt-inducing pose, I could see how much she looked like her mother, something I noticed more and more as time went on. She had her dark brown hair and hazel eyes. She even had her dimples, deep like craters carved into her cheeks. Every time she smiled, I was taken back to the first time I met her mother.

Marie's locker was next to mine in high school. I first met her in ninth grade, and all I could think was that she was so beautiful. The most beautiful girl in the entire school. We'd say hi, here and there. I'd work hard just to make her laugh so I could see that dimple. It paid off, eventually.

"Papa?"

Dani's voice snapped me out of my thoughts, back to a Marie-less reality. "Yeah, honey?"

"Can we hang out this weekend? Maybe go to the movies?" Dani walked over to the table and batted her eyelashes at me.

"You don't want to go with your friends?"

She shrugged. "For right now, you are my best friend, and I want to hang out with you."

I smiled at her, trying not to dwell on the fact that she'd said 'right now'. "Yes, we can hang out at the movies this weekend. Just me and you."

She beamed. Dani never let anything get her down. It could have just been the way she was or maybe it was the fact that she was young and had few worries. Though, she had been through a lot for a seven-year-old. More than any child should have to endure. Yet there she was, still smiling. Making it difficult for me to be sad.

"Now I have to go, but you need to have a great day at school. And I need you to listen to Miss Bonnie and your teachers."

She shrugged. "I always do. Whether I want to or not."

"Well, that's good to know."

"I thought so." She kissed me on the cheek. "You need to have a good day too. Smile more."

"I'll work on that." I didn't smile like I used to, and no matter how hard I tried, I couldn't think of a reason to. Not anymore. Dani made it easy to smile, but once she was out of sight, the smile faded.

I said my goodbyes and headed out the door. I wanted to get to Mrs. Raydor before I went to the clinic. I called my nurse to let her know that I was going to be in late. She sounded surprised.

"Is everything okay?"

"Yes, I just want to check on Mrs. Raydor in Woodvine. She was uneasy before they rolled her into surgery. I just want to make sure she's okay."

"Oh, that's sweet of you. I'll push back your first appointment. Everything else is after lunch."

"Thanks." I kind of felt like I should have been offended by the surprise in her voice. I was a little bit. Just because I wasn't always smiling and trying to start conversations with people didn't mean I wasn't a nice person, especially when it came to my patients. Mrs. Raydor was a nice woman. Her husband died a few years ago, and her son had been murdered a few years before that. She told me all about it the first day I met her. She had a migraine that just wouldn't go away, and she saw my wedding ring when I examined her.

"How long have you been married?" she'd asked.

I had forgotten I was still wearing it. "I'm a widower, but we were married for almost ten years. Together longer though."

She'd nodded slowly. "My Byron and I had been together over thirty years before he passed. Since middle school, really."

"Wow, that's a long time to love someone."

"My whole life, practically. I'd like to tell you the grief goes away, but it doesn't. It comes in waves, sometimes soft, sometimes bone-crushing. There have been days when I couldn't get out of bed, not because I didn't want to, I just… it felt wrong to move without him. To breathe without him. And some days, I think of him, and I just laugh and smile. The grief doesn't go away; I do think it changes, though. I laugh and smile more now than I did when it first happened. Instead of thinking about my life without him, I think about all the things we did together, and those memories make me smile."

"I'll hold on to that."

I wasn't there yet. I smile more now than I did before, but not enough—if I listened to Dani.

"You came to see me?" Mrs. Raydor was still eating breakfast when I walked in. She smiled as she set her spoon down. "I wasn't expecting to see you."

"I just wanted to check in and make sure everything was still going well. Did the surgeon tell you anything?"

She ran a hand through her hair as if checking to see if it was a mess. "He sent me for some test to see if the clot had appeared anywhere else. They didn't find anything. He thinks it dissolved on its own, but he wants to monitor me a little longer and then do the test again. He doesn't think I have a clotting disorder though."

I nodded as she recounted everything he told her. I had been concerned it might have been a disorder, and she would be on blood thinners from now on.

"I haven't been moving around as much as I used to."

My mouth hung open. She had told me she was very active, and she looked like that was true. For an older woman, she was very fit.

"I know. I know. It's been a few months. I just haven't felt like getting around. But I'll get back to it. He thinks the sedentary life that I've been living for the past couple of months might have caused the clots."

I smiled and nodded. For her to have been so active before… she must have been inactive for a lot longer than a couple of months. Maybe she was depressed. She was alone. She lived by herself and had no other children or family in town. I needed to think of a way to help her.

"Well, how are you feeling this morning?"

"Oh! Much better. The pain in my leg is gone."

"That's good, as long as you are feeling good. That's what matters." We talked for a few moments before I headed to the clinic. She seemed like she wanted to talk longer, but I had to get to work. While I felt bad for her, she didn't need my pity, just like I didn't need anyone else's.

My nurse, Nicole, smiled as soon as I walked through the door. "How is she?"

"Doing much better. They think the clot in her leg dissolved on its own. They should let her go home in a day or two."

"It's a good thing you were here, or she would have just gone home. I know Mrs. Raydor. She hates feeling like she's a bother or a burden, so she doesn't bother or burden others with her problems. The pain could have been excruciating and she would have limped home anyway."

I shook my head. "That's what I figured and what I'm afraid of. She seems so lonely. I don't know how to help her with that."

Nicole sighed. "I'll think on it. There's got to be something we can do for her. She's retired, so she doesn't have to leave the house if she doesn't want to."

I headed toward my office and paused, my fingers grazing the knob. Nicole was a nurse practitioner, so she could see patients on her own if needed. "What about us bringing in a receptionist?" I moved toward her desk. "She could take calls and make appointments. It would get her out of the house and around people and let her feel like she was doing something. Not just sitting idly by."

Nicole's eyebrows raised. "That would be a great idea. I'm a little annoyed I didn't think of it myself. But yeah, she could totally do that. And she's so kind and friendly on the phone, she's perfect for that."

"Okay. Once I talk to her surgeon and see how she's doing, and when she is cleared for work, I'll talk to her about it. See if it's even something she'll want to do."

"She will," she said matter-of-factly. The phone rang and she picked it up. "All the ladies want to work here to look at you."

"Is that why you got the job?" I asked as I walked back to my office.

"Hey, I was here before you. I was grandfathered in with the place."

A soft chuckle coasted up my throat. Doctor Malcolm told me that I could fire Nicole if I wanted to when I took the job. He hoped I wouldn't, though. She was a great nurse and the town loved her. But the whole point of me moving to this clinic was to get a fresh start.

I had thought about just cutting ties with her; I really did. I didn't want my first act as the town's doctor to be firing a nurse they all loved and felt comfortable with. They would have really hated me then.

And once I met her, I liked her. Nicole Springer was a tall curvy woman with long braids she kept in a loose bun on top of her head. She was brutally honest but not in a mean way.

"You're hot," she'd said as soon as I walked in. "I'm just telling you what every woman and some men will say behind your back."

"Well, thank you for pointing it out."

She snickered. "Like you didn't know. Now tell me what I need to know about you so I can do my job properly, and I'll do the same."

I learned that Nicole lived with her mother who had a stroke last year but was doing much better and needing less and less care every day. She had two cats, Artemis and Diana, which she named after her favorite anime *Sailor Moon*. She loved anime, comics, manga, and movies that didn't make her cry. She wanted to be a nurse because she liked helping people and making them happy. She had no children and never planned on having any or getting married.

"And before you say I'll change my mind someday, my mind is made up. I like people in the sense of having friends and hanging out. It doesn't get any closer than that."

"Understood. Don't try to set you up on dates."

She'd stared at me for a long moment before laughter burst from her lips. "You don't even seem like the kind of person that could or would do that."

"I really wouldn't. I don't know anyone."

She'd laughed, and then it was my turn. I told her about Marie, some of it anyway. I told her enough to get the gist and about the kid and the nanny.

"I'm so sorry for your loss. If you need me to cover for you because you have to go home, just let me know. I can take over."

"Thanks… what is *Sailor Moon*? Some kind of cartoon?"

The look of disgust and confusion on her face told me instantly I had messed up by asking the question. It caused a ten-minute conversation on the joys of anime and the intricate storylines of Sailor Moon and the Sailor Scouts.

At the end of her speech, the only thing I learned was that Dani might like it. It seemed like something right up her alley: a group of young women with superpowers kicking butt and saving the world.

From then on, Nicole and I were cool. Not best friends but not just colleagues either. She was a great nurse and ready to learn anytime I taught her something new.

Back in the present, she stood in my doorway and sighed. "Alright, your first appointment is here, and he is in a bad mood."

I jumped to my feet. "Might as well get it over with." I followed her down the hall to one of the exam rooms.

"Doctor Elwood."

Elias sat on the exam table, eyes narrowed. He didn't like me much, and truth be told, I wasn't a big fan of his after he yelled at Nicole for asking him too many questions. In his notes, Doctor Malcolm said Elias liked to feel like he was in charge. *He'd have to get over that today.*

"So what is the problem today, Elias?" He had many ailments, but most of them turned out to be nothing. I half suspected he just liked coming in and getting attention.

"My throat is sore. Has been for the past few days."

"Okay. Any other symptoms? Cough? Any pain anywhere?"

He shook his head. "Just like I told you… only my throat. It hurts to swallow."

Huh, this might be a real issue. "Okay, let me take a look. Open your mouth." I took one look at the back of his throat and knew what the problem was. "I'm surprised you still have your tonsils, Elias."

"Is that a good thing?" He glanced at Nicole, who was standing in the doorway.

"Not today. They look swollen. Does this happen a lot?"

"Elias comes in for a sore throat or strep throat a few times a year," answered Nicole.

"Okay. Well, if your tonsils are consistently causing you problems, then we should remove them."

"You mean surgery?" If Elias could have crawled further up the exam table, he would have. Judging by the expression on his face, he wanted to get as far away from me as possible—like I had a scalpel in my hand and was going to carve him up right now.

I threw my hands up in mock surrender. "Don't worry. I'm not doing it right now. You need a surgeon. It's a simple procedure."

"If it's so simple, why can't you do it?"

Touché.

"I'm not a surgeon. But once they are removed, you shouldn't get a sore throat every month."

Elias looked at the door and then at Nicole; uncertainty molded into his face. He didn't like the idea of surgery. And I couldn't force it on him.

"I'll tell you what, I'll write you a prescription for antibiotics for your sore throat. And then you can think about the surgery… for the next time when this happens."

Antibiotics were more appealing than a surgeon. He took the prescription and left. "I probably should have let him stew for a day to think with the pain."

Nicole shrugged. "He'll be back next month, and then you can try again."

My phone vibrated in my pocket. I tore off my gloves before fishing it out of my pocket. "Trouble" by Amy Winehouse got louder and louder.

"Why is that your ringtone?" Nicole leaned against the doorframe.

"It's my ringtone for my brother."

She shook her head. "That's very telling." She closed the door behind her.

I clicked the green button. "Yeah. What do you want now?"

"Is that any way to talk to your favorite brother?"

He wasn't my favorite; he was my only brother. I was stuck with him, whether I wanted to be or not. I guess I should have been thankful. When Marie died, he was there for me and Dani. He helped pick me off the floor and focus back on my daughter. For that, I owed him, but I still didn't want him around. Where there was Isaac Elwood, there was trouble.

"What do you want?"

A soft chuckle rippled through the phone. "I was just calling to say I'll be in your neck of the woods for a little while. I'm stopping through. To see you, sure, but mostly to see the kid. I know she missed her favorite uncle."

"You're her only uncle," I corrected.

"Still counts. Don't be grumpy when I get there."

Before I could say another word, he hung up. I slid the phone back into my pocket, holding my breath the whole way. I loved my brother, but he was bringing trouble with him. I could feel it. I had enough going on.

New job.

New town.

Old wounds threatening to split open.

I stared at the door for a long moment before I opened it. I should have called him back and told him to stay wherever he was. But I didn't. I should have but I kept walking, back to my office to sit at my desk.

Dani loved her uncle, and I wouldn't be the one to take that relationship from her, even though it would bring nothing but trouble, and a mind-numbing headache.

I felt it now, lightly pulsing behind my right eye.

Lucky me.

CHAPTER FIVE

Riley Quinn

"**Y**OU LOOK TROUBLED."

I looked over and found Zelina staring at me. We were walking back to our cars. There was nothing left at the scene for us to look at, and Keith had left with the body. It would be a short while before he had a preliminary report for us.

I was praying for DNA under her fingernails. If he raped her, I hoped he wasn't careful. Most rapists weren't, but the ones who watched *CSI* or were pros at it knew what to do.

"I was just thinking."

"About?"

I shrugged. "Why here? What was he going to do to her here, or did he already do it and brought her here to dump her body?"

"You think that matters?"

"I do. Not sure why yet, though. The scene doesn't seem staged, so why come all the way here? She was tied up somewhere, so why not kill her there?"

Zelina hated it when I tried to get into the minds of people who did horrible things. It was my process. She thought it was dangerous.

"You keep trying to think like a killer. You might turn into one."

"Very funny," I said dryly. I tried to get into the heads of killers because it helped me understand why they did what they did and that helped me catch them. Together we had already solved five murders in town. There were a few unsolved cold cases I wanted to get my hands on, but Zelina wasn't interested. She didn't want to crawl around the dusty storage looking for case files and evidence when we still had active cases now.

It was understandable, but one day… I'd do it. With or without her.

"What are you going to do now?" I asked her.

"Head back to the station and start looking up missing person reports. Someone has to be missing her. You?"

"I think I'm going to take the picture and show it in a few places. Maybe someone knows her or knows where we can find her family."

"Okay. I'll let you know if I find anything."

"Same." I jumped in my car, and we parted ways. My first stop was my mom's coffee shop. Everyone stopped in there at some point during the day. Quinn's Coffee and Bakery was busy. The smell of butter and vanilla hovered around the front door. My mouth watered as soon as I walked in.

My mother waved from the front counter while she talked to a customer. My eyes darted around the room before returning to her and her customer: Doctor Elwood. He had two cups of coffee in his hand, and he was smiling at my mother. His presence was annoying. He looked good, though. White collared shirt and gray slacks. The sleeves of his shirt were rolled up to his elbows. The tip of a tattoo peeked out on his right forearm. Didn't picture him having a tattoo. I couldn't make out what it was. The two talked for a moment like they had known each other for years and were just catching up. Then he thanked her and walked away.

I rolled my eyes as he passed. He could be nice to my mother but clipped with me. What was that about?

"You here for your usual?" My mother tucked a curly black strand behind her ear. Her hair was pulled into a messy bun. She wiped her hands on her cherry red apron.

"That and to ask you a couple of questions."

She looked at me for a long moment, eyes narrowing. "Questions? Interesting. Speaking of questions, have you met the new doctor? You could do with a check-up."

"I'm fine, and yeah, we met."

She leaned forward like I was about to tell her a secret. "Why'd you say it like that?"

"He bandaged my wrist after I sprained it yesterday and he was very clipped about it. Kind of rude."

"Well, he's been through a lot."

"I don't care what he's been through, he shouldn't be rude to his patients."

She looked surprised. "He was nice to me just now and when I met him for my check-up. I'm making your father go next week. That man's got to get his blood pressure under control before it starts spiraling again."

"I thought he had it under control."

"He does until he thinks he can do it on his own and doesn't need any medication, so he stops taking it. But enough about him, what questions?"

"Don't scream." I took out my phone and showed her the picture.

"Heavens. What happened to her?"

"We don't know yet. Do you know her? Have you ever seen her before?"

My mother studied the picture as things moved on around us. Orders were called and claimed. People walked in while others walked out.

"I can't say that I do. She doesn't look familiar. I don't even think she's from here. I've never seen her before."

"Okay. I figured as much, but I still thought I'd ask. I'll keep asking around." I turned to leave. "Oh, can you have the coffee and pastries delivered to the station? I'm going to drive around town and see if someone knows her."

"Sure, hon."

"Thanks, Mama."

I drove around town as slowly as I could, stopping people and asking them if they knew her. No one did. No one recognized her from our little town. It was strange. I couldn't stop thinking about where she had to come from. It had to be one of the neighboring towns. She could have come from somewhere else— perhaps she had taken the bus here. My fingers tapped against the steering wheel. Our first priority was to figure out who she was.

We had to start there. I knew there was someone out there waiting for her to come home. It was difficult to think about. I wasn't a mother, but I knew what it was like to lose someone you loved.

I drove back to the station.

"Thanks for the pastries." Zelina waved a chocolate-filled croissant in the air while she sipped her coffee. "So kind of your mother. She's so good to us."

I grabbed a bear claw out of the box. There was only one, as I was the only one in the station that liked them. They were missing out because it was delicious. My coffee sat on my desk. Black, cream but no sugar. Zelina winced as I took a sip.

"So unnatural."

"I got enough sugar with the bear claw. I don't need it in my coffee, too."

"Just disgusting." She shook her head.

"Whatever. Enjoy your diabetes in a cup."

"Always do." She took a long sip before setting the cup down and finishing off her croissant. Zelina loved sugar. Her top left drawer was filled with candy and snack cakes. It was a serious problem, but amazingly, she was not diabetic. Yet.

"Anyone recognize her?"

I shook my head as I finished chewing. I swallowed hard. "Not that I talked to."

"I figured. Your face was so downcast when you walked in. I figured you came up empty."

"Downcast?"

She looked at me, her lips twitching, fighting a smile. "Yes, downcast. Downtrodden. You know what I mean."

I had to laugh. I did know what she meant. "Did you find anything?"

"I think so."

"Were you going to say anything?"

"I was giving you time to eat your breakfast and drink your disgusting coffee. You need fuel to solve crimes."

I finished the bear claw and got a croissant out of the box. I was so hungry. I chased it down with what was left of my coffee. I swallowed and then smiled. "All finished and properly fueled. Now, what did you find?"

"I think I found our girl." She slid a piece of paper over to me. Our desks faced each other. "It looks like her. I mean, it's pretty close."

I took out my phone. I held the paper next to the picture, and it was similar. The girl in the photo was dead and had been badly bruised due to her fall, but there was something there. She had the same eyes and the same nose. Similar jawline. If it wasn't her, they were related, at least.

"Jade Bailey. She went missing a while ago, with her friend Tiffany Cole. Jade's family filed a report on both girls."

It wasn't ringing any bells. I turned my phone off. "If we go to the family, they will ask us why we are there, and what do we say?" I looked at the missing person's report. "Do we tell them we found a body that resembles their daughter, or do we wait until we get confirmation?"

Zelina leaned back. I didn't want to scare this family and make things worse by telling them about a body that might not be their daughter. But I didn't want them to sit there waiting for her to come home, and she was sitting in our morgue. That would be cruel. Actually, both scenarios were cruel. They shouldn't have to go through this.

"I say we go see the family and see what they can tell us. It might be her, and if it is… well, to know whether it is or isn't, we need DNA. The only way we get it is by going to see the family and telling them about the body."

She was right. I knew that was the answer; I just didn't want to do it. The cases were always harder when it involved kids. It was the part I hated. Someone's life would be changed forever. For better or worse.

CHAPTER SIX

Logan Elwood

I DIDN'T KNOW WHEN HE CALLED THAT HE WAS RIGHT OUTSIDE OF town. I should have, though. He's Isaac. I should have guessed. I handed him the coffee cup outside of the clinic. I didn't want him to go in and meet Nicole just yet. I needed to tell her about him first. There were rules for dealing with my brother. Rules that had to be followed or everything would be ruined.

"Well, that is a good cup of coffee. Wasn't expecting that in this little town," Isaac remarked.

I sighed. Out of the corner of my eye I watched as Riley Quinn got back in her car and pulled away, a scowl etched into her face. She didn't like me much. I still wasn't sure how I felt about her. When I passed her in the coffee shop, part of me wanted to ask her about her wrist. I wanted to make sure she wasn't overexerting herself. She didn't look like she was in the mood to talk though, so I kept walking.

"Who was that?"

"Who was who?" I looked behind me; there was no one there.

"Chick that just drove off. She was hot in an authoritative kind of way."

"She's a cop."

"That explains it. She could arrest me any day."

I took a deep breath. "She might, depending on how long you stay."

"Ouch." He grabbed his chest. "You wound me. I didn't mean to step on your toes. No need to get defensive."

"I wasn't—" I swallowed my words. My brother liked to push my buttons. He knew I wasn't interested in anyone, not since Marie. Riley did have an *I run shit* kind of way about her. And she was pretty. Rich brown hair with the most hauntingly blue eyes I had ever seen. The kind that caught you off guard every time you looked at her. My fingers squeezed around the cup.

"How long will you be here?" the words bumped into each other on their way out of my mouth.

"A little while. I missed the bug. More than I thought I would. Not the fatherly type but I liked having her around. She's pretty cool even though she came from you."

A smile tugged at my lips.

"Had to come from Marie."

"Yeah. She was pretty cool."

"The coolest. And I'm here checking on you too." He nudged me with his shoulder.

"I tell you, I'm okay."

"Yeah, dude, you say a lot of shit. Doesn't mean it's true. You could have gotten your arm chopped off, and you would still tell me you were okay, so I didn't worry. It's annoying and makes me worry more, if I'm being honest. So I had to come and look at you for myself."

I held up my arm. "Still attached."

"For now." He took another sip. "Damn, this is some good-ass coffee. What do they do to it?"

I had to laugh. "Watch it with the cursing while you're here."

Isaac took a deep breath. "Man… I will try my best. I really will. I might slip, though; I'm just letting you know now."

I laughed. He definitely would. I told him where the house was and gave him my key. "Don't lock me out of my house. I'm serious. If I get there and you don't open the door you gotta go."

"I need you to move past that. And have a good day at work."

I watched him walk away. He seemed in good spirits, but then again, he usually was. It still felt like a storm was brewing. I looked down at the coffee cup in my hand.

"I can't go back to the clinic with coffee and nothing for Nicole." I turned around and went back into the shop. I ordered her usual, and headed to the clinic.

She beamed when I brought it to her desk. "Aww, you brought me coffee? That's so sweet."

"I try. Figured you could use a pick-me-up." It was mid-afternoon, and it had been a long day.

"Was that your brother?"

I stopped and spun around. "How did you…?"

"I was walking out and saw you two. I turned around and came back. It looked tense."

"It wasn't, surprisingly, but yeah, that's him. He's staying for a while, so you'll get to meet him eventually."

"You don't seem pleased."

I didn't know what to say. I loved my brother; I really did. He was about the only family I had left, but he was a trouble magnet. He had a hard time saying no to the wrong people. And an even harder time walking away from situations he had no business being in. He had a good heart but made shitty choices.

I was hoping history didn't repeat itself. Not this time. "He's a good guy, just has a hard time…" I didn't know how to finish that sentence.

"We all have family like that. Can't say no to a good time."

"Something like that. He missed Dani, though, and wanted to see her."

"I get that. She's an easy hang." She and Dani had bonded over *Sailor Moon*. She even introduced her to some other anime she liked. I didn't understand any of it, but they both seemed happy.

"That's good to hear, I guess." I sighed as I walked back to my office. "How many more?"

"Four. Next one is in thirty minutes."

"Noted."

The rest of the day breezed by. I was thankful for that. I was so tired by the end of it that it was all I could do to keep my eyes open. I should have gotten an espresso or something stronger.

"Okay, Mrs. Allen. Apply this ointment to the area every four hours. It should clear right up in a couple of days. If not, come back, and we will figure it out."

"Thank you, doctor. I really appreciate it."

"You're welcome."

I watched her walk out the door. Nicole leaned on her desk.

"Have you been working on your bedside manner?"

"No. I think they are just getting used to my bluntness."

Nicole shook her head.

"I am who I am. I'm not sugarcoating anything."

"You gonna come to the skating rink tonight?"

Nicole informed me that the town tried to do things where everyone came together at least once a month. This month, they wanted to go skating. There was a skating rink in town, and everyone was invited.

"I think I'll pass. I don't skate."

"Give you a chance to meet more people. Get that pretty face out there more."

A soft chuckle escaped my lips. "I get that same chance here. Sooner or later, everyone in town will walk through those doors. I just have to wait and see."

Nicole rolled her eyes. "Fine. But I beg you, don't turn into a recluse. It's not cute."

"Sounds nice to me." I headed back to my office to pack up for the night. No one else showed up before we left. I was partly relieved. Ready to go home but not. My brother was there, and I was still waiting for the other shoe to drop. He was planning something, or he needed something. Something else was going on.

I said goodnight to Nicole and headed toward my car. It was a slow drive back to the house, bracing myself for whatever waited for me on the other side of the door.

"Papa! You're home early!"

I swept her up in a big hug, lifting her off the ground for a few seconds. "I am. What is your uncle doing?"

"Watching *My Hero Academia*."

I followed her into the den, where the large TV blared away. Superheroes showcased their strange powers in some kind of competition. "You're watching this?" I pointed to the screen and stared at my brother. He leaned back on the sofa with a bottle of water in his hand.

"Dude, you have the coolest daughter. She's into anime. I love this. One of my favorites; gotta get her into *Naruto* and *One Piece*, though. But *Sailor Moon* and *DBZ* are great places to start. I'm so proud."

What was he proud of? It was just a show. "The nurse I work with got her into this stuff."

"Yeah, I figured it wasn't you. Pop a squat. Sit down."

Dani sat next to him, and I sat next to her. We reclined back and watched what had become one of her favorites in a very short time. She loved superheroes and how strange their powers were.

"It makes you think. Like none of their powers make sense or are useful. So if they want to be heroes they have to think outside of the box and figure out ways to use them to help people."

"I get that," said Isaac. "Some of those quirks make no sense."

"What is it with the kid and purple balls on his head? How is that useful?" As much as I tried to fight it, the show was kind of interesting. It was pretty good. Would I watch it by myself? Probably not, but here with them, it was entertaining. We watched a few more episodes, and then Isaac made us watch *Naruto*. Turned out Dani also liked ninjas.

"Another thing for her to be consumed by." I took our empty popcorn bowls and glasses into the kitchen.

Isaac followed. "Nah, *Naruto* is a good one. It's really about perseverance, you know. No matter how many horrible things happen to you, you just gotta keep moving. Keep fighting. You don't give up until you're dead. And he never does. He fights, and he fights. And he helps people. Not because he wants to be famous or anything. Naruto wants to be the leader of his village not for power, but so they will respect him, and he works his ass off until he achieves that dream. He messes up, he fails, he loses people, but he keeps going."

"Didn't know it was that deep."

He leaned against the counter next to the fridge. "People think it's just for kids but it's not. Animation is just another way to tell a story. And a lot of them are really good. One night after Dani goes to sleep, we can watch *Jujustu Kaisen* and *Demon Slayer*. Definitely not for kids. *One Piece* is a little more kid friendly. It seems like it's just about a kid wanting to become a pirate, gathering a crew and going on an adventure."

"Is that the whole premise of the show?" I placed the dishes in the sink and wiped down the counter.

"Yeah, but at its core, it's about found family, the bonds of friendship, working hard to attain your goals, and overthrowing the government."

"And all those things go together?"

"Oda makes it work."

"You're really into it." I shook my head. I never heard my brother talk about something with such excitement. He sounded like he could talk about it for hours.

"Anime, manga, just different ways to tell stories. And that's what I like. And the fight scenes. I can't wait for you to watch *Demon Slayer*."

He seemed so into it, and so did she. I'd give it a try for them. Well for Dani anyway. Before I could say anything, the doorbell rang.

Isaac glanced in the direction of the door. "It's pretty late. You get the door, and I'll put the kid to bed."

"Thanks."

He disappeared into the den, and I headed toward the door. It was almost eleven. I wasn't expecting anyone. No one came to my house. Not even Nicole. I opened the door. My heart seized in my chest for a moment as my breath caught in my throat.

"Long time no see."

"Jamie." Her name slipped out of my mouth as a rough whisper.

"The one and only." She looked at me expectantly. "You going to let me in?"

"Oh!" I backed out of her way. "Yeah, come on in. You surprised me."

"I know. Sorry to drop by unannounced. But I was missing ladybug and wanted to see her." She clutched the handle of her suitcase in her right hand. "Is she still awake?"

"No. Just put her to bed. How long are you staying?"

"A week at the most. Hope you don't mind."

Even if I did, she knew I'd have a hard time saying no to her. What would people say if I turned away my wife's sister? Not that I cared... well, yeah, I did. More so about what Marie would have said if I turned her away.

It would have upset her. She never turned her sister away, even when she was getting on her nerves, which was often.

"Of course not. Isaac just showed up today."

"Oh! I see. I didn't think he'd be here."

"He missed Dani too."

"She's such a sweet kid."

"That she is." I took her suitcase. "Let me show you to your room." Her room was downstairs. Isaac had already taken the spare room upstairs and I wasn't going to ask him to move. On the other side of the kitchen there was a hallway with three doors. One was a spare room. "Everything in here is new. Just got the bed last week."

"Lucky me."

I set her suitcase near the foot of the bed. "Good night."

She grinned. "Good night, and thank you for having me. Really. I missed you guys."

"Missed you too." I closed the door behind me and headed up to bed.

"Who was that?" Isaac met me on the stairs.

"Come on." I led him to my bedroom and closed the door behind us. "It's Jamie."

"Oh, come on!"

"Shhh!"

My brother threw his hands up in the air. "Why? Why is she here?"

"She wanted to see Dani just like you. She didn't know you were coming, and you didn't know she was coming."

"No." He moved until he was inches away from my face. "I didn't know she was coming. But she knew I was. When I talked to her, she was supposed to be going on a trip to Disney World with her kids and her husband. I told her I was coming to see you."

"When?"

He shrugged. "Yesterday. It was weird that she called out of the blue. We don't talk. I didn't even know she had my number, which reminds me that I need to change it, so this does not happen again."

"Why would she lie?" I leaned against the door.

"I don't know. I'll keep an eye on her for you but… something's not right. Why didn't she go on the trip? She not want me to spend more time with Dani than her?"

I moved away from the door so he could get out. "That might be it. She was jealous. Or maybe she just missed her sister."

"She does look just like her."

I nodded. She really did. More and more every day. It was almost unbearable. Marie should have been here to watch her turn into her twin.

"Night, Log." He opened the door and stepped through the threshold.

"Night Sac."

CHAPTER SEVEN

Riley Quinn

AFTER TALKING TO OUR CAPTAIN, WE DECIDED TO VISIT THE FAMILY.
"I don't see any other option." Captain Marcus Williams sat at his large wooden desk, looking through an old case file. "I hate to say it, but you have to let them know you found a body. If you want them to give you DNA to match it. There is no other way around it. I know it's hard to do but it must be done. And don't forget there is still another girl missing. We can't waste time if we want to find her."

He was right. It was a conversation I didn't want to have but we needed to have anyway.

"I thought so; I just wanted to see if there was another way around it. We'll go visit the family now. Search the house first."

"Ask if it's okay to look at her room before you tell them. It might be one of the parents. I hate to think it, but it might. Watch them and watch how they answer your questions. Body language is just as important as words."

"Noted," said Zelina.

The Baileys lived in the neighboring town. The street they lived on reminded me of the street I grew up on; quiet, with either a swing set or basketball hoop in every other yard. We stopped in front of their home. It was a beige-colored house with a bright yellow door.

"The door is cute." Zelina liked bright colors. After her grandmother died, she redecorated the house, making it brighter, bolder, and a place where patterns went to die.

"Of course you'd like it." The house stood out, the only brightly colored door on the street. I followed behind her as she walked up to the door and rang the doorbell.

The door was yanked open by a tall, burly man with our victim's eyes. My heart sank into my stomach. We had found the right house, the right family.

I held up my badge. "Hello—"

"Did you find Jade?"

My jaw twitched. "We're from the Pine Brooke police department. We need to ask you a few questions about your daughter and her missing friend. Can we come in?"

"Sure." The word practically jumped out of his mouth as he moved out of the way.

The house was just as nice and neat inside as it was outside. Someone was cooking. In the living room, a woman was sitting on the sofa. They were relatively young—maybe early forties. But I could see the signs of stress and grief and tension in the house.

"Is there anyone else home with you all?" I asked.

He shook his head. "Our boys are at a friend's house. Won't get back until later. Have you found her?"

"First, I need you to tell me about your daughter, especially the last day you saw her." I took out my notepad again to write their answers.

"We already gave a statement to the local police," he said. "What's the Pine Brooke PD doing here?"

"We're just following up on an investigation, sir," I said. "Please, if you could just tell us what happened."

"I don't understand why—"

"Matthew, please," Mrs. Bailey snapped from the couch. "If we can do something to help, we'll answer your questions."

I gave a polite smile. "Thank you, Mrs. Bailey. Do you mind taking us through what happened the day she disappeared?"

"Call me Heather. We saw her that morning," she said. "She was in good spirits. She had a test that she had studied for and was eager to take. Nothing seemed wrong."

"Did she always walk home with her friend Tiffany Cole?" asked Zelina.

Heather winced at the name. "Yeah, she did. I told her that girl was not a good friend. She's selfish and rude. She only cares about herself, but Jade likes to see the good in people. She's a good friend to her. They walked home every day."

"Same path?" I asked.

"I believe so," Mr. Bailey answered.

"Can I get a look at her room?" I asked.

Mr. and Mrs. Bailey shared a look before Matthew nodded and led me to the back. Zelina followed close behind. Heather stayed in the living room.

"This is it. Take whatever you need. Whatever you think will help you find her and bring her home." He tapped the door frame twice and walked away, back down the hall toward the living room.

Tears stung my eyes. She looked just like them. Her father's eyes. Her mother's lips and jawline. She was their daughter. I shook my head; a tear rolled down my cheek.

"I know," whispered Zelina.

Jade's room looked like my room did when I was her age. Pink everywhere. Pictures of famous boys I liked and shows I watched. Pictures of me with my friends tacked up everywhere.

Several pictures of her with Tiffany were on the wall. I took two of them and tucked them in my pocket. I also grabbed a hairbrush from her dresser. Her room had a twin bed, a dresser, and a desk. We looked through everything, everything that might lead us to who she met the day she disappeared.

"Think I found something."

I was bent over a drawer in her desk while Zelina checked underneath her mattress. She pulled out a pink and purple journal.

"Let's take that with us," I said, as we finished our search and returned to the living room. Mr. and Mrs. Bailey sat together on the sofa. I exhaled deeply, tapping the hairbrush lightly in my palm.

"Mr. and Mrs. Bailey, there's no way to sugarcoat this. I have to tell you that a body was found. A teenage girl—we have her at the morgue in Pine Brooke."

The sob that erupted from Heather Bailey's lips shook the walls around me. Her husband tucked her head into the crook of his neck to muffle the sound, barely holding it together himself as they held each other.

I sat there holding my breath, trading awkward looks with Zelina. I have never been good with breaking bad news to families. I didn't have to do it often, but it didn't matter how often I had to do it. It never got any easier to see. The sudden way people's faces fell, the way the light blinked out in their eyes as they realized in a single excruciating moment that their daughter was never coming back.

Matthew finally calmed himself after several deep breaths and turned to me. "You're sure it's her?"

"We aren't sure. We can do a DNA test, or you can come down to the morgue to identify her. It's up to you, really." I inched toward the door.

"I'll go," he said. "I'll go."

I nodded. "Okay."

"Umm… How about I ride with you in your car," said Zelina. She looked at me, and I nodded. It was a good idea that he wasn't alone, and I didn't see Heather moving.

"Okay. Let me get my neighbor to stay with my wife, and then we can go."

Heather sobbed into the sofa while he walked out the front door. Her body vibrated against the sofa.

"I'll go to the Coles and talk to them," I said. "I'll tell you what I learn."

"Noted."

I walked out the front door and passed Matthew.

"Was it just the one body?" he asked weakly.

"Yes, sir. So far, just the one."

He drew in a shaky breath. "I see." He headed back toward the house. The parents didn't seem to approve of Tiffany and Jade being friends. They didn't stop her from hanging out with her, but they disapproved. That made me curious.

I also noted, as I walked back to the car, that Tiffany's parents didn't report their daughter missing; the Baileys did in their report. So either they knew where she was, or they didn't care. It was difficult to picture parents not caring about their missing daughter. Difficult to fathom.

The Coles lived in a light gray house with a partially torn-down fence. It looked like someone tried to put it back together but gave up halfway through the endeavor.

I knocked on the door twice and then rang the doorbell. Minutes ticked by before someone finally answered the door.

I held up my badge immediately. "Hello. I'm from the Pine Brooke police department, and I need to speak with you about your daughter."

The woman stepped back and allowed me into the house. She closed the door behind me, and I really wished she hadn't. The Coles' home life seemed drastically different from the Baileys'. For starters, the house was a mess. It was several steps beyond messy. There were clothes everywhere in the living room. It wasn't as if someone was trying to put them away or separate them for washing. They were just strewn about the room for no rhyme or reason, and there was a smell. I couldn't place it, but I didn't like it. When she closed the door, all the fresh air evaporated.

"What about Tiffany?"

"When was the last time you saw her?" I took out my notepad to write down her answer and to give myself something else to focus on.

"Day they say she went missing, two weeks ago."

"Okay. How did she seem? Was she worried about anything?"

"How would I know? Teenagers don't talk to their parents. She seemed fine. I don't know why everyone is making a big deal about this. That's just how Tiff is. She runs off. She always comes back."

I knew there was a chance she might not come back this time, but I swallowed the words. "Do you know her friends? Who does she hang out with besides Jade?"

She shrugged. "I don't know who she hangs out with at school. She never brings anyone home. I've never seen anyone outside of Jade. Like I told the last cops and the Baileys, the girls are fine. They just ran off for a little while. They'll come back."

I sighed and tucked my notepad back into my pocket. "Do you have anything with Tiffany's DNA on it? A hairbrush? Toothbrush?"

She chuckled. "What for?" her arms folded across her chest.

"We found a body we believe to be Jade Bailey, but it could also be your daughter. We need her DNA to rule her out. Well, we might need it. Just in case. Mr. Bailey is on his way to the morgue to identify the girl, but just in case it isn't her, we need Tiffany's DNA."

Mrs. Cole showed the first ounce of emotion I had seen since I walked through the door. She stumbled back and collapsed onto the sofa. "You found a body?"

"This morning. She has no ID or anything, so we are trying to figure out who she is."

My phone buzzed in my back pocket. I took it out and glanced at the screen. I sighed. "It seems like we do not need her DNA."

"It's not her."

"It's Jade Bailey. He just identified her."

A sob bubbled up her throat. "Where is Tiffany?"

"I don't know, but we are looking for her. There was no sign of her at the scene. Can I look at her room?"

Tears streamed down her face as she pointed down a long, dark hall. "Last door on your right."

Tiffany's room was the direct opposite of Jade's. It was plain, with plain white walls and a bed, dresser, and desk. There was no pink, no frills, nothing girly. There was nothing on the walls, no pictures, no posters.

To me, it looked like Tiffany didn't want to get too comfortable in her room. No memories. Nothing to keep her there. She could have run away.

I would have asked her mother, but I doubted she would have noticed if Tiffany had rushed out with a larger bag than normal. Her room was clean, though. Where the rest of the house was a mess, her room was damn near spotless. The desk had been straightened. Her schoolbooks and notebooks arranged neatly.

It was remarkable. Nothing was out of place, which was rare for a teenager. The rest of the house, the rest of her life, was messy, but she kept her room in order. It was probably the only thing in this house she could control.

When I searched through her things, I did so gingerly. I didn't want to make a mess just in case she finally came home. I checked her desk and dresser first. There were some hidden condoms and cigarettes in the dresser, but nothing shocking. I made my way to her bed. Jade hid her journal underneath her mattress. I lifted Tiffany's mattress and found a black journal with a bleeding heart on the cover.

"Bingo." I flipped through it. It was her journal. I finished searching her room and then rejoined her mother in the living room.

"Do you mind if I take this?" I asked, holding up the journal and giving it a little shake.

But Mrs. Cole seemed distant.

"Ma'am?"

She blinked and refocused on me. "Oh. Sure... that's fine... take what you need," she muttered. She seemed to sink even further into the couch.

"Thank you so much for your time. If I hear anything about Tiffany, I will let you know as soon as possible."

She grunted out something that almost sounded like 'thank you', so I left. I felt bad for her. I felt bad for both families. The Baileys knew their daughter was dead, but the Coles were waiting to find out. The waiting was the hardest part. The not knowing. The agonizing uncertainty. The Baileys knew where their daughter was. Even though it was difficult to hear, they knew. But Mrs. Cole was now left wondering if her daughter had shared the same fate and until we found her, I wouldn't have an answer for her.

With the journal, I went back to the station. Zelina was still at the morgue with Mr. Bailey. He didn't want to leave his daughter. I asked her if she wanted me to come down, but she said no.

"I think right now he just needs to sit and let it sink in," she reported. "I'll sit with him for a little while. Keith's almost done with the prelim so you can pick me up when you come down for that."

I told her about the journal, and we reminisced about our journals from high school. I remembered mine, a royal blue cover with strings to tie it closed. I wrote in it every day, sometimes several times a day. I wrote everything in there, but I was never one of the girls who took it to school. I was too afraid someone would take it and read it out loud in the cafeteria like they did in the movies.

"I wrote in my journal every day, but I hid it from my grandmother."

"You thought she was going to read it when you weren't home?" My mother would have never read my journal. At least I didn't think she would…

"Girl, Dominican grandmothers have no respect for privacy. They don't even know the meaning of the word. Read while I'm gone? Ha! She would have had sat in my face and read it out loud so I could hear her. And dare me with her eyes to say something."

I laughed.

"I'm serious. I hid it in a different spot every morning while I was at school. And when I got home, I didn't want to keep it with me because then she would have asked 'why you always dragging that book around. What is it?' And then I'd have to give it to her."

"Did you imagine that entire scenario?"

"I know my people. I'm telling you, we had no privacy. My brother said something about privacy one day, I think she was looking through his drawers or something in his room. She said 'God and I always know what you are doing.' And she said it …like she was certain… like she wasn't exaggerating. It scared me. I still think about it sometimes, living in her house. Still feels like she's watching me."

"She must be so disappointed."

Zelina chuckled. "Rolling over in her grave and ready to fight."

"I'll let you know if I read anything juicy."

"Noted. I'll let you know if her father says anything interesting. I'll try to get him talking, but right now, I'm not too sure he's up to it."

CHAPTER EIGHT

Logan Elwood

OFF TO A GREAT START. THE SILENCE AT THE BREAKFAST TABLE WAS unusual for us. I made breakfast, eggs, sausage, and pancakes. Usually, we talked over our eggs, but now the silence was so thick that I couldn't cut it with a knife. Isaac made a joke about the pancakes, but Dani didn't even break a smile. She could sense something was wrong. Something was off.

I sensed it, too. I couldn't yet put my finger on it, but I never trusted Jamie. Her coming here after she learned my brother was coming to visit didn't sit right with me.

It didn't sit right with Isaac, either. I watched him, as he watched her out of the corner of his eye. Jamie sat at the table, picking over the eggs before settling on the pancakes, completely oblivious to the disturbance her presence had caused.

I understood she wanted to see Dani, but there was a way to do it. I had been keeping my circle relatively small since my wife died, letting in as few people as possible. Very few ventured out this far, and everyone who did called first. Even Isaac called first—granted he was right outside town—but still, there was a way to do it properly. She wanted something.

"So, what are your plans today?" Jamie asked before shoving a forkful of pancakes into her mouth.

"Work," I said.

She nodded slowly. "You work a lot of long hours, don't you?"

"That's what I'm here for," said Bonnie, matter-of-factly.

"Not as long as I used to, since I'm no longer working in the city."

"Hmm..." she pushed her plate away after only taking two bites of the pancakes. "I see. But Dani doesn't get your full attention. That's a shame."

"Well, someone has to work and provide for her," said Isaac. "Not everyone can afford to be a stay-at-home mom with an army of nannies. Some of us have to work."

Jamie looked at Isaac for the first time since she sat at the table. He stared back at her unflinching. They never liked each other. At one point Marie and I thought they would have made a good couple.

They were both flighty and free-spirited. But the instant they met, it was clear they wouldn't work.

"So you're *just* a bartender?" Jamie had said to Isaac the night we invited both of them over for dinner. Her head tilted slightly as she stared at him, taking him in.

"I am. What's wrong with that?"

Jamie smiled, but we all knew it wasn't genuine. It was that fake smile when you were about to hurt someone's feelings, but you wanted to soften the blow. "I mean, it's good if you're putting yourself through college or something but definitely not a lifetime plan. Not for me anyway."

Isaac leaned forward, resting his arms on the table. "And what do you do?"

"Jamie just graduated from college with a degree in medieval literature," Marie had said. She had kept her voice light, trying to lighten the mood, but it didn't work.

"So nothing," said Isaac. "A degree in medieval literature isn't really something you can do anything with. So let me guess, you're the type of girl who wants a man to take care of you so you can stay home and do what you are doing now... absolutely nothing."

The dinner was pretty much over after that. From that moment on, the two did not get along. They never liked being in the same room with each other, and when they were, it consisted of snide remarks and low blows.

"Does that include you? I can't remember the last time you even had a job." Jamie returned to their snide discussion.

Isaac's lips curled into a smile. "I've had several jobs since the last time you had one."

"Well, my husband works hard so he can provide for me and my children. Something you would never understand." She sipped her coffee, assuming that was the last of it.

But Isaac was never to let someone else have the last word. "He works hard because that's less time he has to spend with you. And that is something I fully understand and agree with."

Her smile faltered. Not because what he said was too harsh, but more likely because she thought he might have had a point.

"I bet if you called him now, he wouldn't even answer the phone. He's too busy celebrating his Jamie-free days. The kids are probably in on it too."

I looked at Dani, who had just shaken her head. She was a smart kid. We both knew when to interject and when something wasn't our fight. Jamie and Isaac's disdain for each other was not our fight. I finished eating my pancakes.

Jamie fished her phone out of her pocket and held it up like she was going to call him. Prove Isaac wrong. But she stopped. She stood up abruptly and tossed her napkin onto the table. "I don't have to prove anything to you." She walked back to the guest room and slammed the door.

"She just didn't want me to be right. But I bet you right now she's dialing his number to see if he'll answer. Judging by her attitude for the rest of the day, we'll know whether he did or not."

I rolled my eyes, but he was right. Jamie and Marie were the kind of people who could not hide how they were feeling. This one phone call would color the rest of her day.

"You shouldn't push her buttons like that, Isaac. We don't know why she's here," said Bonnie in a hushed tone. It was good to know that I wasn't the only one who found her sudden arrival suspicious.

"I know. But she keeps pushing mine."

"You haven't learned to let stuff go yet. You're too old to keep falling for this." Bonnie's tone was firm. I suppose she was going to be the adult in the room.

He shrugged. It was clear what she said hit a nerve. Isaac kept his head down as he ate his food. It reminded me of our childhood when our mother scolded him. He could never look her in the eye afterward.

Isaac walked Dani to school while I finished getting ready for work.

"I'll keep an eye on her," said Bonnie as I neared the door. She glanced back at the kitchen. "I might be wrong, but I just have a bad feeling."

I nodded slowly, my eyes fixed on the doorknob. "Yeah, me too." Jamie never did anything nice or thought about anyone but herself unless she was getting something out of it. She'd come because she wanted something.

I trusted Bonnie and knew she would watch her and tell me anything she thought I needed to know. Isaac strolled back to the house as I got in my car.

He leaned against the driver's side window and waited. I rolled the window down.

"Dani seems a little stressed."

"Maybe it's because you keep arguing with her aunt."

Isaac rolled his eyes. "Maybe. Or maybe she thinks something bad is going to happen. I know I do."

My heart sank. I tried my best to give Dani a normal life. Since her mother died… the first year especially had been a struggle. She kept looking for her and waiting at the door, expecting her to come home.

Since we moved to Pine Brooke, we've created a routine. It wasn't the same, but we made it work. The thought of her worrying was like a knife in the heart. She shouldn't have to worry about anything.

"Maybe she sees it as a bad omen," said Isaac. He pushed himself off the door. "I'll watch her, and I'll try to keep my snide remarks to myself."

"I appreciate that. And while you're here, try to look for a job." The engine roared to life.

He chuckled. "Already ahead of you. That coffee shop is hiring." His lips curled into a smirk. I rolled up the window and backed off the driveway.

Figures. He would try to get a job at that bakery in the hopes of seeing Riley. She wasn't even his type. It was a short drive to the clinic. Nicole was already there, of course. She sat at her desk with two cups of coffee; the steam curled into the air.

Her eyebrow shot up as soon as I walked through the door. "What's wrong?"

Nicole seemed to have a sixth sense that could read my emotions. I tried not to get too comfortable around her, but she made it difficult not to talk to her. It was both annoying and nice at the same time.

Since Marie died, I didn't want to let people in. I didn't need them. I just needed Dani. Nicole made it difficult to stay closed off, at least in the office.

"My sister-in-law came to visit." I picked up one of the cups. "She'll be here for a little while."

"Judging by the sound of your voice, you don't seem too happy about it."

"I'm not. Her presence has already changed the atmosphere of my house, and she's only been there for a night."

Nicole nodded slowly. "Okay. Well, put her ass in a hotel if she's messing with your peace."

A smile pulled at my lips. I wish I could have done that. I wanted to—for her and Isaac... but Dani loved her aunt. "She's Marie's sister. I can't just throw her out, no matter how hard I want to. It would have upset Marie."

"I suspect she knows that, and that's why she shows up unannounced."

I shrugged. She was probably right. The morning went by faster than usual. My brain tried to focus on my patients, but it couldn't. It kept spiraling.

Don't think. Don't think. No matter how many times I told myself to stop thinking about all the different scenarios that popped up in my brain, my brain said no and continued on its adventure. By noon, I was ready for a break and something to eat. Mostly, I needed the walk. I needed to clear my head. I tried to focus on other things, but my thoughts kept falling on Jamie and her reasons for being in Pine Brooke. Isaac's presence bothered me as well, just not as much. Isaac wouldn't try to take Dani from me; Jamie would.

Not because she loved her or wanted to take care of her, not because she thought she could take better care of Dani than I could. Solely because Dani was her last link to Marie, the last piece of her sister she could control, and so she wanted her.

The thought lit a roaring fire in my veins. I stalked angrily down the street toward the nearest diner, focusing more on the dark cloud brewing in my mind than where I was going. I rounded a corner and brushed past someone with my shoulder. They scoffed, but maybe they shouldn't have been in my way.

"Hey, what is the—Doctor Elwood?"

A shiver ran down my spine. The sound of the voice stopped me in my tracks. It was that cop who'd come in for her wrist the other day.

I turned around to see Riley there, her expression a mix of shock and fury. "Excuse you."

"Sorry," I managed. It was more of a mumble than anything else. "I wasn't watching where I was going."

She pressed her lips in a line. "Well, make sure you don't make a habit of that. I wouldn't want to have to give you a ticket for reckless walking."

I could tell that she was trying to lighten the mood with a joke, but I could barely even stand to be in this conversation right now. "Sure." I turned back toward the diner and barely made one step before she spoke again.

"Actually, I needed to talk to you."

I sighed loudly and turned around. "What do you want?"

Her eyebrows shot up. "I just wanted to ask you a question, maybe without the attitude."

"I don't understand how you can dislike my attitude so much and yet still go out of your way to talk to me. I am avoidable."

Riley threw her hands up and stumbled back. "Well, excuse me for thinking a doctor could help me."

"You are excused, now, please go away."

Her eyes narrowed at me. "It's a wonder you have any patients."

"It's a wonder you solve any cases. Now excuse me while I avoid you like the plague since my attitude is so disagreeable to you." I turned away. When I reached the door to the diner, I heard her say 'asshole' under her breath.

I sighed as I stepped inside, the cool air mingling with the sweat on my brow.

I shouldn't have done that, I thought as I slid into a booth. My anger at everyone else leaked out. I'd have to rectify that later. Even though she annoyed me, I wasn't angry with her. I wasn't really angry; I was worried. Anxious. Jamie consumed my every thought. I'd have to put it out of my mind for the day. I wouldn't bring up what I was thinking until she said something. If she wasn't thinking about trying to take Dani, I didn't want to put the thought in her head.

Instead, I'd focus on spending as much time with my daughter as possible, everyone else be damned.

CHAPTER NINE

Riley Quinn

"Why is he such an asshole?" I threw my lunch onto the passenger seat next to me and slammed the door. Every time I saw that man, he had an attitude. Sure, a horrible thing had happened to him, and I felt sympathy for him, but why take it out on me? I couldn't understand it. It was like I had done something to offend him or something. I drove back to the police station and made myself at home at my desk.

I was still combing through the journals and waiting for Zelina to call me back. She had gone down to the morgue with Matthew Bailey to wait for the prelim results and to learn any more information on his daughter and where she might have gone the days she went missing.

His grief was so heavy that being in the room with him felt like I was suffocating. Zelina handled grieving loved ones better than I did, so I always left it to her.

I was a faster reader than she was, so it was my job to read through the journals. Jade's journal was full of her thoughts on her family and the people in her life.

She thought they were suffocating her. When you're a teenager, your parent's concern often felt smothering. Asking how you were feeling, what you were doing, and where you were going felt intrusive and unwarranted. The reasons she gave for feeling that way seemed pretty normal. Her parents just wanted to be sure she was safe. And they had made it clear that they didn't like her friend Tiffany. They had nothing against her other friends, though. It was just Tiffany they didn't trust. The reasons they gave seemed solid. Concerns all parents would have. But I imagine if I was in her shoes, I wouldn't feel that way.

I don't know why they keep harping on the same shit over and over. Tiffany is my friend. My best friend. I don't understand why they can't just accept it. Accept her. She has helped me so much over the last few years at school. She is my ally. My only ally these days since the other girls don't talk to me anymore.

Mackenzie started that rumor and now no one wants to be my friend. But I still have Tiffany. I don't know why they can't understand that. They don't think about what I want, only what they want. But if Mom hadn't done what she did, I'd still have my friends.

I stared at the last words on the page chewing on the last bit of tomato from my roast beef sandwich. What had her mother done? What could she have done that would have cost Jade her friends?

I flipped back through the pages to see if she wrote about it. The journal looked like it covered a year's worth of her life. She didn't write in it every day, just when something important happened. Near the beginning, I found it.

She doesn't know that I know, but I do. I wonder if Dad has put it together yet. I'd be surprised if he hadn't. It seems like the whole town knows. She was having an affair with Mackenzie's dad. That's why she hates me now. It's not my fault. I have no control over my mother. I have no control over my life at all. How could she do this to us?

I want to tell Dad, but I think it would hurt him too much. How could he not know? It's all over school.

I leaned back in my chair. It was a nice tidbit of information, but I doubted it had anything to do with her murder. If the whole town knew about it, then it wasn't a secret worth killing over. But if Mackenzie was upset enough about the affair, maybe she would have attacked Jade.

I kept reading.

He knows. They only argue after we go to bed thinking we can't hear them. But I can. Dad sounds distraught every time he talks to her. His voice breaks like he is on the verge of tears. I hate her. If he leaves her, I will go with him. How could she do this to him? To us? What is wrong with her?

My fingers drummed against the table. Her father knew about the affair, but they must have worked it out when they were still together. Would Mackenzie's father kill Jade because her mother ended things with him? It seemed absurd, but I couldn't rule anything out just yet.

I wrote down my possible scenarios on my notepad.

I think they are staying together. While I'm happy Dad isn't going to leave, I don't understand how he can stay with her knowing what she did. Things haven't let up at school. Mackenzie is pissed because her parents are getting divorced. I guess her mom wasn't as understanding as my dad. She left her father and isn't taking Mackenzie with her. She doesn't get along with her dad, so I know she isn't going to like what's happening. She and her mom get along pretty well, so I'm sure she wants to go with her. Since all these changes, she's been taking her anger out on me. I don't get why. I thought we were friends. We were friends. And none of this is my fault. But I guess that doesn't matter. I've become her punching bag. She shoved me into my locker the other day for no reason. I was just walking down the hallway.

It sounded like Mackenzie wasn't good with anger management. She was frustrated, and the only person her age she could take it out on was Jade. She must have been pissed about her mother leaving her. She probably didn't understand why Jade's parents stayed together, and hers had split up—even though they had gone through the same tragic events.

She was angry. *Was she angry enough with Jade to kill her?* It wasn't Jade's fault, but so many times, children had to pay for the actions of the adults in their lives. And those two girls were paying the price, and it wasn't fair. I wondered for a moment if they knew. If the Baileys knew what was going on at school because of their decisions. I'd have to tell them.

I made a note to speak to Mackenzie once I learned her last name. High school girls were irrational, aggressive, and were prone to extreme emotional breakdowns. I knew; I'd been one myself. Maybe, with a combination of social pressures and bullying, one could get mad enough to kill.

I ate a bag of chips while I continued perusing the journal. Something strange caught my attention. It made the hairs on the back of my neck stand straight up. This might be a credible lead.

Mr. Hartley asked me to stay after school today. He's my favorite teacher. He told me how much he liked the book of poems I got him for his birthday. In return he gave me his favorite book of love poems. He even marked his favorites and told me once I read them, we could discuss them during lunch.

My heart pounded in my chest so hard I was surprised he didn't hear it. He's not like the other teachers. He's kind and understanding. He's only twenty-eight which makes him mature but not too old. He still gets how it feels to be a teenager. I feel like he gets me. I spend most of my lunch periods in his classroom.

Jade had a crush on her teacher and judging by his interactions with her, he didn't do anything to deter her. He flirted with her. He gave her poetry, read poetry to her and ate lunch with her most days.

It felt like a date. Just us, eating pasta and talking about poetry. My heart flutters every time he gets close to me. Is this what being in love feels like?

I sighed as I leaned back in my chair. That sounded like trouble. If he was encouraging her, I wonder how far it went. It didn't seem like he was keen to stop it. I added him to the list of people I needed to talk to.

"Bad Boys" blared from my desk drawer. "Yes?"

"The prelim is ready. He wants you to come down to the morgue."

"On my way." I hated going to the morgue. It was part of my job, but it was too cold, too quiet, and too still. The atmosphere was always heavy with grief and someone else's pain. It was too heavy a weight to carry. I never understood how Keith could work there.

Zelina paced near the front door. The morgue was just on the edge of town, as it was shared with the towns close by. "You find anything interesting?" she shouted as I walked up.

"A few things in her journal might prove fruitful. What about the prelim?"

Zelina shook her head. "You aren't going to like what you hear. He didn't tell me what he found," she said, opening the door. "But judging by his heavy sighs and furrowed brows, it's not pretty."

I followed her inside. Keith hated working the cases where the victims were children. We all did. Dealing with death was difficult, but when the body belonged to someone not even eighteen... a barely lived life snuffed out so early made it that much harder to come to grips with.

Zelina believed that all death, regardless of the number of years left, was difficult, especially for the loved ones. I knew she was right, and yet... the death of people younger than me always hit me harder than the others. I followed her down the long corridor. We rounded a corner and were faced with two doors. She opened the one on the end. Keith stood next to an exam table where a white sheet lay draped over a body.

"Nice of you two to join me," he said, a smile on the edge of his voice. "This one is going to be difficult. Just thought I should warn you now."

I braced myself for the details of the crime. I didn't want to know, but had to. For the things I wouldn't want to tell her parents even if they asked—and they always did.

"Understood," said Zelina.

"Okay. I'll start with the marks on her wrists and legs. She was restrained with handcuffs or something metal for a long period of time. She tried to free herself from the looks of it. The metal sliced through her skin and flesh until it reached the bone. From what I can tell, she struggled against the restraints. Her legs, too." He took a long, deep breath. "Now for what you can't see. I'll have to do a full examination later, but her internal injuries are vast. Most of which are from the fall."

"Is the fall what killed her?" I asked. She could have fallen and broken her neck, or her captor could have broken her neck and then tossed her over the edge.

"I believe so. She might have been trying to get away from her captor, stumbled, and fallen over the edge. Her neck broke on the way down. The contusions on her body match what we found on the rocks going down."

"Was she raped?" I asked. I figured that was where this was going and wanted to go ahead and get it out of the way.

He nodded slowly. "She was kept captive for a while. Some of the bruises and wounds had started healing. There's severe tearing... so much so that... it was infected. That might be why he decided to go ahead and get rid of her. She probably had a fever." He sighed as he uncovered her body and spread apart her legs.

Zelina gasped, her hand clamped over her mouth as she turned around. The trauma was evident. The tearing, the bruises on the insides of her thigh, some healed, some fresh. He covered her back up.

"I've had to do quite a few rape kits down here, and this is by far one of the worst I've ever seen. I've taken swabs for DNA, but I doubt we will find any. I scraped underneath her nails, but they were freshly clipped the day she died."

"If he thought to clip her nails, then chances are he made her take a shower," I said.

"A bath, more than likely. Even her toenails were clipped. He was both brutal and careful. And that makes me believe he's done this before."

My heart sank into my stomach. Was he a serial killer? Or a serial rapist? Or both?

"Let us know once you do your full examination. I want to know everything."

He looked at me for a long moment. "Of course. I'll move her to the top of the list, and I'll see if we have any other cases that might match hers."

"Thank you." When I turned around, Zelina was already standing next to the door, waiting for me. I hurried to join her, and we went outside.

"What if he has done this before, but no one has reported him?" she asked.

"Or what if he's good at getting rid of the bodies, and there's no one left to make a report?" I countered.

Zelina neared the car. "I like my scenario better. At least it gives us a fighting chance."

She had a point, and her scenario did as well. Mine was much more bleak and much more likely.

On the way back to the station, I told her everything I had learned so far from Jade's journal and showed her the passages about the teacher.

"This is concerning," she said. She typed his name into her computer. Mr. William Hartley was twenty-eight and had just moved to the area within the last year. He married his wife Alicia five years ago, and they had twin three-year-old boys.

"I wonder where he worked before." Before we talked to him, I wanted to know as much as possible. The more I knew about him, the better I could question him and pick out his lies. If he was flirting with her, chances were he had done something like this before.

While Zelina researched Mr. Hartley, I told her about Jade's ex-friend Mackenzie. She was surprised.

"They seemed so… I never would have guessed she had an affair earlier this year. They must be going to therapy or something to work it out."

"Probably. Mackenzie's mother left, and now she's stuck with her father. Judging by Jade's journal, she's really upset about it."

"Since Jade was raped, I would say she didn't have anything to do with it. Not unless she got one of her guy friends to do it."

I shrugged. "True. But Jade was kept somewhere for a long time. I'd be more likely to believe an adult had somewhere to keep her than a group of teenagers."

"Yeah, that's a good point." She turned her computer screen toward me. "Mr. Hartley worked at a school in New Jersey when he graduated from college. His reason for leaving is not listed, but he only worked at the school for under a year."

I wonder why.

CHAPTER TEN

Logan Elwood

T HE DAY DRAGGED ON AND ON. THE ONE BRIGHT SPOT WAS MY conversation with Mrs. Raydor. Her surgeon was releasing her from the hospital. I went to pick her up.
"You didn't have to do this. I could have taken a taxi or something."
"Of course not." I loaded her into the car. I wanted to talk to her about a job offer. Nicole and I had talked about it. I would mention it, just to plant the seed, and then Nicole would mention it a few days later when she stopped by her home to check on her, and make sure she was taking her pills.
Her working in the office would mean less work for Nicole and it gave me a chance to keep an eye on her. It also gave her something to do during the day which we both suspected was something she missed.

I eased out of the parking lot. "Besides, there was something I wanted to talk to you about."

"Really? Was there something wrong with my scan?"

"Oh! No. Your scans came back clean. I want to talk to you about working in the office with Nicole and me."

"Doing what?"

"Well, as the receptionist. Nicole is a nurse practitioner, so she can see patients on her own. Someone else there answering the phone and making appointments would ease her workload, and if she had more time to see patients, it would ease mine. And you are so personable and kind, you'd make a great receptionist. You'd get to see people, chat with us. We don't really get a ton of phone calls so it wouldn't be super intensive work. But you'd be a welcome addition to the clinic and I bet the patients would love you."

I watched her out of the corner of my eye. She stared at me for a long moment, uncertainty etched in the grooves of her face. "I'd have to think about it."

"That's fine. Take your time. It was just something we were thinking about the other day when we talked about bringing someone else on." I glanced at her. "Take your time and think about it. Get back to me or Nicole."

The rest of the ride back to her house was silent. I couldn't figure out what she was thinking. She didn't seem unhappy about the proposal but not thrilled either. She might have thought we were trying to keep an eye on her. We were, but that wasn't the only reason. The proposal worked well for all parties involved.

Mrs. Raydor didn't like asking for help because she didn't like putting people out. Her working in the office gave me a chance to monitor her health more closely.

Hopefully, she would think about it and realize it's a good idea. I walked her to her door, but she wouldn't let me inside.

"It's a mess in there. I haven't been home in days."

I told her I didn't mind, but she wouldn't hear it, so I left her on her front porch. Only when I backed out of her driveway did she go into her house and close her door. I hoped she would take the position we created for her, but I did my part. Now, it was back to the office.

When I finished for the day, I hurried home to see Dani. But when I got there, she was gone, and Isaac was on the sofa watching TV.

"Jamie took her for a girl's afternoon or some shit like that, she said. Dani seemed excited to go, so I didn't say anything. I figured you wouldn't want to stop her."

My shoulders dropped a little. I was looking forward to seeing her, but he was right. I didn't want to stop her from spending time with her aunt. Jamie was the only living link to her mother, and they should spend time together. I was just afraid of Jamie overstepping like she always did.

I slunk over to the sofa and sat down. Now, what was I supposed to do? Since Dani wasn't home, Bonnie disappeared into her room for some *me* time. Most likely, she was going to watch her stories and snack on some chips.

"You know you could hang out with me," said Isaac. "I am your brother."

I rolled my eyes. We hadn't hung out in a long time. I wasn't really in the mood for whatever he had planned for tonight.

"Come on. Let's do something fun. Let's go to a bar or something. Have fun with your brother." His voice was whiny and annoying, just like when we were kids, and he used to beg me to go outside with him.

"Fine... what do you want to do?"

He turned off the TV; his excitement was annoying but sweet. He bounced onto his feet. "I know just the place."

I was amazed at how he knew just the place, even though he had only been in town for a couple of days. Isaac ran upstairs and got dressed. He came back downstairs, giddy.

"Why are you so happy?" I stood by the front door waiting for him.

"You know how long it's been since we hung out? It's been forever. I'm just happy I get to hang out with my big brother."

I opened the door. I wasn't sure if he was genuine or not. It had been a while, but every time I met up with Isaac, he wanted something. He always needed something. I had nothing else to give, so I stayed away. I missed him... I missed all of them. But I couldn't get close to anyone... not anymore. It was better for everyone if I kept my distance, so I did.

"Yeah, it has been a minute."

"Three years. Not since..."

Not since Marie died. It didn't feel like it had been that long, and yet it felt like it had been an eternity since I had seen her. Not enough time and still too much.

"I'm driving." He snatched the keys out of my hand.

I sighed. I didn't feel like going anywhere. I didn't feel like seeing anyone. I just wanted a quiet night at home. "How about instead, let's walk."

I sighed again. Isaac nudged me with his shoulder. "Don't sigh so much."

I followed him out of the driveway and down the sidewalk. We rounded the corner and just kept walking. "Do you know where you're going?"

Isaac shrugged. "We're just walking, Log. Calm down. Just getting some night air."

I should have known he didn't have a plan. "You started looking for a job yet? How long are you staying anyway?" Isaac never stayed in one place too long. He moved around more than a military family: Florida, Alabama, New York, Washington, Oregon, Virginia, and London.

He shrugged again. "I was thinking about putting down roots here with you guys." He sighed. "I don't know. I'm tired of moving, and I miss you guys. Mostly Dani, but I miss you too."

"Thanks, I think."

"Just tired of constantly being on the go."

Now, knowing my brother, that could have meant a few things. He could have gotten into some trouble and figured no one would think to look for him here since we weren't that close. Or he could have realized it was too difficult being out in the world on his own without any support. Or he could have meant it. He missed us and wanted to be around more.

It was probably a combination of all three. "You tell your mother where you are?"

"You mean *our* mother? Yes, I did. She said she wished you guys would come and visit or call."

"Next time you talk to her, let her know the phone works both ways."

Isaac sighed next to me. My relationship with our mother wasn't my fault. It was hers. She didn't approve of my marriage to Marie and made it known. She never tried to make her feel comfortable or wanted.

"I can't believe you're marrying her. Is she pregnant? Because if she is, that doesn't mean you have to marry her."

She wasn't who my mother had wanted for me. By the time I was sixteen, my mother had my whole life planned out. She knew who I was going to marry and, what my profession would be, and where I would live: a three-story home with a guest house she could live in rent-free.

She pushed me to become a doctor, but it was something that I wanted to do. I couldn't say which came first, her wanting me to become a doctor or me falling in love with medicine. But either way it worked out.

She had wanted me to marry someone from her country club, the daughter of one of her friends. A family of prominence and old money. But I loved Marie. I thought she would come around eventually. I *thought* once she saw how happy I was she would learn to love her too. I thought once Marie got pregnant with her first grandchild, she would warm up to her and want to be involved with my little family.

Not only was she not at my wedding, but she refused to come to the baby shower and the birth of my daughter. She did, however, come to Marie's funeral. She supported her death but not our life together, and that was something I hadn't yet forgiven. If she wanted to talk to me, she'd have to make the first move.

"I get it. I'm just passing along the message. What you do with it is up to you."

He didn't get it. How could he? Our mother was more of a mother to him than me. I got the strict woman who threw her dreams at me and told me to make something of them, so I didn't disappoint her.

He got to make his own dreams. Follow his own path. And she supported him the whole way. He got an inheritance from our grandfather. I was written out of her will when I decided to go against her and marry Marie.

His mother stood by him no matter what he did. No matter how many mistakes he made. I did one thing that she didn't like, and I was written out of her will. I called her *his* mother because that was what she was. She was only a mother to him. How could he understand?

I swallowed my words, not wanting to ruin the silence between us. We argued about her from time to time. Well, we used to. Now, we barely spoke about her with each other. We both understood that she was a sore spot, an unhealing wound between us that was best left untouched if we were ever going to heal our relationship.

He changed the subject pretty quickly. "And for your information, I have been looking for a job. The town is so small, though."

"I think the bar is hiring."

Isaac winced at the comment. "I don't think me working in a bar is a good idea. But I put in an application at the coffee shop, the diner, and the grocery store. I guess we will see."

"That's good." Isaac was an amazing cook. He cooked better than anyone I knew. He was always like that. At the coffee shop, he could work in the bakery or take a job at the diner. Either of those would be good. We made a circle around the neighborhood. The night air was cool and crisp. It smelled like rain was coming. I welcomed it. The rain would help cool off the heat of the day.

By the time we looped by the house a second time, Jamie's car was in the driveway. My shoulders dropped a little. Dani was home. I didn't like the idea of her hanging out with Jamie for a long period of time. I had to keep reminding myself that Jamie was her aunt. Dani was Jamie's only link to Marie. It would be cruel to keep them apart. Marie would have been angry if I stopped them from seeing each other. That was the only thing that stopped me from keeping Jamie away from her.

Marie loved her sister so much that she often ignored her actions. Her love for her sister blinded her in many ways, although sometimes I thought she could see Jamie for what she was and just chose to ignore it.

She was manipulative and selfish. Everything had to be her way. The whole world had to be about her. When I first met Jamie, she was nice and pleasant, but everything changed once things between Marie and me got serious. Jamie came around more and tried to take up more and more of Marie's time. And when she tried to tell Jamie she was going somewhere or doing something with me, Jamie was upset. She acted like a five-year-old who had her favorite toy taken away. It was weird, but Marie seemed to be used to it. It was just how they were with each other. It annoyed the hell out of me, though. Marie had assumed that once Jamie had made a life for herself, she wouldn't be as clingy. She didn't live long enough to see it.

I rushed into the house just as Dani came bouncing down the stairs, grinning.

"Hey, papa. Auntie Jamie took me to get our nails done. See?" She shoved her hands in my face. I pulled them down so I could look at her nails, painted pink and purple with gold half-moons in the middle.

I smiled. "Very pretty. What else did you guys do?"

"Remember, Dani? It's our secret girl's day." Jamie's voice came from behind me. I spun around and saw her standing in the doorway to the kitchen. "Girls got to have our secrets."

I stared at her for a long moment. Dani wrapped her arms around my waist. "Love you. I'm gonna go watch TV with Uncle Sac."

I watched her walk away, and then my eyes returned to Jamie. "Are you serious?" I inched toward her, trying to keep my voice as light and steady as possible.

She blinked and took a step back. "What is your problem? She's my niece, and I can take her to get her nails done if I want to. She wanted to go."

"She's my daughter. You can't take her anywhere without my permission, which you did not have. And what you can't do is tell my daughter she can keep secrets from me. What did you do today?"

"You should have died instead of Marie. It should have been you," she spat. She spun on her heels and walked away.

My jaw twitched. *Who does she think she is?* Isaac eased into the kitchen in the wake of her absence.

"You okay?"

I leaned against the wall. Jamie was trying to turn her against me. I could see how it was all going to play out in my mind. She would suggest outings and places for them to go. And when Dani got all excited about going with her, she would tell her that I said she couldn't go. She'd make herself the fun aunt, and I was the mean father who didn't want her to do anything fun.

I wouldn't let her turn Dani against me.

CHAPTER ELEVEN

Riley Quinn

"Y**OU NEED TO EAT MORE. YOU ARE JUST SKIN AND BONES,**" SAID my mother as she gave me a once-over. It was the start of almost every conversation I had with her. Every time we saw each other, she told me I wasn't eating enough. I knew that I was. I wasn't skinny.

"I'm fine, Mama. I eat enough." I cook all of my own meals and try not to binge on fast food too much, even though I am tempted. Like that night, with the stress of the case, I was tempted to stop by a burger joint and spend at least thirty dollars. But I stopped myself. Instead, I went home for a family dinner. We had them on those nights when we could all get together.

You would think that would have been easy since we stayed in the same town, but it wasn't. My older brother was a coroner in Savannah,

Georgia. He was only home for a few weeks on a much-needed vacation. His last case had taken a toll, and he needed some distance—something I understood.

I stared at Allan on the front porch for a long moment as he pulled from his freshly lit cigarette. He looked like a different person.

His beard was fuller—not bushy and unkempt, but thicker than it was the last time I saw him. Flecks of gray hair dotted his hairline. The lines etched in his face were deeper and more pronounced. He blew wisps of smoke into the air and sighed.

"You thinking about quitting?"

He shrugged. "I don't know. It has crossed my mind a few times, especially lately."

"How bad was it?"

He took another long, slow pull of his cigarette. "I think it was a serial killer. I'm pretty sure, but no one wanted to hear it. One detective listened to me. Just one, but she's just starting out and has no real authority. If no one else gets on board, I think he'll get away with it."

I understood his frustration. Knowing something and being able to prove it were often two completely different things, and sometimes, they didn't go hand in hand.

"Trust your gut, is all I can say." It was all the advice I could offer. I had no standing in Savannah. I couldn't make a call or do anything else to help him. "And make sure you take excellent notes. Your suspicions, who you talked to, and what they said. And if you can record them, you should. At least that way, if they say later on that you didn't do something, or you didn't tell them, you have proof."

"I've been writing things down, but I haven't been recording them. I'll start when I get back. I just have a bad feeling about all of this. I just can't shake it. Something bad is going to happen." His voice was thin and small. He was really worried about this. I wished I could help him. I wished there was something I could do. Judging from our previous conversations, there was nothing concrete; everything he had was circumstantial, but there was a clear link between the cases. The similarities were too difficult to ignore.

"You two gonna stay out here moping, or are you going to come back inside and eat?" My mother phrased it like a question, but we both knew it wasn't one. Allan pressed his cigarette into the metal frame of the porch as I stood up. I pulled him to his feet.

"Thank you."

She opened the door wider so we could enter and then closed it behind us. The house smelled like roasted meat and garlic. Mama loved garlic; the more, the better.

I followed Allan to the dining room, where everyone waited for us at the table.

"'Bout time." My father sat at the head of the table as usual. He looked tired, as if it took everything in him to sit there with his eyes open. The rest of the family crowded around the long, gray wooden table. I had two brothers and a sister. Allan sat next to me, Dillon across from him, and Ayala next to him. My mother sat next to my father, as always.

There was a quick prayer before the food was passed around. I was starving, which was typical when I was stressed. It always made me hungry. Not really hungry... more as if I felt like I had to eat or snack on a bunch of stuff at the same time.

I'd been told it's called emotional eating. I tried to stop, but in some of the more difficult cases, it was hard to let go of the habit. The food made me feel better for a little while, anyway. My mother made pot roast with potatoes and carrots, and a mountain of garlic. She also made rice, gravy, and my grandmother's famous biscuits.

The biscuits alone were worth the interrogation I knew was coming. I had two helpings of roast and gravy with rice, four biscuits, and I popped the potatoes in my mouth like they were chips. I felt Allan's eyes on me. He noticed everything, even if he didn't comment on it.

"Rough case?" he whispered.

"We have no leads and a missing girl, and Oceanway PD hasn't been cooperative, so yeah, it's pretty rough. We cannot interview suspects just yet until everything gets cleared up with the school." Before I came back, there had been some trouble with the school in the next town over and the police. I didn't know the particulars, but ever since, the police department has had to clear any interviews or visits with the principal and coordinate with the school's security.

Our captain was trying to coordinate with the principal so we could do things on friendly terms. But as a last resort, we could go to their homes and interview them there.

I wanted to talk to Mackenzie and Mr. Hartley. It would be easier to interview her away from her parents. Mr. Hartley... it might be easier to interview him at home. Or at the school away from his wife...

Either way, we were waiting. I hoped it wasn't long.

"When do you go home?"

"This is his home," corrected my mother.

I rolled my eyes. "He knows what I mean."

Allan chuckled. "End of the week. The break has been good, though. Almost forgot how it was to sit around and do nothing. It's nice."

"I can't wait until retirement," said my father. He talked about retiring every week. He could retire, but we all doubted he ever would. He liked working too much to let it go. He liked having something to do every morning, somewhere to go. My mother rolled her eyes at his comment. We never talked about him retiring unless he brought it up. He knew we didn't believe him. A smile pulled at his lips when he spoke about retiring.

I glanced at Allan, who shook his head. One of these days, he might retire. He'd surprise us one day and just stay home without a word or any fanfare. He was like that. He wouldn't want a big fuss, and after a week or two, he'd find another job because the boredom was too much.

"It sounds nice," I said.

Ayala laughed. "You guys work too much. You need to take more breaks." She was a teacher, so when school was out, so was she. She got most of the summer off and major holidays; the rest of us didn't. However, she didn't make a lot of money and had to deal with kids all day, which was something I didn't envy.

"Yeah. We do need more breaks. Maybe a family vacation," said Allan.

I laughed. It was unlikely that any of us could agree to go to one place together. My mother would end up picking the place and making the arrangements and then complaining that she had to do everything herself, while we quietly complained about being in the place that she chose even though we didn't want to go.

No one said anything about the family vacation; my mother quickly changed the subject.

"So, what is this new case you're working on?"

I shoved the last piece of a biscuit into my mouth. Everyone's eyes were on me. I swallowed hard and chased it down with a sip of tea. "Missing girl was found in the woods."

My mother's eyes lit up. She loved all things true crime, books, podcasts, and TV shows. My father once joked that if something ever happened to him, my mother would do it.

"I thought that might be your case. That poor girl and her family."

"Yeah, notifying them was difficult. Now we are just looking for leads and interviews."

"I know there's more to it than that," said my mother.

"I will not be your fix for true crime. You'll have to read about it in the paper."

"Who reads the paper?"

Allan laughed next to me. Dillon chuckled while Ayala shook her head. She was always asking me about my cases. Most of them weren't interesting enough for her. But this one… she would be on my ass every day trying to get details.

Dinner went by as usual. We ate, and the children, now grown adults, helped put the food away and clean the kitchen. After a couple of hours in the living room talking and playing cards, it was time for me to go home. I was tired and had an early start tomorrow.

After a good night's sleep, I woke up before six, made coffee, and sat outside watching the water… and Luna running around chasing birds and butterflies.

The whole short ride to the station, I ran through the crime scene in my head. The position of the body, the vacant look in her eyes, the footprints in the dirt.

Honestly, I was starting to think she wasn't pushed. It was easy to stumble off the cliff in the middle of the night. Especially if you were frightened and running away from someone. Whoever took her might not have killed her, but they had taken her and held her captive for weeks. That still made them responsible for her death in my book. And we still needed to find Tiffany.

We needed to talk to her friends at school. I walked into the station two minutes before Zelina. She pulled her long dark brown hair into a messy bun.

"You look like you had a late night." I eyed her from my desk.

A slight smile eased across her lips. "I did have a late night."

And that was all I would get out of her. The male officers might have swapped stories of conquests and long nights, but we didn't. Zelina wasn't the kind of woman to kiss and tell, and I wasn't the kind of woman who asked questions that were none of my business. I didn't press her, and she didn't offer any details. I was curious, though. I swallowed my curiosity.

"While we are waiting for permission to go to the school, I want to search the area where the body was found. I feel like there's something we might have missed." I looked at Zelina waiting for her take on it.

"You think Tiffany might be up there?"

I shrugged. It was possible. He could have gotten rid of both their bodies, and maybe Jade got away. "I feel like they must have been taken together for them both to go missing around the same time."

Zelina nodded slowly. "Yeah. He could have gotten rid of Tiffany first, gone back for Jade, and somehow she was able to run away. Or maybe he still has Tiffany."

That was plausible. He could have gotten rid of one girl and kept the other for whatever reason. Maybe Jade caused trouble… although she didn't seem like the type. If anyone was going to give him trouble, it would have been Tiffany. She seemed the rebellious sort. Jade seemed like the kind of girl who would do whatever anyone asked of her. The kind of person who went along to get along. She wouldn't have wanted to rock the boat. The only way she would have run away from her captor was if she saw it as her only way out. She knew he wasn't going to let her go. If she didn't run, then she was dead. Turned out she was dead anyway.

"Or… maybe he knew she had an infection. Jade was getting sicker, and it wasn't like he could take her to the hospital or get her any antibiotics. Maybe that was why he was going to get rid of her and leave Tiffany behind."

"Now that is possible." Zelina glanced at the phone on her desk. "Yeah, another search might be warranted. A wider search. We still don't know how long she was running or where she was running from."

She picked up the phone and made a call for the techs to meet us there. We needed to do a wide search, and it would be handy to have them in too just in case we found something. If Tiffany hadn't gotten sick like Jade, chances were she was still alive. Judging by the evidence on her body, he kept her for the two weeks she had been missing. The fact that he didn't kill her right away told us a lot about him. He liked to hold on to his victims and make them suffer.

Two weeks was a long time. And if she hadn't gotten sick, who could say how long he was originally planning to keep her. We needed to find the person as soon as possible.

We informed the captain of where we were going. I popped my head into his office to see if he had heard anything from the principal.

"I haven't heard back yet. I'll let you know once I do. I imagine it shouldn't be a problem, but I still want to be sure. I'll call you when I know more."

That was his way of saying 'I'll let you know… don't ask me again'. Granted, I hadn't asked him that time, but I understood what he wasn't saying.

He and the principal had known each other for a long time. She might be more amenable to his asking than ours. Technically we didn't need her permission, but it would make things easier in the future. He told us to let him handle it, so I would go along. We had something we needed to do anyway.

"I don't like the look of that sky." Zelina stared up at the clouds as she walked to the car. I looked up.

The clouds were dark and looked heavy. My heart sank a little. That wasn't a good omen.

"We need to hurry up and see if there is anything we can find before it's all washed away."

CHAPTER TWELVE

Logan Elwood

MARIE ALWAYS LOVED IT WHEN IT RAINED. SHE'D OPEN THE WINdows and watch the rain beat against the house. She loved it. Said it was calming. Thunderstorms were also a favorite of hers. Dani must have gotten that from her. As soon as she saw how dark the clouds were on her way out the door, she got excited.

The morning was tense. An awkward silence hung in the air like a thick blanket. Isaac made breakfast, and while it was good, as it was so often, it was difficult to enjoy it with Jamie sitting across from me next to Dani.

"Just kick her out! Dude… it's your house. Your house, your kid. You don't have to let her stay here." Isaac placed the dishes in the sink with the help of Bonnie.

"You know we don't see eye to eye on a lot of things, but I agree with your brother. You don't let someone treat you like that in your home. She said you should have died instead of her sister." She shook her head. "What kind of person says shit like that?"

I blinked. Isaac's head snapped toward Bonnie, his lips twitching into a smile. She didn't curse, and the fact that she did made him giddy.

They were right, but I couldn't bring myself to do it. Truth be told, there were moments when I thought she was right. I should be dead instead of Marie; it would have been better that way.

Dani should have her mother. She'd be better off if she was raising her. And I knew Jamie was taking advantage of my love for her sister. Of course she was… that's what she did. And yet, even though I knew that, I still couldn't bring myself to kick her out. I kept thinking about Marie and what she would have wanted. She would have wanted us to get along for the sake of Dani; that's what she would have liked. And since I knew that, I'd try my best to do it even though some days Jamie made it impossible. I think she did it on purpose. She wanted to get me all riled up so I'd do something I shouldn't.

I had some problems with my anger in my teenage and college years, but all of that was behind me now. And it would stay there. She left shortly after Dani walked to school.

The house felt lighter without her in it. A dark cloud hovered in every room when she was there. It was so uncomfortable that Isaac and Bonnie either stayed in their rooms or outside on the patio. She was ruining the dynamic of my home and she didn't care. She probably didn't even notice how her presence affected everyone.

I was ready to go to work once Dani was at school. I looked forward to it just to get out of the house.

"What are you doing today?" I asked Isaac as I grabbed my bag and headed for the front door.

"I was thinking about going to the diner and seeing if they let me try out for the job. You know, showing them my skills may help me get the job."

"Okay. Don't bother Bonnie if you don't leave the house. She gets paid to watch Dani, not babysit you."

"Understood. I'll stay out of her way. You have a good day, and try to stop worrying. Jamie can't do anything. She doesn't have any legal standing. Relax."

I sighed. He was right, and yet I couldn't relax. I couldn't stop thinking about her being here and why. I knew she wanted something, and it wasn't just about spending time with her niece.

But that wasn't the only thing roaming around in my mind. I was too snappy with Riley when we bumped into each other at the diner. She had a question for me, and instead of being polite or concerned, I snapped at her. My anger and attitude got the best of me. I wasn't even mad at her. It was just all this shit with Jamie.

I needed to figure out a way to make it right. I couldn't say why it bothered me so much, but it did. What if it was a serious health question or about her wrist? It's literally my job to answer questions like that and I messed it up. Granted I was off the clock, but still.

Nicole sat at her desk typing something on her phone. She looked up when she saw me. "I sent our adventurous young patient another picture. If genital warts don't gross him out enough to wrap it up, he might be a lost cause."

"Has he responded to any of them?"

She checked her phone. "Mostly just throwing up emojis. I told him I'd rather he was throwing up than throwing something else around."

A soft chuckle escaped my lips. She had a point. If that kid didn't stop what he was doing, he was going to catch something worse than chlamydia. I figured him for a visual learner so these pictures might do something. I hoped they did.

"How was your night?" I asked.

She shrugged. "Same as all the others. Yours? Did you go out?"

"Walked around the neighborhood with my brother for a bit."

"That's nice. It's good that you guys are hanging out. Spending quality brother time."

I wiggled my head from side to side. She was right. It had been so long since we just spent time together. Whenever we did, we had to do so outside of the house. Our mother always seemed to want to pit us against each other whenever we were together. "Yeah, it was nice."

"Sister-in-law still in town?"

I rolled my eyes.

"I'll take that as a yes. Maybe she'll leave soon."

"Hopefully." I opened the door to my office and tossed my bag inside on the floor in front of my desk. "Who's first today?"

"Mr. Long. He said he was having some issues with his heart. I told him he might do better at the hospital. He said it wasn't that serious."

"Not that serious?"

She shook her head. Two braids slid from her ponytail and fell in front of her eyes. She tucked them behind her ear. "That's what he said, and he's had two heart attacks before, one mild and one massive."

"Yeah, I guess he would know better than anyone what it feels like. As soon as he gets in, check his blood pressure."

"That's what I was thinking."

People who have had heart attacks or strokes are much more likely to have another one. They are at risk of high blood pressure, so if that is what it is, we need to get him on some medication before he has another more fatal condition.

I was informed about Charles Long when I first started. Doctor Malcom gave me a rundown of his more complicated and stubborn patients, and Mr. Long was one of them. He hated taking medication and wanted to stick to his home remedies. Which sometimes worked, but for high blood pressure, we needed to get it down immediately before it caused other issues.

I'd have to work on my delivery with him. I went into my office and worked out what to say. While I waited, I went through his file. He had a mild heart attack three years ago. His massive heart attack happened last year. That was concerning. I wondered if he had been following his diet and getting any exercise.

Nicole knocked on my door an hour later. "Mr. Long is here, and he is… he's not happy. And his blood pressure is high."

"How high?"

"170 over 103."

I blinked. That's too high. "Okay. He's not going to like this conversation." I grabbed my stethoscope and hung it around my neck. Mr. Long was in the third exam room. He sat on the exam table with a scowl on his face. It was clear he had not been sticking to his diet. Last year, during his massive heart attack, he was almost three hundred pounds, and from the looks of it, he still was.

"Good morning, Charles. I hear you're having chest palpitations. How long has that been happening?"

He shrugged. "A week or two. Feels like my heart skips a beat or something. It's weird. But there's no pain. Not like with my heart attacks."

"I see." I sat on the stool across from him. "Your blood pressure is too high. And that can cause palpitations. After someone has had a heart attack or stroke, they are at risk of high blood pressure and having another cardiac event. You survived the last two, but if we don't get your blood pressure in check, then you might not survive the next one."

Charles's eyes went wide. It was like it just occurred to him he could die the next time. He cheated death twice, so he probably thought he was lucky that it wasn't a big deal.

He took a deep breath. "I've been trying. I just can't stay motivated to lose the weight. My wife has tried everything to motivate me. I might stick to it for a couple of weeks but then I… I don't know what happens."

"I understand that. It's something so many people go through. So here's what I'm going to do. Our first priority is lowering your blood pressure. We need to get that under control. So I'm going to write you a prescription for a blood pressure medication. Take it once a day in the morning. I know you don't like taking medication, and while I understand that, it is necessary right now. But if you show me you can lower it on your own, starting with weight loss, then we will see if we can wean you off of it."

He sighed. "How much weight should I lose?"

"Well for each ten pounds you lose will bring your blood pressure down a few points. Let's get it lowered first and then we will see if we can get you on a weight loss program that you can stick to. How does that sound?"

He shrugged. "I guess I have to, so I'll do it."

"Good." Nicole handed me a script pad, and I started filling out the prescription. "What's something you like to do?"

"Mostly sitting on my ass watching TV. Lately, anyway."

"Okay. What's something you used to like doing?"

He ran a hand through his short blonde hair. "I used to love hiking and swimming when I was younger. Too out of shape to do it now."

I handed the script to him. "Those are both things you can do to lose weight. With hiking, start slow. Short hikes until you get back into the groove. And swimming is great for weight loss."

"There's a pool at the YMCA," said Nicole. "There's classes and everything."

"You need to start small and work your way up to bigger things. So, on top of that prescription, I'm prescribing swimming twice a week. At least ten minutes."

He nodded his head. "I think I can do that."

"Okay. We'll do this for a month, and then when you come back, we'll see what we are working with."

"Okay, doc."

After Mr. Long left, another patient came in with almost the same problem. High blood pressure was almost pandemic, especially in this small town. Mrs. Rose had high blood pressure and was just coming in to see if she still needed the medication. She did. Her blood pressure was still high, and she had the occasional dizzy spell. I sent her for testing to see if we were dealing with just high blood pressure, or perhaps a blockage in her arteries.

"Lot of heart issues in this small town."

Nicole chuckled. "Yeah, we're mostly meat and potato eaters here. There are a lot of health issues, especially in the older ones. Once they retire, they just kind of sit around all day—most of them, but not all. Which I get. When I no longer have something to do one day…"

I laughed. We'd have to do something about *one day*. Get people more active, and maybe their health will improve. Some people are more apt to work out with a group of people than at home alone or take a walk by themselves.

"You look like you want to change that."

"I think we should try and do something. Heart health is important, and the best thing for it is a good diet and exercise. Might not be able to control their diet but we might be able to do something about the exercise."

Nicole smiled. "Look at you trying to get out and do things for the community."

My smile waned. That wasn't at all what I was trying to do. My plan for when I came here was to lay low. Do my job and go home to my daughter. I didn't want to get involved in the community. I didn't want to open up to people or get to know people, but that plan had pretty much gone to shit since I met Nicole.

She made it difficult for me to stay to myself, which Marie would have liked. She would have hated the original plan. If… if she was here, we would have integrated into the town by now. People would have wondered if we had lived there this whole time. She was that kind of person, welcoming, easy to talk to, and never met a stranger.

For me… everyone was a stranger unless we were blood-related, and some of them were strangers now, too. My cell phone vibrated in my back pocket. I sighed when I looked at the screen.

"Why is that ringtone the theme of *Psycho*?"

I looked up. Nicole was staring at me, a ghost of a smile on her lips. "Because it's my mother." I declined the call. She was only calling because Isaac was staying with me, and he was probably ducking her calls. We had nothing to say to each other. Not now anyway, I was working.

"Alright, who do we have next?"

Nicole stared at the schedule. "Lunch, we have lunch next. I'm starving, and I could really use a coffee. Let's go to the diner."

I shrugged at first but then I remembered Isaac was trying to get a job there and it might be worth going. I wondered if he was really trying or if he was just telling me he was. It was hard to say with him. I wanted to believe he was sincere about putting down roots and wanting to build a different life, I just wasn't sure about trusting him.

"You need to give people the benefit of the doubt." Marie used to say that damn near every day. I don't think she understood how hard that was.

"Okay. Let me put some files away, and we can head to the diner."

"Okay. But make it snappy."

CHAPTER THIRTEEN

Riley Quinn

BY THE TIME WE ARRIVED AT THE CLIFF, THE RAIN WAS A TORRENtial downpour, its relentless assault on the car creating a harsh, unyielding rhythm.

"I don't think we'll be finding anything out here today," said Zelina.

I thought we could wait it out. The rain came on suddenly, and I thought it would go away just as fast. It happened sometimes in California when it did rain. But I was wrong, and Zelina was right. The rain did not let up by noon. We decided to go to the diner and get something to eat and wait for it to let up a little.

"Did the forecast say anything about a storm coming?" I asked as we bolted from the car into the diner.

"Not that I remember."

THE GIRLS IN PINE BROOKE

The door closed behind me. The place was packed. It looked like everyone in the vicinity had the same idea: If you have to take shelter, you might as well do it where you can get something to eat.

"You can sit here!" A woman waved at us. Well, she waved at Zelina.

"Oh, that's Nicole." Zelina grabbed my hand and pulled me over to the booth.

"I guess we all had the same idea." Nicole slid over, and Zelina sat next to her.

I positioned myself on the edge of the booth next to her boss, the doctor with an annoying attitude. He didn't even look up when he slid over, closer to the window, like he couldn't stand to sit next to me.

I moved in a little, but I stayed as far away as I could. Zelina eyed me as the waitress returned to the table with two more mugs and menus.

"Do you two know each other?" asked Zelina once the waitress had walked away.

"We've met." I opened the menu and held up to block my face from Zelina's gaze. This was going to be a conversation later; I just knew it.

"I take it, it didn't go well," said Nicole. She looked at her boss, whose head was also buried in a menu.

"I guess not," added Zelina, who I could see was sharing a look with Nicole. I sighed behind the menu. I wasn't really looking at it. I got the same thing every time I came here. And she knew that.

"Usual?"

I nodded as I closed the menu. Everyone else ordered, and she took the menus and walked away.

"Shouldn't you two be working on a big case or something?" asked Nicole.

"We were trying," said Zelina. "The rain washed us out, as well as the crime scene. We couldn't even get to it." She sighed. "There'll probably be nothing left, once we can get out there."

I sighed. She was right. We should have gone earlier.

"Damn. The rain was pretty sudden. We just happened to be on our way here when it started pouring." Nicole tried to keep the conversation going.

Rude doctor didn't say anything, too busy staring out the window to be bothered with our little conversation. Nicole kept glancing out the window like she was expecting him to contribute. He didn't even look at her.

I took out my phone and started flipping through it, trying desperately to ignore how good he smelled—like eucalyptus, clean and fresh—and how broad his shoulders were.

Zelina and Nicole started talking to each other and ignoring our silence. I focused on my phone. I hadn't noticed when he moved in closer. His elbow brushed against mine, causing me to look up.

"Oh, sorry. Wouldn't want to be *disagreeable* to you," I snapped.

I expected him to fire back just as hard, but I was surprised when he sighed. "I'm sorry about the other day. I was mad about… something else, and I shouldn't have taken it out on you."

"Hope you sorted that something else out."

He gave me a weak smile. "I'm trying. I really am, but it looks like it will be around for a while. In any case, that doesn't mean I had to blow up at you like that."

I chewed my bottom lip for a moment. "Apology accepted, I guess. But dude, you got to work on your bedside manner."

"Yeah, I keep telling him that." A man walked over to the table with a wide grin on his face. "He's not a people person."

"He's working on it," said Nicole. "A lot better than he was when he got here." Nicole smiled at her boss.

A smile tugged at the corner of his mouth. He tried to shake it off, but I saw it. The man standing by the table looked like Doctor Elwood, but not quite. They shared the same nose and strong jaw.

"This is Logan's brother, Isaac. He's in town for a while." Nicole made the introductions.

"Nice to meet you all. And it will be a while." He gestured to his apron. "I got the job." He grinned.

The doctor smiled a wide, toothy grin. "That's great. They gave you a tryout?"

"Yeah, that was this morning. The owner liked my food and hired me an hour ago." He took a small bow. "And I will be making your food this afternoon."

"Don't put anything in mine."

He pointed at his brother. "I will try, but I make no promises."

Before Logan could say anything, his brother walked away laughing.

"He's going to put something in our food?" asked Zelina.

"Yours? No. Mine? Probably."

A soft chuckle bubbled up my throat. I'd put something in my brother's food, too, if I was making something for him. Nothing nasty, but something I knew he didn't like.

Zelina and Nicole continued their conversation while we waited for the food to come.

"What did you want to ask me?" His elbow brushed up against my forearm.

"Doesn't matter any longer. I asked my brother. He's a coroner."

He nodded slowly. "I wanted to do that at first."

"You have the disposition for it."

Logan's lips curled into a smile. "Not the first time I've heard that."

"Why didn't you?"

His smile faltered for a moment before disappearing completely. There was a story there.

"My mother told me there wasn't enough money in it. Said I should go with something else."

"My mother wanted me to be a lawyer."

He chuckled. "You have the disposition for it."

It was my turn to laugh. "I do like a good argument. It's one of my favorite things to do. But defending criminals was not for me, and prosecuting them didn't seem like much fun. I like solving puzzles, and I get to do that now. What happens after is someone else's problem."

"It figures arguing would be a pastime for you. Makes total sense now."

I laughed. "I know, right?"

The waitress returned with our food. I ordered a corned beef sandwich with roasted vegetables. Zel ordered a Cobb salad with sliced turkey and grilled chicken. Nicole ordered a burger and fries with fruit and Logan ordered a burger too… only he got roasted vegetables instead of fries.

He eyed our plates and then slowly nodded his head.

"Does this meet with your approval?" asked Zelina as she poured her dressing over her salad.

He smiled. "Yeah. It's all pretty healthy. Right now, at least."

Nicole laughed. "We were just talking about the town and our many heart issues. I told him we are mostly a meat and potatoes town."

Zelina laughed. "Yeah. This is just lunch. I don't know what I'm having for dinner tonight, but it's not this."

He laughed. "We need to do something about that."

"What, like weekly community hikes for the town? I don't think a lot of people would be interested," I noted before I began eating. The roasted broccoli, cauliflower, potatoes, and Brussels sprouts were seasoned perfectly.

"Something like that. Most of the patients I'm getting have some type of high blood pressure or heart issue. Should try to do something to get everyone up and moving."

"Might make it a game." Zelina stuffed a forkful of salad into her mouth. "Like a weekly treasure hunt or something. Stash a prize in town, and people have to walk around to find it."

His eyes lit up.

"Yeah, that would be fun. But you gotta make sure the price is worth getting off your ass and walking around for. I'm not hiking all over town for a pen or a key chain," I said.

Zelina pointed at me with her fork. "Exactly."

"That sounds like a plan," said Nicole. "I'll look into how we can set it up. Maybe we can get people to donate prizes like free swim classes or free coffee and doughnuts for a week."

"Should probably leave out the doughnuts," I said. "Defeats the purpose."

She laughed. "Good point. Yeah. I like this idea."

By the time we finished our food, it was still pouring rain outside. Lightning lit up the sky as the wind picked up.

"Yeah, I don't think you two are getting back to that crime scene today," said Nicole.

I sighed. That plan was a bust. Trees shook as the wind whipped around them.

"We should head back," said Logan. He paid for our meal. Said it was his way of apologizing. I slid back into the booth and next to the window. Before I could say anything to Zelina, I felt someone slide into the booth next to me. At first, it thought it was Logan. Maybe he forgot something, or maybe they decided not to go back in this weather just yet. But it wasn't him.

"Hi, Miley," said Zelina dryly.

"Hello, detectives," Miley grinned from ear to ear. It was a startling picture. Miley was known as the town gossip. If something happened in town, she knew about it. She knew everything. No one knew how or where she got her information from, but usually, she was right.

"I heard you two caught a difficult case."

"And who did you hear that from?" I asked after I finished my sandwich.

"Can't reveal my sources, but I hear it is a doozy. No leads? Do you know who the girl is yet?" She leaned forward with her elbows on the table.

Zelina mimicked her posture. "Would we tell you if we did?"

Her smile evaporated. "I'm just trying to help you."

"How are you trying to help us? By exchanging information? If you knew something… if you could, you would tell us what you knew without needing anything from us." I looked at Zelina, who smiled. Miley always wanted information from the police. I wondered what she was going to do with it. Extortion? She didn't seem like the type. I think she just liked knowing something no one else knew. It made her happy.

Her life was filled with nothing really. She lived far from her family, and she had few friends, because she kept spilling their secrets to everyone. Gossip was all she had. But I wouldn't be feeding her today.

Finally, understanding we weren't going to tell her anything about this case or any other if I could help it, she got up and went back to her table. I sighed with relief. I could finish my meal in peace. Miley eyed me from her table as she shoved a French fry into her mouth.

"She's not happy."

"Seriously? Can we just eat in peace?"

Zelina leaned back against the cushion. Then Kyle Richards appeared. He was like Miley, only he got paid for his research and acquiring stories. He worked for the local newspaper and spent a lot of time in this diner looking for a scoop. Just about everyone in town at some time or another ate at the diner. It was a good place to go hunting.

He slid in next to me. "I already know who the victim is, a Jade Bailey. We are running the story in the morning. Care to give us any details?"

"If you are running the story in the morning, then you already have all the details you need," I said. I finished the last of my lunch and pushed the plate away.

"Can't hurt to ask."

"But it can hurt to run the story. A family is grieving, and another is—"

I kicked Zelina in the leg underneath the table. We hadn't talked about Tiffany because we didn't know if she was missing or if she just ran away. It was possible she was taken at the same time as Jade, but she could have run away before then.

"Another is...?" He leaned forward.

Zelina waved her hand dismissively in his face. "Please go away and let us finish our food."

He smiled before sliding out of the booth and walking away. He irked me in so many ways. I understood he was just doing his job, but there was a way to do it. The Bailey family shouldn't have to see a picture of their daughter in the paper. Not before they even got to bury her.

On the other hand, the paper might scare up a lead. I doubted it, but it would be welcomed if it happened. He'd have all the details he wanted soon enough. The police department leaked like a faucet. He'd have all the information he wanted in a week or two. I just wished I knew who was feeding him and Miley information, and why.

A loud bang outside silenced the crowd eating lunch. I jumped up and leaned against the window, trying to get a better look at what was going on outside. The wind whirled trash around while the thunder roared. Rain slashed the window.

"It's getting worse," said Zelina. Lightning crackled in the dark sky. The lights flickered for a moment and then came back on. I looked at Zelina. We wouldn't be doing anything else today.

The lights flickered again, but this time, the lights went out.

"Saw that coming," I said.

Zelina groaned. With the lights out, everything stopped. Couldn't look up anything. Couldn't—

"Phone lines are down!" yelled the waitress as she set the phone back down on the hook. "Sorry. It looks like the lights are out all over town."

The sound of glass shattering was distant and alarming. Something must have flown into a window. It was too wild out there to investigate. I leaned back in the booth, checking my cell phone. It was out, too. Now, all we had to do was sit and wait for everything to be over.

Two hours later, the rain turned to a drizzle with thunder every few minutes.

"Well, that's something." I stood up. The power was still out, and the phone lines were still down. They would be for a while. Once everything went out, it took a little while and sometimes a few days to get everything back online. I headed outside to check the damage. The drizzle had lightened up even more. Tree branches were scattered all over the street. Tree limbs had landed on cars and buildings.

The loud crash from earlier turned out to be a large tree limb crashing into the store next door. It busted the window and looked like it went straight through the store all the way to the back.

We needed to go into clean up mode and the whole town would have to pitch in. I turned to Zelina who'd stepped up beside me. "Okay. Well, we need to get started with clean up and see who needs help and if power is down all over. Mike's should have some generators."

The clean-up took days. The neighboring towns were also hit. We helped them, too, but it took us until Saturday. With everything down, no work could be done anyway.

The storm had been a surprise to everyone, including the weatherman on the local news, who apologized once the power was back on.

"I should have seen it, and for that, I am so sorry. So many of you count on my forecast to plan your day, and I can't even imagine the panic the storm caused."

He sounded sincere. My mother thought it was stupid for him to apologize.

"What is he apologizing for? He's not God; he doesn't know everything. Sometimes the machines don't work. At least no one was hurt."

She was right about that. Surprisingly, no one was seriously hurt. Tree limbs and trash cans were blown all over the place. Crashed into windows and landed on cars, and there were a few people who had minor scratches and dents from debris floating around, but nothing major. So at least there was that. But the storm paused our investigation. We couldn't even interview the families or our suspects because it was all hands on deck cleaning up everything.

When we did finally get back to the cliff it was clear the rain had washed so much away. There were no more footprints, but thankfully we had taken molds of the ones that were there before.

"Let's just walk in the opposite direction," I said pointing to the cliff. It had been so long since I had been out there, but I knew the teens still used it for parties and making out. It was so out of the way no one could hear the loud music… or hear you scream.

Zelina and I walked straight back from the cliff, scanning the ground for anything that was not washed away by the storm. Both of us knew we weren't going to find anything.

"You know there are already rumors as to who killed her," said Zelina as we walked.

I tried not to pay attention to rumors; there were so many in a small town, and some were unwarranted.

"Is there now? And who is that?"

"Mr. Gil."

I stopped short. It had been so long since I heard that name. Mr. Gil was old when I was in elementary school. It was a surprise to hear that he was still alive.

"He does live around here." I pointed to the path between the trees. "All the way back there. He doesn't come out much or at all, really."

"Yeah, that's what I heard. I'm not saying he's the killer, but maybe he heard something or saw something."

"It's worth a shot. We'll follow the trail, and we'll end up at his house."

Zelina nodded. Mr. Gil was the town boogeyman. When I was younger, everyone was afraid of him. Even adults. I could never figure out why. I always assumed it was something that happened before I was born, but the more I thought about it… he was just different. He wasn't a people person and didn't like people in his house or around his property. He kept to himself. And even though the teenage kids were always messing with him, he never turned any of them in. He never reported the rocks or toilet paper being thrown at his house. He didn't do anything. From what I could tell, he just wanted to be left alone.

We followed the winding path through the trees until we came through an open field. "On the other side of this field, through those trees, should be his house."

"He lives on the edge of town."

As we neared the trees, I heard shouting. It was distant at first, but it got closer and closer with every step. *Who would be yelling all the way out here?*

It was two voices. One shaky and the other angry. My heart sank into my stomach as my body lurched into a run.

CHAPTER FOURTEEN

Riley Quinn

As I cut through the trees, Mr. Gil's home came into view. It looked the same: old and raggedy, and it was in desperate need of a remodel. It looked old and run down when I was a kid, and it hadn't changed a bit. Zelina picked up speed when she saw it.

Two men were on the front porch, one near the front door and the other on the steps pointing a gun.

I recognized him instantly: Matthew Bailey. As I neared the steps, I drew my weapon.

"Mr. Bailey!"

He spun around. "He killed my daughter. He did it. Everyone is saying it was him. Why haven't you arrested him yet?"

"There's no evidence he did anything. I know you are grieving, and it's hard to see straight. But I want you to listen to me for a moment… Mr. Gil is at least seventy years old. Look at him." His head spun around to the old, shaking man near the front door. Mr. Gil looked like it hurt him to breathe, let alone walk. "Do you think someone that frail could get your daughter into a car, drive off with her, and rape and torture her and then drag her to the woods? Does he look like he has that much strength?"

Matthew watched him for a long moment, and then the gun lowered. "Why haven't you found who killed her yet?"

"I'm so sorry Mr. Bailey. We are trying but it's not going to happen overnight." I took the gun out of his hand and handed it to Zelina. She grabbed Mr. Bailey while I walked over to Mr. Gil, who had already ducked back into his house. He watched me walk up the steps through the glass door.

"Hi, Mr. Gil. I think someone should take a look at your face." His cheek was bruised, and his lip was busted. He had bruises on his hands and upper arms.

"I'm fine. Don't worry about me." His voice was hoarse and shaking. "Just get him off my property. I'm sorry about his daughter, but I didn't have anything to do with it."

I glanced at Zelina, then back at Mr. Gil. "Do you want to press charges?"

"No! Just make him go."

I nodded slowly. "I'm going to bring someone up here to take a look at you. I'll be back."

I walked over to Zelina and Mr. Bailey. "He doesn't want to press charges. Don't come back up here. Let us do our job."

His shoulders slumped as he walked to his car.

"Guess we can head back to town now. I didn't find anything, but at least we were able to stop this from getting any worse."

I nodded and followed her back down the path. We drove back to town. I dropped her off at the station and headed to the clinic.

Logan was leaning over the desk talking to Nicole when I walked in. He looked up and forced a chuckle, but there was no humor in it. "Detective?"

"Doctor."

"You know, I was only joking before. I don't think Isaac would put anything in your food."

It took me a second to remember the joke from the other day. I shook my head. "Actually, I need your help with something."

Logan traded glances with Nicole. "Actually, I'm kind of busy…"

I looked around to the empty lobby and gestured wide. "Doesn't seem like it to me."

He groaned. "I'm not a coroner. I don't work with dead bodies."

"I promise you, the patient is alive."

He sighed. "What do you need?"

I explained about Mr. Gil and how he was beaten up but wouldn't leave his house.

Logan disappeared into his office and came back with a bag. "Alright, let's go. Hopefully, he'll let me in."

"Yeah, hopefully."

The ride was silent. He didn't seem like he was in a good mood, and I didn't want to push it. I didn't really feel like arguing. I just wanted to finish this and go home. I swallowed my words and my comments, which was so hard to do. I was curious about what or who in his life was pissing him off so much. His brother?

"Someone lives here?" he asked as I pulled up to the house.

"It's always looked like this… ever since I can remember. His wife was dead before I was born, and my mom said his life went downhill after that. She died, and then his newborn son. He was never the same." I opened the car door and jumped out.

"Yeah, I get how that changes everything." He slammed the car door behind him

My heart sunk a little for him. I didn't know the details of what had happened to his wife, but I didn't want to ask—and I definitely didn't want to participate in all the gossip around town.

I knocked on the glass door and then waited. I heard Mr. Gil shuffling on the other side.

After a long moment, the door opened. "What now? I told you I wasn't pressing no charges."

"I understand that. I told you I was going to bring someone to look at you. This is Doctor Logan Elwood. He's new in town."

Gil stared at him for a long moment.

Logan attempted a smile. "I'm not going to bite, but I do need to clean the cut on your lip and look at the bruises on your head and arms. I'll be quick."

Gil turned to me. "I do this, you'll leave?"

I nodded.

"Fine." Instead of inviting us in, he stepped out onto the porch and sat down on the metal chair next to the front window. "Do what you need to."

"Okay," Logan said slowly. He walked over and started examining Mr. Gil. He had a busted lip and some cuts and bruises but it seemed like he was going to be okay. He refused to go to the hospital to get his head examined.

"My head is fine."

"Okay." Logan didn't try to push. Mr. Gil had made up his mind, but he wasn't leaving. He bandaged up the cuts, gave him some Tylenol, and Mr. Gil went inside without saying another word.

"Thanks," I said as we walked back to the car.

"I take it he doesn't leave the house much."

I got in the car and closed the door. "Not since his family died. My mom said he stopped leaving if he didn't have to. When he was working, he went to work and then went home, and there was nothing else."

"Grief is a strong emotion. Crippling, even."

"Yeah, it does change you. Changes everything," I said softly. I could tell he was going through it, so I put on a smile. "Who has you in such a bad mood? You brother do something? You want me to arrest him?"

He chuckled. "Nah, surprisingly, he's behaving himself. Now, if you can arrest my sister-in-law, that would be great. Hold her indefinitely."

"I'll see what I can do. You need me to take you back to the clinic?"

"No, home is good. I'm taking my daughter to the movies."

"Oh, that's nice. Daddy-daughter day. My dad and I used to do that."

"Yeah, I try to spend as much time with her on the weekends as possible. Today is our day."

"Well I'll try not to disturb you for the rest of the day. Unless I'm arresting your sister-in-law."

He laughed. I dropped him off at his house and then drove back to the station.

"Where did you go?" Zelina sat at her desk, arms crossed, eyes narrowed.

"I took the doctor to check on Mr. Gil. He wouldn't go to the hospital, but his bruises and scrapes were treated."

"That bruise on his cheek was pretty bad."

I shrugged. "Couldn't force him to go, so I did what I could." I sat at my desk. "Learn anything new?"

"We have been cleared to talk to the kids at the school on Monday."

"Good."

"Parents have been notified, and if they don't want us speaking to their child, they need to sign a note. So far, it looks like it will be okay. Mr. Hartley will be available to us. The principal doesn't believe he had anything to do with it. He was her favorite teacher."

"I bet he was. I wonder why…" I had no proof he was doing anything with her, but the flirting and the poetry were suspect. It was at least worth a few questions.

I couldn't wait until Monday. The weekend went by fast and uneventful. I stayed home and mostly just cleaned. I cooked my meals for the week—well, my dinner, which consisted of baked chicken, roasted vegetables, and jasmine rice. Sunday night, I packed everything into my container and shoved it in the fridge. Then I ordered a pizza because I didn't feel like eating what I cooked, and I didn't want to cook anything else.

I went with the large meat lovers supreme, so I could have some vegetables… and a large glass of wine. Then settled in to watch a show about vampires, which was how I ended my night.

The next morning, I was up an hour earlier than usual. I read over the journals so I could refresh my memory on what I had read, and what had pissed me off. I wanted it to be fresh in my mind before I talked to Mackenzie and Mr. Hartley.

Zelina and I talked over the case last night, as we so often did. Either when I couldn't sleep, or she couldn't sleep, we'd call each other and talk everything out. It helped me see the case from her perspective as well as mine.

"I'm just not seeing Mackenzie having a dog in this fight. I mean, Jade was brutally raped. What kind of young girl—"

"You forget how cruel young teenage girls can be. If she wanted her to suffer like she was suffering, I think there was no limit to what she could do. Or have someone else do it for her. She might have watched."

Zelina took a deep breath. "Okay, point made. I'm still not seeing it, but I will reserve my judgment for when we talk to her."

"And I respect that. I'm judging everyone now, and when I meet them, because—I just am."

She chuckled. "The parents are still throwing me off, though. Even if your daughter ran away a lot, the fact that she could go missing for a couple of weeks and you don't even think about filing a report is insane to me. I just don't understand it. How could they just sit on their hands while she was missing?"

"I don't know. It was so weird being in that house. Part of me felt like she planned on leaving, you know. I looked at her room, and she definitely seemed like a planner. She could have looked for a way out. I would have."

We were on the line for a while, trying to figure out how one disappearance related to the other. By the time I went to bed, I had nothing.

It was odd, and it was difficult to say if they were together or not. And that was what bothered me. Did Tiffany leave on her own, or was she taken with Jade?

We made it to the school during first period, and the principal, Claudia Moreno, was waiting for us in the office when we arrived.

"I've talked with your captain, and he assured me this will be handled delicately."

I nodded. "I understand. We just have a few questions for their friends. Try to figure out what happened when they left the school."

"It's shocking. I still can't believe it. Jade was such… I mean, if this happened to Tiffany, I would have believed it. It wouldn't have surprised me at all. But Jade… she…" The principal shook her head. "I just can't believe it. The whole school is stunned. Anyway, you can talk to the students in the counselor's office," she said as she opened the door and waved us in.

CHAPTER FIFTEEN

Logan Elwood

Something about Mr. Gil piqued my curiosity. It wasn't that I believed he was capable of such a heinous act; his frailty seemed to contradict that. But there was something he was hiding. His weakness and his undernourished appearance all seemed to point to him not taking care of himself.

And the fact that he didn't want me in his house—either it wasn't clean or maybe he was a hoarder—might explain a few things. But the front of the house was neat and well taken care of. Someone had to cut his grass. It couldn't have been him. Maybe there was someone helping him. I hoped there was because he needed it.

I walked into the house, ready to see Dani. It was our father-daughter day—just us. It also gave Bonnie a break for the day, something she needed.

"Hey Papa, Auntie Jamie is coming with us."

My blood froze in my veins. "What??"

"Auntie Jamie wants to come and hang out with us."

Jamie bounced down the stairs behind her, grinning. "I haven't been to the movies in so long. This should be so much fun."

"Don't you take your own children to the movies?" I asked, trying to remove the anger in my voice.

"They aren't really into it. You know they are younger than Dani here. Hard for them to sit still for a twenty-minute show, let alone a movie." She chuckled softly.

"Can she come, Papa?"

I sighed. "Sure, why not." Dani looked so excited about her coming with us. I couldn't say no. I'd try to make the best of it no matter who came with us, but she knew it was our day. "Well, let's get going, shall we." I opened the door and let them both walk through. Before I could step through the threshold, I felt two firm hands on my shoulders. I spun around.

Bonnie stood behind me. "Try to make the best of it. She's trying to make it seem like you need her to help take care of Dani. She wants to be the fun aunt for some reason. I'm not sure what's going on, but don't let the hussy out of your sight. And don't let her get under your skin. I got the feeling she's going to try."

I nodded and walked out. She closed the door behind me. The two of them were already in the car when I got in.

"First movie and then food," said Dani.

"Yup."

The movie was not as interesting as I thought it was going to be. Dani wanted to see *Planet of the Apes*. The movie had come out decades ago but was being reshown in the local theaters. She was excited to see it, and I was too. I had watched it with her mother. But my mind was swirling with angry insults to Jamie. I sat on one side of Dani, and she sat on the other.

After the movie, we jumped into the car and headed to the diner to get something to eat.

"I'm surprised what passes for entertainment in a small town and their small-town movie theater. What did you think of the movie, Dani?"

"I liked it, Aunt Jamie. It was a little scary, but it was interesting. Makes me wonder if it could really happen."

"You three?" Isaac's eyes settled on Jamie first, narrowing the longer he looked at her.

"You work here, Uncle Sac?" Dani stared at him with large, questioning eyes.

"I do. I'm a cook. Just got the job the other day."

"That's where you've been going when you're not home. I told Miss Bonnie you had a lady."

"And what did she say?" I asked.

"She said she doubted that. She said Uncle Sac didn't have any game."

A smile pulled at my lips.

"I hope you avenged me," said Isaac.

"She might have," I said. "If she knew what game meant."

Isaac's shoulders slumped forward. "Gotta teach her more stuff. So is this your daddy-daughter day excursion?" he looked at Jamie.

"Daddy, daughter, and aunt day." She smiled at him. He rolled his eyes behind Dani.

"I'll leave you to it." Isaac walked away. Jamie asked Dani a question, and the two started talking.

My phone vibrated in my back pocket twice. The number wasn't saved on my phone.

Unknown Number: Sorry, I can't arrest your sister-in-law. No warrants out, and I looked.

Unknown Number: Sorry, this is Detective Quinn. Numbers pass around in a small town; got it from my mother, who got it from someone else. Sorry if it seems weird.

A smile bloomed on my lips. Riley actually looked her up, which surprised me. I saved the contact into my phone before typing out a response.

Me: Maybe you can get her on a technicality. Is being an incredibly annoying third wheel on my date with my daughter a crime?

Riley Quinn: Not in the state of California, at least.

Me: Damn.

Another text popped up while I was typing, this one from Isaac.

Isaac: I am definitely putting something in her food, don't you worry.

I hadn't been worried, until he said that. He couldn't mess with the food. If someone caught him, he'd get fired. I appreciated the sentiment, though.

Me: Leave the food alone. Don't get fired, but thanks for the thought.

Before I slid it back into my pocket, it vibrated again.

Isaac: I'll think about it. Might fart on her burger, haven't decided yet.

I wouldn't be ordering a burger, that I knew. I deleted the last two texts just in case something happened. He still didn't like Jamie, and I understood why.

Dinner seemed to breeze by. The most important thing was that Dani was happy. She beamed while she ate her chicken pasta and broccoli. She giggled while she talked to her aunt and her uncle, who couldn't seem to stay in the kitchen.

"You want to see what the kitchen looks like?"

Dani grinned as she took his hand without another word.

"We need to talk," Jamie said as soon as Dani was out of earshot. "Not now, but we do need to talk soon."

I looked at her, but her eyes were fixed on the kitchen doors. She was determined not to look at me. My heart sank into my stomach. Part of me felt like I knew what she wanted to talk about. I saw it coming.

I took out my phone and sent another text to Riley.

Me: Thanks for trying. I appreciate the thought. Have to work on another plan for now.

A few minutes later, my phone vibrated again.

Riley Quinn: Let me know what your plan is and if I can help. I owe you after your help today.

A chuckle escaped my mouth. At least I knew there was someone on my side just in case something happened. It made me feel a little better.

After Isaac took Dani on a tour of the kitchen, they returned with an ice cream cone.

"I should have known you were giving her some sugar this late."

Isaac shrugged. "Yeah. You knew this was going to happen." Dani grinned, chocolate dripping from her chin. She took a napkin and wiped her face. "It's really good."

"It looks like it." I put some cash down for the food. "You ready, daughter?"

She beamed. "Yup."

Jamie took her by the hand and led her out of the diner. I looked at Isaac, who shook his head. "This is going to be a conversation later."

"You know Mom called me?"

Isaac's eyes were as wide as saucers. "No! I didn't know. I wonder what it was about. I'll run interference for you. I'll call and ask what she wanted, and I'll tell her you were busy."

"If she's trying to do a visit—"

"I'll tell her not right now. You have enough going on. I'll let her know."

"Thanks, Sac. I'll see you tonight."

"Got it."

Jamie and Dani leaned against the car while Dani ate her ice cream. "Is Uncle Sac coming home with us now?"

I shook my head. "He's still working. He'll be back tonight. You want to go for a ride around town?"

She nodded. And so we did. I took all the quiet streets and looped around several times until she fell asleep in the back seat, her mouth sticky with chocolate ice cream.

CHAPTER SIXTEEN

Riley Quinn

MACKENZIE EVANS WAS THE FIRST STUDENT ON MY LIST—THE only student, really. I had so many questions I wanted to ask her about Jade since she and Jade had once been friends. It was clear that Jade's attacker was male, but that didn't mean Mackenzie couldn't have set everything up.

"Truth be told, it's more on Mackenzie's part than Jade. I don't think Jade wanted any problems with her. She wanted to still be friends. I think that's why when she did something to Jade, she didn't say anything," said the counselor. "I heard about it from the other students. I tried mediation, but… Mackenzie's just so angry that I couldn't get through to her. I doubt anyone could. She's just pissed about her mother."

"But it's not Jade's fault," said Zelina.

THE GIRLS IN PINE BROOKE

"True. I understand that, and you understand that, but they are children. She can't lash out at her father or her mother for leaving. Jade is the closest she can get to those involved in the situation. So Jade became the focus of her anger."

It was clear that everyone in town knew about the affair, which was unfortunate. It followed Jade wherever she went. She was suffering the consequences of her parents' actions and that wasn't fair. I understood what the counselor was saying, but that being said, it still didn't make what Mackenzie did okay. She should have found another way to channel her anger. A better way. A less destructive way. She was a teenager but that wasn't an excuse for making others' lives miserable.

The principal and the counselor put together a list of students who knew or hung out with both girls. Tiffany was still missing. She wasn't in school, or home, but we still weren't sure that she had been taken with Jade either. Until we knew otherwise, we needed to act like she was kidnapped with Jade.

Mackenzie was the first student to walk through the door with a scowl on her face. She looked exactly how I imagined her: shiny blonde hair, bright blue doe-like eyes, and a cruel smile. She smiled when she walked in, which I found strange. Jade, who had been her friend at some point, had been killed, and she was smiling. *I guess she didn't care about her after all.*

"What is this about, Ms. Claudia?" Mackenzie glanced around the room slowly. Her eyes lingered on me for a long moment before focusing on Zelina. "Did I do something wrong?" The smile on the edge of her words was unnerving. She acted like she had no idea why the police would be at the school.

"These are the police," said Ms. Claudia slowly. She stared at Mackenzie like she was waiting for her to ask another question.

I cleared my throat. "We are here about the murder of Jade Bailey. We heard you two were friends."

Mackenzie looked at Ms. Claudia and shrugged one shoulder. "We used to be friends, but that was a long time ago."

I wedged myself between her and the counselor, forcing her to look me in the eyes. Her face soured. She had this oblivious look on her face like she couldn't understand why we would want to speak to her. The look on her face was irritating.

"It doesn't bother you that she's been killed?"

Mackenzie looked at the wall to my left as she answered. "Should it? People die every day. I don't cry about those; why would I cry about her."

"She was your friend. Are you a psychopath?" I asked.

Her eyes met mine and narrowed slightly. "Of course not. I just don't care about her, that's all. She's dead, so what? I had nothing to do with it. It's not my problem."

"Okay. But you were picking on her and picking fights with her up until her disappearance. This makes you a suspect in her disappearance and her murder."

Her eyes went wide like it had just sunk in why we were there. Her arms folded across her chest. "You can't be serious. I didn't kill her. I didn't even notice she was missing. I don't care."

"You kept starting shit with her, though… you must have cared about her. You must have noticed when she wasn't around for you to mess with."

She blinked. "I didn't care enough to notice."

"She's dead," said Zelina. "You two were as thick as thieves, and then her mother screwed your father…"

Mackenzie's face distorted in anger.

"Broke up your happy home, and you took your anger out on Jade even though it wasn't her fault. You were friends, and your parents screwed that up. And you want us to believe that you don't care that she's dead?"

"Why are your eyes so red?" I asked.

Her eyes flickered toward me. The whites were a light shade of pink. Her eyes were slightly puffy. She had been crying; it was only evident when you got closer to her. Mackenzie stepped back.

"Your entourage isn't here," said Ms. Claudia. "You can cut out your attitude. We know—I know—you cared about Jade even though you want to act like you don't. We won't tell anyone, but they need to know who did this to her."

Mackenzie leaned against the door frame, her arms crossed around her small frame like she was hugging herself. "I don't know what you want me to say," she whispered. "Yeah, I was a bitch to her… I was just so angry… but I didn't kill her. I didn't have anything to do with this."

I sighed. Part of me believed her now. "When was the last time you saw her?"

She shrugged. "Couple of weeks ago, I think. I stuffed her in a locker. I didn't see her after that."

"Okay," said Zelina. "Is there anything that we should know about Jade? Was she dating anyone? Did anyone other than you have a problem with Jade?"

She shrugged, her eyes glued to the floor. "I don't know. I don't think so. She kept to herself lately. Just her and Tiffany, now."

"Why is that?" I asked. I had a feeling I knew the answer to that question, but I still wanted to hear her say it.

She swallowed. "After everyone heard about her mom and my dad, things kind of went downhill from there. We stopped hanging out with her. If her mother was a slut, she's probably one too."

"You know she's not," admonished Ms. Claudia.

Mackenzie stared at the wall for a long moment. "I don't know anything. People lie. Everybody lies."

"Is that why you stopped hanging out with Tiffany... because she wouldn't stop talking to Jade?"

Her head snapped back in my direction. "I never hung out with Tiffany. Jade might not have been a slut, but Tiffany definitely was. She would screw anything that showed her an ounce of attention, it was disgusting."

"I think Tiffany knew what it was like to be ostracized because of an unproven rumor. She befriended her and stood up for her when needed," Ms. Claudia interjected.

"Unproven rumor?" Mackenzie rolled her eyes. "Yeah, right."

"What was the rumor?" Zelina turned toward Ms. Claudia.

The counselor glanced at Mackenzie. "A senior claimed he had sex with Tiffany. Told everyone that she practically jumped him and begged him to do her. Tiffany said it never happened. He had tried to sleep with her, but she turned him down. That pissed him off, and he started spreading all those rumors. At least that was what she told me."

Mackenzie gaped at her. Apparently, she hadn't heard Tiffany's side of things. She probably never cared to ask.

"Based on his version of events, everyone took it and ran with it. Started calling her a whore and all that. Her family is pretty poor and has been known to get into trouble, so that didn't help. Tiffany does like older men, but I think that's because she's looking for a way out of town, and they can give her that."

"I don't know anything," said Mackenzie. "Can I go?"

"You don't know if there was someone that Jade would have gone away with? Someone she would have trusted to take her home if she didn't want to walk? Someone she would have run to if she was in trouble?"

Mackenzie's shoulders dropped a little. "She didn't have to run to anyone if she was in trouble. She had her parents. She had her dad. She always said she could turn to him instead of her mom."

"Did they not get along?"

She sighed. "I wouldn't say that, although, after the incident, things got intense. She just... she was always closer to her dad than her mom. I don't know why. They just always seemed closer in comparison to my dad and me. If she was in trouble or afraid, she would have called her father or gone to him. And he would have helped her, no questions asked." She shook her head. "I wish my dad was like that. Now he's just a drunk that likes to—" Her bottom lip eased in between her front teeth.

"Is there someone else you can stay with?" I asked. She looked at me, a long, hard look. It was like she was seeing me for the first time.

She shrugged. "No. I wanted to stay with my aunt, but my dad won't let me. Says I can't leave him too."

"If he wanted everyone to stay around, then he should have kept it in his pants," said Zelina.

A ghost of a smile kissed her lips. "Yeah, well, here we are."

I glanced at Zelina for a moment. "We will see what we can do about that. No point in you both being miserable because of his actions. You shouldn't have to pay for his sins."

Mackenzie's face softened. "Thanks." She chewed her lip for a moment. "I'm really sorry about Jade. I... I was such a bitch; I don't know why. She didn't deserve it."

I nodded. It was the first time since she walked in that she said something with even an ounce of feeling. Ms. Claudia opened the door and walked her out of the room. I turned around and looked at Zelina.

"She had to have been taken from the school or on the way home. She walked home. Someone could have stopped her while she was walking."

"She and Tiffany walked together; maybe it was someone Tiffany knew, and Jade went along with it."

The door opened again. Ms. Claudia stepped into the room with a male student following close behind. She closed the door behind him. "This is James McGaven. He's friends with Tiffany."

"Have y'all found her yet? She's never gone this long."

James' long black dreadlocks were pulled into a loose bun on top of his head. He wore black-rimmed glasses that he pushed up his nose.

"I'm sorry, no, we haven't. What can you tell us about Tiffany? Where would she have gone?"

He exhaled loudly. "I don't know. Usually, she ran off when things with her family got rough. She didn't like being there. She was beyond ready to get out of this town."

"Was it the town or her family?" asked Zelina.

I understood the urge to run away. I wanted to get away from my family, too, when I was a teenager. I just wanted to get as far away from this small-ass town as possible. But when things got tough, and the world knocked me down on my ass, I ran right back... to this small-ass town. As hard as I tried to get the hell away, I ran right back when I needed to. And it was here for me. And so was my family. But not everyone had that. My family was close at times, a little too close.

Tiffany's—they didn't even look for her when she didn't go home. Weren't even concerned because she had run away before. Once she left, I doubted she was coming back.

"Both. People in town aren't really nice to her because of her family. Her dad's been in and out of prison, and then her older brother and cousin killed those people a few years ago, and that just brought a bunch of shit down on her. She got the brunt of it. Her family is full of bad seeds, and therefore, she must be a bad seed too. But I promise you she's not. She's a good person."

"Do you know where she would run to? Is there someone she stays with when she needs a break?" asked Zelina.

"Me. When things get hard at home, she sneaks into my house. Well, she used to sneak, but now she just knocks. My mom knows she's there and lets her stay as long as she needs to. She's not at my place. She didn't call me or ask if she could come over. I don't know where she is."

"Is she seeing anyone?" I asked. Maybe she decided to stay at a boyfriend's house instead of his.

He shook his head. "Nope. She was when school started. Eddie Greer. They started dating during the summer."

"Why'd they break up?"

He shook his head. "His parents figured out who she was and about her brother and her family. His mother said her son wasn't dating a delinquent. Made him break it off. And so, I guess, to get brownie points; he told the guys that she was too easy. He didn't want to be with a girl who would give it away so easily, even though she only gave it to him because he kept begging for it."

I glanced at Zelina. "Yeah, that's usually how that works. And let me guess because he said that, a senior figured she was easy and tried to get with her. And when he couldn't, the rumor started."

James nodded. "Exactly. It's like you were there. He's the reason all these rumors got started. But after that, she hasn't really dated much in school—not like people think she does. She tries to keep to herself. Mostly, she's into older guys—guys that can get her out of this town. That's it."

"Did you hear anything about people bullying her? Threatening her?"

James nodded. "Yeah, she would get a lot of it. A lot of threats because of what happened to her family. You know. Kids just saying stuff to be cruel." Even as he said it, though, he furrowed his brow, seeming to be lost in thought. "But... the last day she was at school, she got a note shoved into her locker. It seemed to really freak her out."

I cut my eyes over to Ms. Claudia. She didn't seem surprised.

"I'm aware of some of the notes she received," she said. "Unfortunately, as much as we try to stop bullying, there's only so much we can do."

"Can you take us to her locker?" I asked James.

He nodded. "She's next to mine."

We walked down the hall until we came to the locker. Ms. Claudia pulled out a key and opened it, and James's eyes went wide.

"You can open our lockers?"

"Why don't you return to class, Mr. McGaven. We'll take it from here."

The kid looked at me pleadingly, as if I could convince her to let him stay, but I shook my head. "I promise. We'll do everything we can to find her."

I handed him my card and he slumped away.

I returned my attention to Tiffany's locker. Much like her room at home, it was organized and neat. Which made the crumpled piece of paper at the front of it even more obvious.

Zelina quickly snapped on some gloves, reached in and smoothed it out, then looked at me.

On the paper, in jagged, red letters, it said:

Their blood is on your hands.
You will pay.

CHAPTER SEVENTEEN

Riley Quinn

I turned my attention back to Ms. Claudia. "What happened with Tiffany's family?"

Her face soured immediately. Her shoulders dropped as she backed away and then rounded her desk. A heavy sigh escaped her lips as she sat down. Her hands clasped in front of her and rested on her stomach. "That is a long story... well, a series of long stories, actually. Long, seemingly never-ending stories that have swept through the town and landed at poor Tiffany's feet. I'm not too sure about her younger brother and what he's dealing with." She sighed.

"What happened?" I prodded. She acted as if she didn't want to tell us what was going on. I inched toward her desk. "What was it exactly?"

"Where to start... Well, her father has been in and out of prison for years. Robbery. Assault. Sexual assault. I think he's in prison now, actually."

"What about her brother?" asked Zelina.

Mrs. Claudia took a deep breath. "He was a good boy when he was younger. I don't know what happened as he got older. His teen years, he was in and out of trouble. Well... to make a long story short, he and his cousin killed two families."

"Two families?" I looked at Zelina as she eased down into a chair across from the desk.

"Yes. In a nice neighborhood. They broke into the homes and killed the families that lived there. Raping both of the mothers. Ten people in total. They didn't try to get away with it or, you know, not leave any evidence behind. There were fingerprints and DNA all over the place."

"They wanted to be caught?" I asked. "Why would they do all that? Did they know the families?"

"Nope. Never met them. They just picked a house and went in, and then they picked another one. No plan. No reason. Nothing. They wanted to kill, so they did. At least that's what the police said."

My ears pricked up at that. "Do you not believe that?"

Her eyes darted from me to Zelina. "I don't know. He was... I don't know. Some people said he did it. Others say he was set up."

"Why would someone set him up?" asked Zelina.

She shrugged. "I don't know. The rumor is that Larry had nothing to do with it. That he wasn't even there, and neither was his cousin. Rumor is that it was the Sheriff's son, Michael, and a friend of his who did it, and his father covered it up and blamed two boys who were known to get into trouble."

"You think it's plausible?" I asked.

She smiled tightly. "There is also a rumor that Michael has raped before. I don't think any charges were filed or anything. But rumor has it that he has done it before, and maybe he did it again. I don't know, and without evidence, I can't say whether I believe it or not. I do know Larry has never said he was innocent. He never said anything."

"He didn't confess?"

She shook her head. "He didn't say anything ever. He never helped with his defense or tried to proclaim his innocence. Nothing. It was really strange."

"What about his cousin?" asked Zelina. "Did he say anything about what they did?"

"Never got the chance. He was killed in jail while awaiting trial. Larry didn't even try to blame everything on him after he was dead. I mean, he was killed before Larry went to trial; his lawyer could have blamed it all on him and said he was afraid and went along with what his cousin wanted. I don't know if anyone would believe it, but it would have been some kind of defense."

I looked again at the note. "So Tiffany gets the brunt of the blame for all that?" To me that didn't make any sense. She didn't have anything to do with what her brother or her father did. It had nothing to do with her so why blame her? She was a child.

"Apparently. The Moore and Hayes families were well-loved. They had been part of this town almost since its inception. Their roots run deep, and the town is filled with cousins by blood and marriage. Yeah, they take it out on the family, and Tiffany gets the brunt of it. I think that's why she wants to leave so badly. I would."

"Yeah, me too. That's incredibly screwed up." I glanced at the door. I wonder if what her brother did had something to do with her being missing. Was that why she and Jade were taken?

"We'll be taking this for evidence," Zelina said, putting the note in a plastic bag. "It could be nothing… but it's worth a shot."

Claudia nodded nervously. "Thank you."

"Um… we need to speak with one of the teachers. Mr. Hartley. Is he available now?"

She blinked, her lips pressed into a hard line. "Oh, right."

"Unless you can think of any more students we should talk to."

She glanced down at her list. "Well, not really. The other names were in their classes. But no one saw anything. The most I was able to get from them was that they saw Jade walking home with Tiffany, as always."

"So the girls were together when they left the school?" I asked.

"That's my understanding. It was just any other day. Jade waited by Tiffany's locker. Tiffany joined her and then the girls were on their way. Now where they went once they left school grounds remains a mystery."

"Okay. Well, thank you for all your help."

"Of course and if any students come forward with information, I will let you know." She glanced down at her watch. "Mr. Hartley should have a free period right now. I'll walk you to his class." She jumped to her feet. I opened the door, and she walked out with Zelina following behind her. We walked through a maze of hallways until she stopped at a light green door. "Here we are." She knocked on the door twice before turning the knob. "Mr. Hartley?"

We followed her into the room. My jaw twitched at the sight before me. Mr. Hartley was perched on his desk. In front of him was a teenage girl seated at a student desk. Her back straightened when she saw us. I wasn't sure what I was looking at. The way he sat on his desk and the way she leaned forward both looked like they had been caught doing something they shouldn't have been doing.

She looked alarmed. The student stood up. "Um. Hi, Ms. Claudia."

"Miss Calloway. Shouldn't you be in the cafeteria?" Claudia looked at Mr. Hartley for a long moment. "These detectives need to speak with you about Jade Bailey. Come with me, Miss Calloway." Judging by the tone in her voice, it was clear Miss Calloway didn't have a choice in the matter. She swept her books into her arms and stomped out of the room without protest. Ms. Claudia closed the door behind them.

I stared at Mr. Hartley. He looked younger than he was. I understood why some of the female students might get swept up in his pale blue eyes and strong features. He ran a hand through his short black hair.

"I don't know what I can tell you about Jade. I didn't even know she was dead until I saw it on the news. I was concerned when she stopped showing up to class. She's one of my best students. She always came to class. She stayed behind. She was an excellent student."

"You were concerned, but you didn't try to contact anyone or alert the authorities. You didn't call her parents?"

He shrugged. "I didn't think it was my place to inform the police. I figured her parents would have done that, and they did. So I was right there. But other than that, I don't know what to tell you. She was a good kid, a sweet girl. She loved books, and reading was her main hobby. She loved poetry."

"I heard that she loved poetry." I glanced at Zelina. "You used to give her poetry, right? Love poems?"

Mr. Hartley glanced toward the door. He folded his arms across his chest. "Um... she asked what my favorite type of poetry was, so I loaned her a book. That was it."

"Of course. But you spent a lot of time with her. It's been difficult trying to find someone who actually spent a lot of time with her. If we could find her friend Tiffany, we could ask her, but she's missing, too."

He straightened. "She is? I didn't know that. I haven't seen her in class, but unlike with Jade, that isn't too unusual. She runs away a lot, but she always comes back. Are you sure she's missing?"

"We aren't sure. We haven't been able to locate her, and her parents don't know where she is. She went missing around the same time as Jade. And back to Jade... so I was reading her journal, and she talked about you a lot. A *lot*. She was infatuated with you." I inched closer to his desk.

He smiled a bit stiffly. "You know, teenage girls..." He chuckled. "They become infatuated all the time. It doesn't mean anything."

"Yeah, I know. But in her journal... the way she writes, she seems to think you were flirting back. Like you returned her feelings. I just wanted to ask you about that. If you had any ideas on why she might have felt that way."

He moved back behind the desk and sat down. "I don't know what to tell you. She was my student and nothing more. She might have been desperate for attention and clung to every ounce I gave her, but it wasn't anything improper on my end. I gave her some poems and nothing more. It's not as big of a deal as you are making it out to be. Trust me."

I looked at Zelina; she stared back at me.

"Sure. So everything was all in her head?" asked Zelina.

"Apparently. And I have to say I don't like what you two are insinuating. I would never date or flirt with a student."

"You looked a little cozy with the student who was just in here," said Zelina. I was glad I wasn't the only one that thought that. It looked... it felt like we had walked in on something we weren't supposed to see. They looked like they had been caught. It gave me an uneasy feeling in the pit of my stomach. Something was wrong. I was glad Claudia was with us when we walked in. The tone of her voice before she left said something wasn't right here.

"Well, I'm sorry you took it that way. We were just going over what we read today in class, Macbeth. Shakespeare can be difficult for this generation to understand. She was having a difficult time doing the homework, so I was just breaking it down for her. That is all."

That wasn't what it looked like. They were having a deep conversation, one that required him to sit on the edge of his desk and her to lean forward. Macbeth didn't do that.

"If you say so," I said. "But we are going to have to ask you a few more questions before your next class comes in. Have you been to Pine Brooke in the last week?"

"That's where she was found? What the hell was she doing there?"

I understood his surprise. I was curious as to why she was in our town myself. How did she go from walking home in her town to ours? If someone took her to the hill to get rid of her body and they came from this town, that made sense. The killer wouldn't want to get rid of her close to home. In another town, it made it seem like it wasn't connected to anyone here.

"Yes, that's where she was found. Were you there this past week?" I asked again.

His fingers drummed against the desk for a moment. "No. I was here... or at home. I usually am on most nights; you can ask my wife. I don't appreciate where you've taken this conversation. I've done nothing inappropriate with any of my students. All I am doing is trying to be the best teacher I can be. That is all."

"What can you tell us about Tiffany?" I asked, trying to get him away from being so defensive by asking questions about someone else.

He sighed. "She's definitely troubled. A good student if she would just apply herself. I think everyone kind of believes that her family is bad because of what her brother did, and everyone in her family must be equally horrible. She leans into that bad girl image instead... trying to prove them right. It's almost as if... if you think I'm like this, then I'm really going to be this person. She's not, though. I don't think she is. But I think she does it because of how she's treated."

"Almost like her suit of armor or something," said Zelina.

"Exactly. She does it to keep people at bay and to... I don't know. She likes to pretend that she has the toughest exterior, but I've seen her crying in the library. She wouldn't say what was wrong, but... I feel so bad for her sometimes."

I felt bad for her now. She was missing. She was somewhere and no one seemed to care, not even her parents. That was insane to me. James cared, but he was still a child and there wasn't much he could do right now.

"Okay. Thank you for your time," I said. Zelina eyed me as I walked to the door. I knew what she was thinking, but we had nothing to arrest him for. No proof, nothing. Sure, it looked like he had inappropriate relationships with his students, but without proof from a complainant, there was nothing to be done right now. And that was beyond upsetting. He was doing something. I knew it. I felt in the pit of my stomach. Something wasn't right about him. Something...

I knew. Zelina knew it. Ms. Claudia probably knew it now. Hopefully she would look into it. She could talk to the students during school hours. They already trusted her so it would be easier for her to get information out of them.

"Come on, Z," I said. I opened the door and stepped out into the hallway. Zelina followed me a moment later, annoyed.

"I know. I know," I said when we got back in the car. "But we have nothing to hold him on. A hunch is not evidence."

She sighed as she stuck the key into the ignition. She knew I was right. "But more importantly, I want to know more about Tiffany's brother and his case. I'm thinking someone might have wanted revenge and Jade was just collateral damage."

CHAPTER EIGHTEEN

Logan Elwood

I couldn't get the image of her smug face out of my mind. I was halfway into my day, and I couldn't get over how she looked at breakfast. Like she had done something or said something funny. Jamie had a permanent grin on her face that made both Isaac and I uneasy.

She insisted she walk Dani to school. Dani seemed so excited about the idea I couldn't say no.

"That woman is taking too many liberties," said Bonnie in a hushed tone as soon as the front door closed. "I don't want to speak ill of your family—"

"We don't like her either." Isaac leaned forward, resting his head in his hands. He and Bonnie had become friends or rather friendly since he had turned up almost unannounced on our front step. She liked him even more now that he got a job.

"I wouldn't say *we* don't like her."

"I know you wouldn't." He leaned toward Bonnie. "That's why I said it. "She—"

I looked at Isaac as he leaned back in his chair. "Never mind."

"What?"

He jumped to his feet. "Nothing. I got to get ready for work and so do you."

Bonnie's eyes narrowed. I glanced down at my watch. He was right; I needed to get a move on.

I was almost late for work, but I made it with a minute to spare before my first appointment. Even though I was at work, my mind kept drifting back to the breakfast table.

"How long have you had this type of headache?"

Mrs. Stokes sat on the exam table wearing sunglasses and a faint smile. "A few days now."

"And how intense is the pain?"

"Worst pain… worst headaches I've ever had."

I pushed all thoughts from my mind. The worst headache she ever had was concerning. "Is it just a headache, no other symptoms?"

"No. Just the pain on the right side of my head."

"Okay. Nicole is going to take your blood pressure while I take a look at your eyes."

Nicole wrapped the blood pressure cuff around her bicep, and I fished my flashlight out of my pocket. I used the light to look into her eyes. There was a delayed reaction to her right pupil, and it was slightly dilated.

"Okay." I turned the flashlight off and slid it back into my pocket. When I looked up, Nicole was staring at me, eyes narrowed and her jaw set. Something was wrong.

She turned the monitor so I could see the screen. My mouth went dry instantly.

"Okay, we need to get you to the hospital. Can you lift your arms up for me?" I tried to remove the panic from my voice. If I stayed calm, then so would she, but now wasn't a calming time. It was time for fast action.

She raised both her arms. While her left arm went straight up the right one wavered, the tips of her fingers only making it as far as the top of her ear. She looked at the arm.

"That's not right, is it?"

I shook my head. "No, but we're going to get you to the hospital so we can fix it."

"It would be quicker to drive her," said Nicole. I agreed. Mrs. Stokes' blood pressure was 212 over 172. She was having a stroke. Nicole gave her some medicine to stabilize her while she was on the way. I jumped into the car after we helped her into the back seat. Nicole stayed behind just in case someone else showed up for an emergency.

I sped down the highway to Woodvine. As soon as I pulled up to the ER, an ambulance was pulling out. I jumped out, leaving the key still in the ignition. I opened Mrs. Stokes's door just as a nurse rushed out of the double doors.

"This is my patient, Elaine Stokes; she's having a stroke. Blood pressure 212 over 172 with a persistent headache on the right side of her head, delayed pupil reaction, and inability to raise her right arm."

While I spoke, the nurse signaled for two men and a gurney to come outside. We strapped her in, and they took her away. "I'll park, and then I'll come right in," I said as they wheeled her away, panic frozen into the grooves of her face. I jumped back in the car and drove through the parking lot until I found a parking space near the front.

I sent a text to Nicole on my way back to the building, telling her we made it.

Nicole had called Mrs. Stokes' daughter as soon as we left and let her know which hospital we were going to. I didn't want to leave her alone—she already looked so frightened. And I wanted to be there for her daughter to explain what was going on.

Mrs. Stokes had two aneurysms. One surprisingly large. The surgeon allowed me to look at her MRI, and we both explained it to her and her daughter before she went into surgery. One of them had ruptured and caused a slow bleed on her brain; if she hadn't come in when she did and had gone to bed like she was planning, she wouldn't have woken up again. The surgery was going to be a long one, lasting anywhere from six to ten hours. I called Nicole and told her what was going on while I waited in the waiting room with Elise, her daughter. She kept her purse clutched tight to her body, her right leg vibrating in anxiety. When I finished the call, I slid into the seat next to her.

"I know this is difficult right now, but try to stay positive," I said. I didn't want to tell her that everything was going to be okay. I knew all too well how that wasn't true. Anything could happen on the operating table. Anything could happen while they wheeled her back to her room. Anything could happen in the nights after the surgery. It was never a certainty. But I didn't say that. I didn't dwell on the fact that her surgeon gave her a thirty percent chance of survival, and even then, he wasn't too optimistic. I didn't dwell on what could go wrong or how long it should take.

Instead I just sat next to her. And I would for as long as it would take to ensure she wasn't alone.

The surgery took seven hours. My heart practically jumped out of my chest when her phone started ringing. She looked at me wide-eyed as she pulled it from her purse.

"Hello?" Her eyes closed as tears streamed down her face. "Really? She's okay?"

I leaned back as she hung up the phone. "Everything go well?"

She nodded slowly. "He said that she came through it alright, but we won't know the extent of the damage until she wakes up. He said the other aneurysm was small, and so he wasn't worried about it right now because it hadn't ruptured yet."

"That's good."

"What if it does?"

I inhaled deeply, the smell of sanitizer filled my nose. "Well she will probably be on blood thinners and an aspirin regimen for a while. That might help the smaller one dissolve and no surgery would be needed. But the fact that he isn't worried about it tells me she isn't in any danger from it right now. And that's good. Let's just focus on what is and not what could be."

She nodded. "You're right. He said we could see her in a little bit. A nurse will come and get us unless you have somewhere to go."

I looked at her. She had her mother's eyes, big and light brown and scared. Not just scared but worried and hoping I wouldn't leave. I glanced down at my watch. It was almost six o'clock. "No, I'm here. I want to see her before I go anyway." I wanted to see how she'd come out of the anesthesia and if she had her motor skills or not. She had a stroke, and that was something serious. It could affect her in so many ways.

We waited another thirty minutes, and then a nurse, bright-eyed and soft-voiced, appeared out of nowhere in front of us. "I can take you now, Ms. Stokes."

We both jumped to our feet. She led us through two thick double doors, a long hallway, and then round a corner. we stopped at a sliding glass door. She opened it and we stepped inside. I stayed back while Elise walked over to her mother and grabbed her hand. She kissed her fingers, and Elaine lifted her head, smiling at her daughter. I noticed there was a slight drooping to her face. Elise noticed it too.

"All in all, she's doing okay," I called Nicole as soon as I got back in my car. "There is some muscle weakness on her right side, but her memory seems to be okay."

"That's a relief. I've already closed up for the day, so you can go ahead and head home."

"Thanks." It was after ten when I finally walked through the door. Isaac was still on the sofa. He perked up when he saw me.

"What happened?"

"Patient was having a stroke, so I had to take her to the hospital. Dani asleep?" I collapsed onto the sofa next to him.

"A few hours ago. Tried to wait up for you but it was past her bedtime and Bonnie wasn't having it." He glanced toward the kitchen. "Saved you some dinner though."

I was hungry, but I didn't feel like getting up. "I'll get it before I go to bed."

"I think Jamie was waiting for you too. She was pacing around here a few minutes ago before she finally went to bed."

It had been a long day, and I didn't feel like dealing with her bullshit. "Glad I missed her." We watched a little TV together. I opted for a sandwich before bed instead of heating up leftovers. I crawled into bed close to midnight.

"Did something happen yesterday?" asked Dani as soon as I sat at the table for breakfast. "You got home late."

"I know, and I'm sorry. A patient was having a stroke, so I had to take her to the hospital. And then I sat with her daughter during the surgery because she was scared, and she didn't have anyone else."

"Is she okay?" she stabbed a piece of sausage with her fork.

"I believe so. She will be. The surgery went well."

"But still, you miss so many dinners," said Jamie. She sipped her coffee slowly.

"He's saving lives," said Dani.

"And I understand that, but your life is important too."

The whole table remained completely still except for Dani, who kept eating her eggs. She paid Jamie no attention. I glared at her, and Jamie smiled.

"I'm just saying she is important. She should be the most important thing in your life, just as my kids are to me."

"And yet here you are away from your own kids for so long," said Isaac.

"Well, I felt like Dani could use a mother figure for a couple of days. Someone to spend time with and give her what she is missing."

My fork slipped out of my hands. "I need to get to work." I stood up and kissed Dani on the forehead. "Have a good day and behave yourself."

"I will, Papa. I always do."

"You too, Isaac."

"I usually don't, but I'll give it a try."

I rounded the table.

"Hey, how come I don't get a kiss on the forehead?"

"I'm not kissing you, Sac!" I called back as I headed to the front door.

"That's not fair!"

"I'll give you a kiss, Uncle Sac; come here."

I sighed as I reached for the doorknob. It was about to be the longest day in history.

The morning whirled by. Nicole and I both wondered if time was moving faster today for some reason. For lunch, she went home and ate with her mother while I was at the diner.

"Hey, how's the sister-in-law?"

The sound of her voice brought a smile to my face. Something I hadn't done all day. I looked to my right, and Riley Quinn sat by herself in a booth. I walked over to her.

"Still around," I said as I slid into the booth. "Still around."

"And that does not make you happy?"

I shrugged. "What was it you wanted to ask me the other day? I keep thinking about it."

A smile tugged at her lips. "We found a body... I guess I wanted to know how long it would take for someone to starve to death."

"You think the person starved to death?"

"No. We know she fell off a cliff and broke her neck on the way down, but someone was keeping her for two weeks. I saw pictures at her mother's home and she... when I saw her, she was emaciated. I mean, in two weeks, she looked like an entirely different person. You could see her bones. And the M.E. said she had an untreated infection."

"Hmmm, well, without food, you can last almost three weeks but that is only if you are staying hydrated. While the body can survive without food for a little while, it can't survive without water. Without hydration, maybe a week, maybe less."

"Yeah, that's what my brother said. Maybe he was keeping her hydrated."

"But with an infection, it might not have been enough. And that's assuming she could keep anything down."

"Right..." Her fingers drummed against the table.

"Stumped, huh?"

She smiled. "Yeah, I am. I just can't stop thinking about her and her family, her missing friend, and her creepy teacher."

"That's a lot to unpack there."

"We're still investigating. I just stopped in to pick something up and take it back to the station. Haven't left our desk in a couple of days."

"Yeah, I get like that sometimes. I get so focused on something that the rest of the world ceases to matter. That's why I had to get out of ER medicine and find a more stable practice."

"Can't be consumed by puzzles anymore?"

I shrugged. "Not since my wife died. I have a nanny, but I don't want to put more pressure on her than I have to. I wanted to focus on my daughter, and in order to do that, I had to make a change. However, there are complicated cases here, too. And ones that require a lot of attention."

"Small towns can get complicated."

"Yeah, I wasn't expecting that." I glanced through the menu on the table. "Full of surprises."

Riley smiled. It was a real, genuine smile, not just a polite one that she usually put on. It made her blue eyes sparkle. "Well, I'm glad we can keep you on your toes."

I chuckled nervously. "Yeah."

A waitress walked over and set a large bag down, packed with smaller bags and white containers. My eyebrow raised slightly as she caught me staring at the bag. It was a lot of food for just her and her partner.

"We'll probably be at our desk until dinner, and I'm not making two trips." She smiled as she stood up.

"Good luck."

She smiled. Those blue eyes nearly blinded me. "Yeah, you too."

CHAPTER NINETEEN

Riley Quinn

"Here you go." I placed Zelina's bag, with her burger and fries, on her desk. She smiled and nodded a thank you. She was on the phone, like she had been when I left. it seemed like a calmer conversation this time, so she must have been talking to someone else.

I sat in my chair and took my fries and turkey club out of the bag. I was so hungry I could have eaten anything. I skipped breakfast that morning, opting to go straight into the precinct to start on our research.

Someone, for some reason, believed Tiffany was at fault for the murder that her brother Larry had committed. Could she have been the mastermind? It was unlikely, but it was the only direction I had to go in. It didn't help that Larry was full of surprises, and had an extensive arrest record for someone so young.

THE GIRLS IN PINE BROOKE

He started getting arrested when he was fourteen. Mostly breaking and entering. Zelina was thinking maybe he escalated to murder. The unusual thing was that it wasn't a robbery at all—it was just cruel, sadistic, murder.

It took some negotiation, but we finally got the files on both murders. The Oceanway police seemed hesitant to hand it over. Our captain had to talk to theirs before they would give it up.

I thought that was curious. "Why the pushback on two murders that were solved? I don't get it."

Zelina shrugged. "You know how territorial officers are. You wouldn't want anyone looking over our cases. Same rules apply. They just don't want us to mess with their work, especially since the case is solved."

When she said it like that, I understood it, but still, something didn't sit right with me; when we walked into that police station, three officers locked eyes with us immediately. They rose to their feet and walked over before we could figure out which way to go.

"What do you two want?" asked the one in the middle. He was tall and slim with large dark eyes and short brown hair.

"He means, how can we help you?" asked the one on the left. He was shorter than the one in the middle, with sharper features and short blonde hair.

"We are looking for the officers that worked the Larry Co—"

Before I could even finish his name, the three men backed away with their hands up. It was like saying his name was taboo.

"What do you want with it?" asked the officer in the middle.

I held up my badge. "We're working a case, his name came up. We just wanted to look at the murder files to get a better understanding of his case and what happened. see how it ties in."

"It doesn't. It doesn't link to that case, and nothing does. It's over and done with. That's all you need to know."

I stared at the man in the middle for a long moment, and then all three backed away. I looked at Zelina, who shrugged. "Let's talk to the captain and see if he can smooth this over. We probably should have started there," she said.

She had a point. While we walked away, I couldn't help but wonder if they were getting rid of what we needed. There was something so strange about that precinct—how quiet it got when we walked in, how those three officers spoke to us, and how they reacted to hearing his name.

Our captain spoke to their captain, and the files were brought over the next day. It looked like everything was there. *But how could we know for sure?*

"Don't second guess them until you have a reason to," said Zelina, recognizing the look on my face. She didn't like going against fellow cops. To her, it set a bad precedent. I understood the feeling, but I didn't share it. If the cops were bad or doing bad things, they needed to be called out for it. Something about the way the Oceanway police had handled both this case and the disappearance of the two girls left a bad taste in my mouth. But I wasn't sure that was what was going on, so I kept my thoughts to myself.

I waited until I finished eating before I started looking at the files. I heard the crime scenes had been pretty bloody. So bloody, those houses had to be torn down; the blood stains on the walls would never come out. I didn't know how true it was, though.

I finished the last of my sandwich and fries and chased them down with a soda. I waited a few more minutes to let my food settle into my stomach before I opened the files.

"You and your weak stomach," said Zelina, a laugh on the edge of her voice.

I rolled my eyes. "My stomach isn't weak. I just don't want to throw up."

"That's what that means."

"Shut up." I guzzled the rest of my Sprite. Zelina laughed. I did throw up easily; it was probably not the best job for me and my weak stomach. My first big murder case involved a body that had been sitting in a shed in June for at least six weeks. The flesh had been purple and soft like over-ripe fruit. I saw something on her arm, and when my gloved finger touched the skin, maggots oozed out of the cut.

I had tried to swallow the bile that bubbled up in my throat, but I couldn't. I ran out of the shed before I contaminated the crime scene. I threw up in the bushes, and Zelina never let me live it down. She brought it up a lot in the following weeks and still finds a way to work it in every now and then.

For weeks I could still smell the body. I could see the maggots oozing from the lacerations. New flies filling her eye sockets. I hoped the pictures in this file were nothing like that, or I was going to show Zelina how weak my stomach really was.

I opened the file and started with what led to the police showing up.

Annie Moore was supposed to go over to her friend's house Thursday night but never showed up. Her friend's mother, Rebecca Thorne, tried calling the family several times, but no one answered the house line or their cell phones. She grew worried and went over to the house; when she saw the cars in the driveway, she called the police immediately.

Okay. So one of the daughters was supposed to spend the night at her friend's house and never made it over. I flipped through the file and found the M.E. report. The Moore family had probably been dead for at least a week. I flipped back to the front of the file for the summary.

Officer Pat Green and Officer Joseph Hernandez were the first on the scene. Officer Green checked the front door while Officer Hernandez went around the back to check the back door. The front door was locked. Officer Hernandez shouted for his partner. The back door was unlocked. Upon entering the house the smell of decomposing bodies alerted them that something wasn't right. Hernandez called for backup while Green began to search the house.

Two bodies were found in the primary bedroom. Twin girls were found in another bedroom, and an older boy was found in a bedroom across the hall from the bathroom. Blood was smeared all over the walls. Mrs. Christina Moore was raped sometime before death.

My stomach soured. That's a horrible thought. I wondered if her husband was dead before they attacked her. The order in which they were killed was uncertain. They probably killed the parents first, or at least the husband. Then they might have incapacitated the wife and kept her in the bedroom while they moved through the house.

Perpetrators were in the home for a while after the murders. The dishes in the sink were fresh, juice on the counter, and the shower had been used after the murders, as evidenced by the blood in the drain and the damp towels.

So they stayed a while. Larry's parents didn't look for him? *They didn't look for Tiffany either.* If they stayed in the house for a few days, the bodies were upstairs, so they didn't have to see them. But why stay that long? Why stay long enough to eat and take a shower?

"Claudia said the boys made no efforts to conceal the fingerprints or their DNA during the murders. But I don't understand why they would stay in both houses for as long as they did. That doesn't make sense to me."

"Maybe they didn't have anywhere to go." Zelina flipped through the file she had. "I mean, they must have been covered in blood. They couldn't ride around town like that."

"Okay. I get that. But I'm looking through this and they never found their clothes at either crime scene. So they changed their clothes and then took their bloody clothes with them? Did they bring clothes with them in case they had to change?"

Zelina tapped her pen against the desk. Her mouth opened and closed twice before she said anything. "That is a good question. They might have brought clothes with them, or they took clothes from the house."

I nodded slowly as I flipped through the file. "But nothing was taken from the house."

Zelina sighed. "Okay. So where did the clothes come from? And is it important?"

I leaned back in my chair. I couldn't say whether it was important or not right now. It made me curious. More than curious. Something felt off about it. Where had the bloody clothes gone? Did they burn them? That would have been smart, but if they made no other efforts to conceal their crime, they couldn't have been that smart.

"That is weird." Zelina tapped her pen against the desk harder. "Let's keep looking through the files and see what else might seem out of place."

I nodded and flipped through to the end of the file where the crime scene photos were. Part of me didn't want to look at them, but I knew I had to. I wanted to see the placement of the bodies. The twin girls were found in the same bed. Staring at the photo, it looked like they might have been scared and had gotten into bed together to feel safe. They were tucked in with the stuffed bears, one pink and one purple, next to them.

Who would do that? Make sure the girls were comfortable before they were killed. The older boy wasn't in his bed but next to it. He was on the floor between the wall and his bed. The window had been opened. He must have tried to get away and was caught. The blood splatter evidence told us the window was up before he was killed.

Mr. and Mrs. Moore were found in their bedroom, in their bed. The duvet tucked underneath their chins. They must have been moved after their murders. They looked so peaceful, almost like they were sleeping. It was uncanny. There was another picture with the duvet pulled away. Underneath that blanket, the blood stain was evident. They were covered in blood, so much so it was difficult seeing where their stab wounds were.

"I wonder if they raped her and then put her back in the bed..."

"Or maybe they raped her in the bed. Next to her husband's dead body."

I sighed. I guess that was possible. But if they raped her while she was dying, they would have been covered in blood. Head to toe. "Maybe they stayed long enough to wash their clothes."

Zelina blinked. "Seriously? Yeah, that makes sense. They took off their clothes, stuck them in the washer, and waited for them to be done."

"Okay, now that doesn't bother me as much. I still want to know what they were thinking. What was the point of this?"

Zelina shrugged. "They never spoke. Larry didn't even speak during his trial. He didn't get on the stand."

"I'm going to look up his lawyer and see if he will speak with us."

Zelina closed the file. "Why are we doing this?"

I sighed. "Something isn't right. I get the feeling that in some kind of way this is all related and I want to know how. If Tiffany was being blamed for what her brother did, maybe someone tried to hurt him by hurting her. And since she and Jade were always together, she got caught in the crossfire."

"I guess that's possible if someone in the extended family wanted revenge." Zelina pondered aloud.

"Claudia said the families still live in the town. See if you can find them."

"Will do."

I searched for Larry's lawyer, Noah Jameson. His profile online had a photo. He was in his mid-forties, with graying black hair and gray eyes. And he was handsome. I dialed his number hoping he remembered the case. He probably would, it was a difficult case to forget. It was the kind of case that lingered in the back of your mind no matter how you tried to stop thinking about it.

"Hello?"

"Hello, this is Detective Riley Quinn. I'm looking for Noah Jameson."

"This is he."

"Hi, I need to talk to you about a client of yours."

He exhaled slowly and paused before he said anything. He wasn't eager to talk. "Okay... what client?"

"Larry—"

Dial tone.

I pulled the phone away from my ear and stared at the receiver for a long moment before hanging up. I can't believe he hung up on me. Before I could even get a word out.

"He hung up on me!" My voice came out in a loud shriek. Zelina winced.

"Seriously? I guess he takes client privilege very seriously."

"I barely had time to say his full name. All I said was Larry, and the phone line clicked. What kind of shit is that?"

A smile pulled at the corner of her mouth. "Nobody wants to talk about this guy. It's weird, though. I mean, has he only ever had one client named Larry?"

"Exactly. How did he know who I was calling about? I can't believe he hung up on me." I stared at the phone as if daring it to ring. He surprised me. I made a note of where his office was. I held up the note so Zelina could see it. She laughed.

"Okay. We should definitely stop by unannounced."

I smiled. "We should. Did you find the families?"

"Yeah. A few members of the Moore family still live in Oceanway. But a few members of the Hayes family moved to Pine Brooke, a few months ago. I guess they didn't want to stay in that town anymore. I get it. If members of my family had been brutally murdered, I'd have to move somewhere else, too. I didn't think I'd move to the town next door, though. I'd have to get further away. Maybe another state.

Maybe another country. "Let's see the Hayes family, since they are closer. I'm curious about how they feel about what happened."

"Their family being killed?" asked Zelina.

"About Larry and the trial and everything else that happened. I want to know if Larry did know the family. It just seems strange to me that he and his cousin killed them, and the official story is that they didn't know each other. In such a small town... that's not sitting right with me."

CHAPTER TWENTY

Logan Elwood

"I have to tell you something." Isaac slid into the booth across from me.

"Shouldn't you be working?" I glanced at the counter, where the waitress who took my order was filling the coffee pot. "Every time I come here, you aren't working."

"Relax, I'm on break. And like I said, I need to tell you something important. About Mom."

My heart sank. Whatever he had to say about that woman was not going to be good. It never was, especially if he was saying it to me. She didn't like me, and my indifference toward her really set her off.

"Okay," I said, bracing myself.

He chewed his bottom lip for a moment. That was one of his tells when he had bad news. I leaned back, bracing for whatever was about to come my way.

"She wants to come visit."

"I thought you were going to squash that," I whispered in a harsher tone than I had planned.

"I tried. I really did. I told her you had a lot going on right now with taking over the new practice. You didn't need any extra people being here and crowding you. I told her that you and Dani were still trying to get into a routine in this new town. And I thought I had her, but then Jamie and Dani came into the kitchen giggling, and she heard them over the phone... it got her all riled up. She believes you need help with Dani, and... if you do, it should be family that helps you take care of her. Not strangers." He said the last part quietly.

"She is a stranger."

He winced at that, but it was true. Dani didn't even remember her. I trusted Bonnie with my daughter. I did not, however, trust my mother. I wouldn't trust my mother with my house, let alone my child. She couldn't be trusted around children. She didn't know how to talk to them or interact with them. She damn sure didn't know how to raise them. If she ever got her hands on Dani, she would ruin her, as she had ruined us. We both knew it.

"I'm sorry. She's still not settled on coming. She wanted to talk to you about it first. But just in case she decides to come I figured I'd go ahead and give you a heads up.

I swallowed hard, pushing back the bile rising up my throat. She always ruined things. Always. It never failed. "Thanks. I appreciate you trying."

"I'll keep trying the next time I talk to her. She wants to see Dani. At least that's what she said."

"Seven years too late," I grumbled as he slid out of the booth. His hand squeezed my shoulder for a moment before he walked away. My brother and I got different versions of my mother. Mine was the controlling, manipulative version, who only thought about what she wanted and forced me to live the life she wanted me to live. He got the understanding and loving version. I guess in me she saw that the first version didn't work, so she had to adjust. But the second version didn't work either. Isaac still loved her, though, and he still talked to her. Not because he felt like he had to but because he wanted to.

"She doesn't have anyone else, and I would hate to be that old and have no one too."

I understood that, but I didn't have it in me to be as forgiving. While he loved her, he still saw her for what she was. So when I refused to talk to her, he understood why and didn't push the issue. Now she was pushing it. I couldn't have her here with Jamie. I couldn't deal with both of them at the same time. I'd have to take Dani and move to a different state if that happened.

That's a good idea. I'd tuck it in my back pocket for later. The waitress returned with my food and drink but my stomach had soured. I wasn't hungry at all anymore. I packed it up to go and left heading back toward the clinic.

Why now? Why were they both coming at me at the same time? Were they so desperate for someone to give them love or attention that they had to encroach on my life out of nowhere? Part of it was about Dani. She's a great kid and a joy to have around. But I couldn't help but think part of it was about getting back at me.

Jamie has never forgiven me for Marie's death. Granted, it wasn't my fault; the truck sped through a red light and hit my car on the passenger side. But I was driving, so in some kind of way, it had to be my fault. And I couldn't blame her for that line of thinking. I felt that way for a long time. If I hadn't been driving, I'd be the one dead, and she'd be here. If I had done what she wanted and just stayed home, none of this would have happened. I was the one who wanted to go out to dinner instead of ordering in. If I had listened to her, she'd still be alive. Marie liked staying home when she was pregnant. It was more comfortable, but we hadn't done anything or gone anywhere in months, and I felt like we were due for a fun night out.

My decision killed my wife and almost killed my daughter, and that was something I had to live with. Jamie still blamed me, but my mother didn't care. She hadn't come to our wedding and only came to her funeral. She didn't hold Dani while she was there, and she didn't stay long. Just long enough to say that she was there. That she made an effort. That was how she was.

She sent Dani a few birthday cards, but they were never on the right day. She sent her gifts she thought she should have. Princess frilly things that were covered in pink. But Dani didn't like any of that. My mother would try to mold Dani into who she thought she should be instead of letting her become her own person, and I couldn't have that.

Just because she was getting old and was afraid no one would care if she died didn't mean she could just barge back into my life... into our lives... to fill some void. I didn't want to talk to her, but I'd have to set this shit straight. Sometimes, just the sound of her voice made my head hurt.

I walked back to the clinic and set my food on my desk for a moment before putting it in the fridge. I slumped into my chair just as the door opened.

"How was your lunch?" Nicole stared at me for a long time, waiting for me to answer. "That bad, huh."

I nodded slowly. "If I talk about it, I will scream. How was your lunch?"

"Great. My mother said hi. She's having some trouble with her sinuses, so she wants to stop by tomorrow."

"Okay. What kind of trouble?"

"I think it might be a sinus infection, but she wants to see a real doctor to be sure. Not that she doesn't trust my judgment and all that."

A smile bloomed on my lips. "Did she really say that?"

She nodded. "Sure did, and not for the first time either."

My lips curled into a smile. "I know it's not supposed to be funny, but it is."

She rolled her eyes. "Yeah, I know. She cracks me up." She looked back at the front door and paused. "You have another appointment in an hour and then two more after that."

"Alright." I grabbed my lunch back out of the fridge and stuffed a fry into my mouth, my appetite slowly returning. I couldn't wait for the day to be over so I could go home. I called Elise, Mrs. Stokes' daughter. She sounded perkier when she answered the phone, which told me her mother was doing a lot better.

"Yes. she's doing great. Her right side is still weaker than her left, but they want to put her in physical therapy to help with that. She's talking, eating, and her memory is pretty good. Some missing spots like before she came to the hospital, but overall the surgeon is impressed with her recovery."

"That's great. I'll be by in a couple of days to check on her. Tell her I said hello."

"Will do. Thanks, Doctor Elwood."

I muddled through the afternoon appointments pretty well. Nothing serious. But then, while I was sitting at my desk filling out paperwork, I pulled my phone out of my desk drawer to find a text message from Riley.

Riley Quinn: Do you ever have any patients from Oceanway?

Me: Not really. I think they have their own clinics over there. Why do you ask?

The text had been lying there, unread, for over an hour. But she replied right away. As if she had been waiting for me to respond.

Riley Quinn: Just seeing if I can follow up on some paper trails. But there's probably nothing you can do anyway. Oh well.

Riley Quinn: Are you having a good day?

That was weird. Was this a case-related conversation or did she just want to chat?

Me: Yeah, it's not so bad. Thankfully, no complications from the emergency I had the other day. If we hadn't taken her in for surgery that night, she would have died.

Riley Quinn: That's so cool. I don't really get the chance to save lives much. Usually when I get handed a case, the person's already dead.

Me: You get to bring them justice, though. That's important too.

Riley Quinn: Yeah. But just every once in a while, it would be nice to see some happy endings, you know?

My mind flashed with memories. Marie. She was supposed to be my happy ending. But she was gone. And even if somehow I got "justice" for her—whatever that meant—it wouldn't bring her back.

Me: I know.

∼

I pulled into the driveway and sighed. Turning the car off and removing my seatbelt, I sat back in my seat. I was home in time for dinner, but I didn't want to go in just yet. Jamie was there, and so was the heaviness that followed her. She was the only person that didn't know she was unwanted. Or maybe she did know and just didn't care. I didn't want her to come here and wreak havoc on our lives, but I didn't feel like I could turn her away.

It would have broken Marie's heart if I was mean to her sister even though she deserved it. I needed to be nice for Marie's sake. For Dani's. So I would. I would bend myself into all different kinds of shapes to make Dani happy. And to keep her with me.

I fixed my face, put on my best smile, and swallowed all the harsh words threatening to leap off my tongue. I would be nice and pleasant. And I wouldn't blow up at anyone for any reason. Tonight would be a good night as long as Dani was there.

"Papa!" Dani ran from the sofa and wrapped her arms around me. "You're home early. Everyone okay?"

I nodded. "Yeah, it was a good day, so I was able to get off early tonight. No one had to go to the hospital for emergency surgery, so that's something. How was school?"

"It was great. Auntie Jamie came to school today and ate lunch with me. It was fun."

My eyes locked on Jamie. She didn't tell me she was doing that today or ask my permission. I stared at her for a long moment before sitting next to Isaac. "Well, I'm glad you had a good day. That's what matters. Isaac nudged me with his elbow, but I ignored him.

"Alright. Dinner is served."

Isaac jumped to his feet before anyone else could move and followed Bonnie back into the kitchen. She was an amazing cook, and I understood his excitement. The scene made Dani laugh. She bounced up next to him and followed him into the kitchen. I followed them, ignoring Jamie. She wanted to get a rise out of me, and I would not give her the satisfaction. This wasn't about her; it was about Dani and only Dani. I sat at the table next to Bonnie, who sat next to Isaac. Jamie made sure to sit between me and Dani like I knew she would. But that's okay. She was my daughter and mine alone. Jamie could never mess with that.

We ate our food in relative silence. A few conversations here and there but nothing in depth. I didn't really have anything to say to any of them. Dani twirled her spaghetti with her fork and stuffed it into her mouth and smiled. She loved spaghetti, it was her favorite food, which was why Bonnie made it often.

"That was really good as always, Miss Bonnie." Dani grinned.

"Well, baby, I'm glad you liked it. As always."

Dani laughed.

"Yes, it was really good. More vegetables would be nice but still... good." Jamie's voice hung in the air.

The table went silent. Bonnie looked like she wanted to curse Jamie out, and had Dani not been there she might have. We finished eating and cleared the table. Isaac and I washed the dishes and put them away while Bonnie got Dani ready for bed.

"I'm glad you are home," said Dani. "I miss seeing you before I go to sleep."

"I miss seeing you before you go to sleep, too. I'm sorry when I miss it."

"It's okay. You're helping people. That's your job, and it's important."

I smiled as I pulled the covers up to her chest. "It is important. But you are important too. I hope you know that."

"I'm your entire world. I know that."

A chuckle bubbled up my throat. "That's right. My entire world. Love you, kid."

"Love you too, papa." I handed her a stuffed bear her mother had gotten her when we were setting up her crib. She held it close, and I kissed its forehead and hers.

She giggled.

I closed the door behind me and headed back down the stairs to see Isaac. But he wasn't there. He must have gone up to bed and didn't tell me, just like him. I walked into the kitchen, and there she was. Jamie. She sat at the kitchen table with her hands clasped on the table in front of her, resting on an envelope.

She stood up slowly. "Listen, I don't want this to be an argument. I don't want to argue with you, and I don't want any yelling around Dani. But this is a conversation that needs to be had." Her voice was slow and measured. She was purposely trying to control her tone. "And I want to have it with you, but I don't think you are ready. So, I am going to give you these papers to read over. Once you do that and it has time to settle then we can have a conversation and talk about everything." She handed me the papers and walked away without saying another word.

I had something to say, but when she started talking, my mind went blank. What was in that envelope? That was all I could think about. I turned it over in my hands over and over again. I shook my head. I wanted to open it, but something told me not to. *Don't do it here.*

Instead of opening it in the house, I walked outside and closed the door behind me. If I opened it in the house, I was going to go ballistic, and then Dani would wake up and get scared and wonder why we were fighting. And all of that would just prove Jamie right. That was the last thing I needed. I got in my car and slammed the door, but I didn't pull out of the driveway.

I opened the envelope and removed the stack of papers. My eyes stopped at the first line.

Petition for Custody of Danielle Elwood

CHAPTER TWENTY-ONE

Riley Quinn

Jamal Hayes stood on the porch, watching us as we walked up the driveway, his chocolate-colored eyes narrowing the closer we got. He didn't know who we were, but it was already clear he didn't want to speak with us.

"What do you want?" His voice was harsh and loud.

I smiled and held up my badge. His eyes didn't soften. "We want to ask you a few questions about the Hayes murder case. Just a few questions."

"Why?" he inched closer to the edge of the step. "Why now?"

I shrugged. "We have another murder case, and we think it might be related."

He chuckled. "You can't be serious. Your new case has nothing to do with us."

THE GIRLS IN PINE BROOKE

Before I could say anything, the screen door burst open. An older black woman stood in the doorway eyeing us. She pulled her robe closed.

"What is all this noise out here? Why are you yelling, Jamal?"

Jamal looked back at his grandmother. Before we drove to the house, we did our research. Jamal, his grandmother Celestine, and her son Booker all lived in this house. Booker was at work, so we knew Jamal and Celestine were alone in the house.

"Cops, nana. They want to talk about the case."

"Just a few questions," I add softly.

Celestine eyed me carefully, her eyes softened. "Come on in."

"Nana?"

"Boy, I don't need your permission for who I let in my house. Come on now."

I walked past Jamal and followed her into the house. Zelina followed close behind. We got farther than I thought I would. Now, I needed to think of some questions to ask. I had a few.

"Have a seat."

We followed her into the living room. She pointed at a soft leather sofa and took a seat in the rocking chair facing the TV.

"Alright. Ask your questions. I don't know why you would have any. The case is over and done with."

"I understand that. I just have a couple of questions I'm hoping you can help me with. Do you believe that Larry Cole killed your family members?"

"Of course not. That boy ain't have nothing to do with it."

I blinked. I looked at Zelina, and my mouth hung open. She was a very honest and upfront woman. She said it so matter-of-factly like she had said it before.

"Could you elaborate, please?" I leaned forward.

"Well, I knew Larry. I knew him well. He was a troubled boy, I know. He had a lot of troubles, especially dealing with his family. But he wasn't any killer. He didn't have it in him. I knew that, and everybody else knew that, too. But the police were adamant that he was the killer. Said they found all that evidence. I didn't believe it then. And I still don't."

"So he did know the family?" I asked. I had heard he had never met the family. He never knew them.

She shrugged. "People said that he didn't, but people say a lot of things. I don't know who started that rumor. Henry Moore tutored Larry; that was how they knew each other. He was always over there at their house and eating with the family. He was a good kid; he just fell in with the wrong crowd. He was looking for something he wasn't getting at home."

"I wonder why people say that."

She rolled her eyes. "Damn if I know."

"The police started that," said Jamal from the doorway. "I know that. Everybody knows that."

"Okay." Zelina looked at me. "Wow. I don't know what else to say. Except I was not expecting this."

Celestine laughed. "Yeah. I don't think he did it. I feel so bad for his cousin. He was killed in jail. I don't think either of them had anything to do with it, but nobody asked me what I thought."

"The police came to say they caught the boys responsible, and they told me their names. And when I said I didn't think they would do this, I was told they were the guys. And that was it."

"So they weren't even open to investigating other leads?" I asked.

"To them, there were no other leads. It was the two of them. End of story."

My jaw twitched. "When was this? I mean, how soon after the murders did they come to you?"

"The next night. I heard their bodies had been found dead that morning, and the next night, they caught the guys. I didn't even think that was enough time to investigate, but what do I know?"

"I think you're right," I said. "What else can you tell us about the case? Did they have any problems with anyone?"

She shook her head. "Not that I know of. They were quiet people. They kept to themselves and raised their children. I don't know—there was an issue with the Moores, but I don't know any specifics. My son wouldn't talk about it, so I don't know what it was."

"Whatever it was, I find it interesting that both families were killed," I said.

"Me too."

"Have you had any contact with anyone from the Moore family?"

"Nope. Nothing. Not a peep."

"Why did you move?"

She shrugged. "I just couldn't stand being there anymore. Larry did not kill my baby boy. I know that. And the police know that. So if he didn't do it, then the killer is still wandering around that town, and I couldn't stay there knowing that. I couldn't look at those people every day and know what they've done. I just couldn't do it. All the stares and whispers. I just couldn't take it anymore."

I gave her my card. "If you can think of anything else that might shed some new light on the case, please let me know. Call me anytime."

She took the card and stared at it for a moment. "I will do that. I'm glad someone is finally looking into it. That boy staying in jail for something he might not have done is not fair—not fair at all."

"Yeah, you're right. Do you know his sister Tiffany?"

"Of course. She's struggling. I feel so bad for her. Her parents offer her no guidance or support, or love. It's not their fault, though I don't think they have it in them. Especially her mother."

"Why do you say that?"

She sighed. "Well, her mother was fourteen when she started dating her father, and he was twenty-three."

"What?" Zelina's voice went up two octaves. "Twenty-three?"

She nodded. "Mm-hmm. I don't know how that all started. But she got pregnant when she was fifteen. She was a baby herself. And he... he likes them young."

"Do you think he might have done something to Tiffany?"

She shrugged. "She never said anything, and neither did Larry. But that doesn't mean he didn't. That family and their secrets. They have a lot of them. That could be one of them. I know she doesn't like being home."

"Does she ever come here?" I asked.

"Sometimes. I knew her family back when we lived in Woodvine. She visits sometimes when she doesn't want to be home. She's a good girl, just a little lost. She's still trying to find herself, but she doesn't think she'll find it here. And I agree with her. Hard trying to figure out who you are when you live in such a small town where everyone thinks they know you."

I nodded. I agreed completely. Sometimes the best thing you could ever do was getting away from your family and the place you grew up for a little while. "Have you seen her lately?"

Celestine leaned back in the rocking chair. "It's been a couple of weeks, I think. Sometimes, she runs off and stays with somebody when she doesn't stay here. I don't know who it is this week. But I've been keeping an eye out for her."

"Okay. Well, if she contacts you, please give me a call. No one has seen her in two weeks."

She nodded. "I'll call you if I hear from her."

I stood up, and Zelina followed me to the door. As soon as we got outside, I took a deep breath. It was the first time since we went inside. It didn't go at all how I thought it was going to go.

I expected the Hayes family to hate Larry and Tiffany. I expected them to carry so much animosity toward them, but that wasn't at all what happened. She still talks to Tiffany. She still believes that Larry had nothing to do with the murders. And if she believed that, I wondered as I walked back to the car if anyone else did too.

How did the Moore family feel about it? I got in the car and paused. Zelina stuck the key in the ignition, but she didn't turn it.

"That went a completely different way than I expected."

"Sure did," I said quietly.

"What do we do with this information?" she asked.

What could we do? Celestine had a feeling but no proof. She believed he was innocent but without proof we'd never get him out of prison. And this case wasn't ours. It wasn't what we were supposed to be investigating. This case was about Jade, and Tiffany—who was still missing. That was our focus. But this was something I wanted to revisit when this case was over.

"Could the cases still be connected?" The engine roared to life, and she backed out of the driveway.

"I don't know. I mean, if someone wanted revenge it wasn't them. Maybe the Moores see things differently. The Hayes left because they felt like Larry didn't do it and they didn't want to be part of living in a town that would send an innocent man to prison. But the Moores are still there."

"So maybe they believe that they did it. And wanted to take it out on Tiffany and her family." Zelina nodded slowly. "I think I could see that. This is starting to get messy and cluttered."

"I know. Finding Tiffany and solving Jade's murder is still our main priority. We have to focus on that and do that first. Whatever else happens, happens."

"Understood."

Zelina drove to the station. I wasn't sure what I wanted to do when I got there. We stopped by the lawyer's office, but no one was there. He probably left as soon as I called, assuming we'd stop by after he hung up on me. I'd see him, though. He was going to talk to us eventually. I'd make sure of it. But first, we needed to find Tiffany. And Jade's killer.

"Okay. We need to get back on track. I don't know how much further we can take this connection to Larry's case. What can we do with regard to Tiffany?" Someone had to see her somewhere. I mean, she couldn't just disappear out of thin air. "Can you take another look into Mr. Hartley? There is something so off about him. I don't trust him, and I don't like him. While you do that I'm going to read more of Tiffany's journal. Hopefully there is something in there that could tell us where she might be."

"Okay. There has to be something on him. He had to have done something at some of his other schools. I just refuse to believe this is new behavior for him."

"I second that." I pulled Tiffany's journal out of my desk. I removed the bookmark from the middle of the book and started reading. Unfortunately, there hadn't been much there in the last three times I'd gone over it. I don't know what I was looking for. Would she have just said the names of the boys she was dating, or the places she could possibly hide out in?

I groaned. "I don't know where to go from here. This journal isn't nearly as useful as Jade's was. Honestly, I can barely even read some of what she's saying. It's... random meaningless words."

Zelina reached out her hand snapped impatiently. "Let me see."

I laughed. "What, you have a sudden idea?"

"I do, actually. Now gimme."

I shoved the book over to her. She flipped through several pages humming and muttering to herself for several minutes.

"Are you going to tell me what you're looking for?" I asked.

"Give me a second..." She grabbed a notepad and scribbled quickly, flipped a couple pages back, then nodded quickly.

I craned my neck over to read her notes. "What is this?"

"It's a code."

I slammed the desk. "Of course!"

"Remember how I told you my grandma would have read my diary out loud to everyone? Sometimes, if I was afraid she'd find my hiding spot, I'd start writing in code. I understood it, but to anyone else, it looked like..."

"Random meaningless words," I finished for her.

"Bingo."

"So what have you found out?"

She shook her head. "Still cracking it. But it sounds like she was dating someone. I'm seeing a lot of references to 'him'. He took me out today. He got me a fake ID. He took me to the clinic in Pine Brooke. He brought me flowers."

"Any name?"

"Not one that I can find yet. Sounds like she *really* didn't want anyone to know. Even in the code she's not spelling it out."

"Wait, hold up. He took her to the clinic? The clinic here?"

"That's what it says."

"If she lived in Oceanway, why would she come to Pine Brooke for a clinic visit? And why would her boyfriend even take her there in the first place?"

Zelina shrugged. "Maybe a pregnancy scare? Maybe she didn't want anyone in her town to know? She was already having such a hard time with her family..."

"Sounds like we need to pay a visit to our friend Doctor Elwood," I said.

CHAPTER TWENTY-TWO

Logan Elwood

MY HAND SLAMMED INTO THE STEERING WHEEL SEVERAL TIMES. What the hell was she thinking? Along with the custody papers, there was a letter. She had the nerve to write me a letter trying to explain her side of things. My body went hot as if fire pulsed in my veins. I knew this was coming. Deep down, I had a feeling she was going to try and take her from me because she wanted to be closer to her sister, and Dani was the only link she had left. I saw it coming.

Dear Log,

This letter shouldn't come as a surprise. You know and I know, Marie would have wanted her to be with me if she was not able to take care of her. It just makes more sense. Girls need their mothers. They do. Fathers are great to have, but a young girl needs her mother more growing up. Marie knew that and I think deep down you know it too. You can't fill that void in her life. you just can't and you never will.

I'm the one who knew Marie the best. I could tell Dani about her mother. I could raise her the way Marie would have wanted. She would be loved and cherished if she lived with me. I'm not saying you don't love her. I can see that you do, and when she comes to live with me, you can visit occasionally. But she needs to be with a mother who understands her.

Right now, you work so much that you don't have time for her. Dani should not come second to your job. I'm not working, so I could devote all the time and care needed to raise her. I know that when you think about what is best for Dani, you will come to the same conclusion.

I know you will. This is what Marie would have wanted.

All my love,

Jamie

How the hell could she think she knew my wife better than I did? *This is what Marie would have wanted.*

The hell? Marie wouldn't have wanted me to be away from Dani. She would have never consented to Jamie taking her away from me. Can she do that? I stared at the letter again. Willing an answer to appear on the page. How could she be this dense?

She only wanted Dani because she wanted to be closer to her sister. She wanted to mold her in Marie's image instead of letting her be her own person. Dani would be miserable living with her. What about her other children? What about them? Where are they going to be? Is she going to take care of them too?

My hands gripped the steering wheel. I was glad I went outside. If I had read this letter in the house, I would have screamed. I would have choked the life out of her, and that would have caused a completely different set of problems. I stayed in the car for a couple of hours, reading the papers over and over again. She really thought she was more entitled to my daughter than I was. What kind of bullshit was that? How could she be so delusional?

Why was I surprised? Isaac wasn't going to be surprised, and neither was Bonnie. We all knew she was here for a reason; we just couldn't figure out what it was. Well, now I knew. When I went back into the house, it was after two in the morning. I went straight to my bedroom and closed the door. If I saw anyone right now, I would scream.

When dawn finally came, I kissed Dani and told her to have a good day before skipping breakfast and heading straight to work. I didn't want to talk to them right now. I didn't want Dani to hear me raise my voice at her aunt. I didn't even look at Jamie. I felt her staring at me, but I kept my eyes on Dani and then on the floor as I walked out.

First things first, I needed to find a lawyer and have them look over this paperwork. My old friend Ricky might be able to do it, or maybe I knew someone, but I hadn't talked to him in forever. Not since we moved. He tried to reach out, but I wasn't—I cut so many people off, and most of it wasn't on purpose. I just didn't want to talk about it. I didn't want to talk about the accident, or what I was going to do next, or any of it. My friends kept trying to be there for me, but I kept pushing them away, and he was one of them.

His number was still on my phone. I had gotten rid of some, but others I just couldn't. I sent him a text before I walked into the clinic. The cool air mingled with my sweat and sent a shiver down my spine.

"You look pissed." Nicole sat at her desk, watching me. Her eyes narrowed. "Who pissed you off this morning?"

"I've been pissed since last night." I set my stuff down in my office. Nicole jumped to her feet immediately and followed me in. She leaned against the door frame.

"Keep talking. Do I have to fight someone? Because I will. I mean, I don't like to throw hands, but I will."

A smile tugged at my lips, but I fought it. I wasn't in a smiling mood. I fished the envelope out of my bag and handed it to her.

"What is this, and why is it so thick?"

I slumped into my chair while I waited for her reaction.

"No, the hell she didn't."

"That's exactly how I felt."

Nicole stared at the papers moved open. "I can't believe her! She can't take Dani away from you. She can't. She'd have to prove you are an unfit parent, and she can't do that."

"Her argument is that I work too much, and the nanny is raising her more than I am."

Nicole shrugged. "Isn't that her job? That's literally what you pay her for, and how many nannies does miss thing have?"

That was a good point. I hadn't thought about it last night. Jamie had nannies. Two I believe. What about them? She didn't even raise her own kids, how was she going to raise mine? "That is an excellent point. Thank you."

"I can't believe she would do this and blame it on your wife's memory. I can't believe she'd use her sister's death as a way to steal her child."

That wasn't that big of a surprise to me. I did expect it. That was how she was. Jamie was cold and calculating, and she wanted what she wanted. And she always wanted her sister. Marie was like a toy, and she refused to put it down. I wouldn't let her use Dani in the same way she used her sister.

"Have you told your brother about it yet? I know he's gonna be pissed. Shit, I'm pissed, and this ain't got nothin' to do with me."

I shook my head. I wanted to tell Isaac, but I needed to think it through a little more. Isaac loved Dani. If something happened to me, I would trust Isaac—with Bonnie helping him, of course, to take care of Dani. He loved her like she was his own. And she loved her Uncle Sac. They had been close since she was born. He helped take care of her in the early days. It was a wonder to watch. He knew what to do when I felt like I was drowning. That time together helped us repair our relationship. I saw him in a completely different light.

If Jamie took Dani away, Isaac would lose his mind.

"I still need to think through some things before I tell him. I contacted a lawyer friend of mine. I'm hoping he gets back to me later today. I want to know if it is even possible or if she's just trying to start shit."

Nicole stood up straight. "Honestly, I think it is. I think she can at least file a petition for custody. That doesn't mean it will be granted. Only if she can prove you are an unfit parent, and she can't. You are a great father. You're great because you love your daughter, and you understand you can't do it on your own, so you got help." Nicole shook her head and headed back out to the front of the office. "That floozy."

I chuckled. "I needed that." I stuck the envelope back in my bag. "So, who do we have today?" I called out.

"Looks like we have a walk-in…"

I frowned. What? I never took walk-ins first thing in the morning.

"Come on back, ladies," Nicole said, and before I knew it, I was face to face with Detectives Riley Quinn and Zelina Carter.

I groaned. This was not what I needed right now. "Can I help you, detectives?"

"You might be able to," said Riley. "I need to ask about one of your patients."

I was glad to see her, I guess, but I bristled. "You realize I can't really tell you much, right? Doctor patient confidentiality."

Riley held up her hands. "I know, I know. We're not asking for details. I just need to know whether you saw Tiffany Cole within the last month."

Nicole frowned. "The missing girl?"

Riley nodded. "We have reason to believe she came here."

"I thought she was from Oceanway."

"She is. But our trail specifically led us here—to the Pine Brooke clinic."

"She would have come with a boyfriend," Zelina supplied. "We think it could possibly be related to a pregnancy scare, or other sexual activity."

I racked my brain, trying to remember any time I would have dealt with a case like that. "Not... not that I can think of," I admitted. "I don't really deal with teenage pregnancies so much around here. We can check the records, though."

Riley smiled. "If you could, it's kind of urgent."

I rolled my chair over to the corner to quickly dig through the file cabinet. Nicole was already going through the one in the opposite corner.

"I'm not seeing Tiffany Cole in here..." Nicole said.

"We think she may have come in with a fake ID. Almost certainly without insurance."

"How am I supposed to find her if she had a fake ID?" I asked.

"Don't you guys scan the IDs? You could look at the pictures."

"I'm not gonna look at every single picture in every single file," I said. But then, the very next file I opened, I frowned. Something about it was familiar. "Can you show me the photo of Tiffany real quick?"

Riley pulled it up on her phone and showed me. I looked down and nodded, then pulled the file out on my desk. "She came in here, all right. But she used a different name."

"Who was it?"

I hesitated for a second. Was I allowed to tell?

"Look, I know there are confidentiality rules. But this might be our chance to find a missing girl. If there's anything you can tell us, that would be a huge, huge help."

"Technically, if she used a fake ID, it's our duty to report medical fraud," Nicole pointed out.

"Right." I nodded and took a breath, then flipped the file open. "Looks like our patient— Tiara Kohl—"

"Real original," Zelina muttered.

"—came through with her boyfriend, about three weeks ago. They got tested for several STD's and we discussed birth control for her."

"Who was the boyfriend?" Riley asked.

I flipped through the file. "Looks like his name is... Boston. Boston Craster."

Riley and Zelina traded glances. I could tell whatever I'd said was a huge lead for them.

"Thanks, doc. We'll get out of your hair now," Riley said.

They bustled out of the office quickly and immediately sped out of the parking lot before I could blink.

"You're welcome," I said.

Nicole laughed.

The rest of the day passed pretty smoothly.. I had nearly forgotten the situation with Jamie until I got a call from my old lawyer buddy, Ricky.

"Long time no talk."

"I know. I know. I'm an asshole. I'm sorry."

"Nah, man. I get it. You were going through a lot and trying to put the pieces back together. Sometimes, you have to do it alone so you can do it in a way that works for you. I get that."

I smiled. "Thanks, man... for understanding."

"So what's up? How's Dani?"

"That's why I'm calling you. Marie's sister Jamie wants custody of Dani. She said that's what Marie would have wanted."

"For real?"

"Yeah. But that's the thing. Marie knew her sister was flighty. She wouldn't have trusted her with her daughter. Maybe for a weekend, but not eighteen years. Is it possible? Can she get custody?"

Ricky went silent for a long moment. "Family law isn't my thing, but I know a great person to refer you to. I think she can, but that's based on my limited knowledge of family law. She can petition the court if she believes that you are an unfit parent. There will be an investigation, and if they find that you are unfit, she can get custody. She probably made the petition hoping you wouldn't want to go through all of that and just hand her over."

"I would never."

"I know. I know. I'll text you the number. Now, Bernie is a little weird, but he's good at what he does. And he always does what's best for the child. That is his only priority. I can't believe—you know what, yeah, I can believe... who am I kidding."

"That's what I said. I was surprised, but I wasn't. This is her to a T. Now I have to tell my brother, and I know he's going to be pissed."

"Sac staying with you?"

"Yup, and so is Jamie."

"Hold up… how you gonna live in my house while plotting to take my daughter? Who does that?"

"I know. I was trying to be nice because it's what Marie would have wanted."

"Yeah, to hell with all that. First, and I hate to say this, but Marie is dead… what she would have wanted should not factor into your decision when it comes to your daughter, because she is not here to tell you her wishes. Secondly, Marie knew her sister. She knew Jamie better than anyone, and when she stepped out of line, Marie called her out. Marie would have cussed her out over this. This is about you and Dani, and only you and Dani. Marie isn't here to make any decisions. Stop letting that be a factor. And no one should make you uncomfortable in your own home. Anyone that does has gotta go."

I sighed. He was right. Ricky was always the voice of reason. He had a way of breaking things down in the simplest way, and I appreciated it.

"Kick her out so I can come visit you."

I laughed. "Dani might like that. Two goofballs in the house."

"We would keep her entertained." He paused for a moment. "Alright Log, I gotta go to a meeting. I'll text you the info and you call me and let me know what's going on. I will come down there."

"Thanks."

He was right. It was my house, and I needed to do what was best for me and Dani. I knew how much Marie loved her sister, but he was right about that, too, and I didn't even think about it. Marie did call her out when she overstepped, which was often. She was quick to do it in a calm and loving way, but the message was always clear.

I drove home, ready for whatever was waiting for me on the other side of the door. Bonnie and Dani sat on the sofa watching TV, Isaac was in the recliner, and Jamie was in the kitchen.

"Bonnie, can you take Dani to get some ice cream? Since she's been so good."

Dani beamed and jumped to her feet. "I'll get my shoes." she was out of the living room before Bonnie could get to her feet.

"Everything alright?"

"I'll explain it to you when you get back. Just take your time."

She nodded and walked away. Isaac watched me from the recliner. I waited until they left and was halfway down the driveway before I said anything.

"Am I in trouble?"

Jamie eased out of the kitchen into the living room. "You thought about my proposal."

I threw the envelope into Isaac's lap. "How *dare* you stay in my house while trying to figure out a way to take Dani from me! Who the hell do you think you are?"

"I am her aunt, and I should have her. You can't take care of her properly. You are never home. You have a nanny. She spends more time with the nanny than with you."

"Who do your kids spend more time with? Their nanny or you?"

Jamie placed her hands on her hips. "Why are you getting so defensive? She can come with me; you'll still see her. But you'll be free to live your life. You can do whatever bachelors do."

"I'm not like you. I don't only think of myself. I'm not a bachelor; I'm a widower, and that little girl is my only priority. And you will not take her from me."

"Exactly," said Isaac.

"You also won't stay in my house rent-free while plotting to steal my child. You need to pack your shit and get out of my house tonight. There are plenty of hotels you can stay at, or you can go home and take care of *your own* children."

"Hear, hear," said Isaac.

Jamie scoffed. "You aren't seeing reason. I have to be the one to take care of her. I'm the only one who can raise her the way Marie would have wanted. It has to be me. And if you were thinking of someone other than yourself you could see that. You can't raise a child on your own."

"I'm not on my own. I have Bonnie and Isaac. These are people she loves. We all take care of her, and love her, and you want to snatch her away from the only home she has ever known to what… boost your ego? You make everything about you… but not this. Dani is not about you. She is a human being and not some doll you can mold into whatever you want her to be. She is not Marie, and she never will be. Whatever you want to make right with your sister, you are too late."

Tears filled her eyes, but she angrily shook them away. "I will get custody because I can show I have a better more stable environment than you do. A sad lonely man, who doesn't like people and is still grieving his dead wife. That's a miserable lonely environment to raise a child in. And a judge will see that. So no, I'm not leaving this stupid town without Dani."

I crossed my arms. "You're not staying here."

She balled her hands into fists at her side. "Fine. I'll find a hotel. This is happening whether you like it or not so get on board."

"You can have her over my dead body."

Jamie chuckled. "Okay."

I stood there and watched, never taking my eyes off her, until she gathered her things and stormed out the door.

CHAPTER TWENTY-THREE

Riley Quinn

"Boston Craster," I said with a groan as we peeled out of the parking lot. "How old is he these days?"

"Twenty, I think," Zelina said. "I haven't seen him down at the station lately."

"Me either."

Boston was well known in town, especially by law enforcement. He was always getting into trouble for something or other. Never anything too serious—shoplifting, trespassing, criminal mischief, that sort of thing. He was always getting into fights with other teenage boys and hanging around places he shouldn't have been. The fact that he had apparently been dating the underage Tiffany Cole was troubling.

Was he responsible for her disappearance? Was he the one who also held Jade captive and killed her?

I turned at a light toward the only grocery store in town. "He still work at Channey's?"

"As far as I know, yeah."

We barreled down the road to the small store and I didn't even have to wander the aisles to find the manager out front.

"Channey's Grocery, how can I help you?"

I held up my badge. "I'm looking for Boston."

She scoffed. "Join the club. He has been so frustrating lately. Didn't show up *again*."

"Has he been unreliable the last few weeks?" I asked. "Well—more unreliable than usual?"

"Been a huge pain in my rear. He's calling in a lot, and when he is here, he's distracted. He promised he'd be here this morning, and he called in yet again. Fifth time he's called in sick in two weeks. He's about to get fired."

Zelina looked at me. "Tiffany has been missing for two weeks."

"Do you have his home address?" I asked.

The manager faltered. "I don't know..."

"Call it a welfare check," I told her. And technically, it was. It just wasn't Boston's welfare I was interested in checking.

Did he do something to Tiffany? Or was she still with him? Was she hiding out at his house because she didn't want to go home? The manager gave us the address; we thanked her and headed back out.

We decided to follow up with Boston's father Tory, who was a truck driver. Hadn't seen him around since the night of the storm when he helped with clean up.

Everyone in town knew Boston because of his father. Tory was the kind of neighbor that was always there to help if you needed it. Whatever it was, if he didn't have it, he could find it or knew someone that could do it. My mother's car once broke down on the side of the road leading into town when he was coming home, and he fixed it for free so she could get to where she was going. He was always doing things like that for people.

His son, on the other hand, was a disappointment—he was nothing like his father. Boston only did things that benefitted himself. He was all about Boston... and no one else. He was rude and obnoxious and always getting into trouble. I felt bad for Tory. He worked hard building up his reputation in the town and his son soured it every chance he got.

He probably hated his father and went out of his way to make him look bad. The way I heard it, from my parents of course, Boston only got the job at the grocery store because of his father. His father put in a good word for him, and the owner took him on as a favor. Before that, Boston was busy smoking weed and hanging out with his friends after graduating from high school.

And now he was on the verge of losing that. "We need to go to his house and see what he's up to."

"I wonder if he's holding Tiffany hostage or something," said Zelina as we got back into the car. "If he did something to Jade, maybe his intention was to only get Tiffany, but since they were always together, he had to take her too. She was getting sicker because of the infection, and he decided to take her somewhere so he could kill her and hide her body."

It was a credible summary of what could have happened. It made sense, yet something about it didn't fit. Why would Boston take both girls? That was the thing I couldn't wrap my brain around. I couldn't understand the why. Did he have a thing for Tiffany? Did he want to take her, but she didn't want to be with him? There had to be more to the story than that.

I shrugged, and Zelina shook her head, her dark curls falling right above her eyes. She said I tended to overthink things. That might be true. I liked looking at a scenario from all different angles. It was my process, and it annoyed her, which made it that much better. I wanted to imagine what happened from every possible angle until something either felt right or stood out or accounted for the evidence at the scene.

There wasn't much evidence at the scene where Jade died, which was interesting. There might have been more evidence if we had been able to examine the scene before the thunderstorm hit, and then had to pause our investigation to help the clean-up. Boston, as usual, was nowhere to be found, but his father showed up, and he was always there when we needed him. When anyone needed anything, he was there.

I wondered for a moment if Boston hadn't shown up because he didn't care or because he had a tied-up Tiffany in his house, and he didn't want to leave her by herself. It could have gone either way. I leaned more toward Tiffany being the reason.

Boston lived in a house on the edge of town, close enough to still be considered part of the town and yet far enough away that sometimes, I forgot it was out there. His car was in the driveway, so I knew he was home. He lived on a plot of land his father had given him to get him out of his house. He got a trailer and parked it on the land. His father wanted him out of the house but still couldn't stop taking care of him.

Parents were like that. No matter how old you got, you would always be their baby. Boston took advantage of that. At least, that was what my mother said.

"He knows how much his father loves him. He's all he got left. He takes full advantage of that hole in his father's chest. He knows what he's doing. He pulls on his heartstrings all the time. His father is a pillar of this town, and there he is, getting arrested again for pot and driving drunk. And you know he will bail him out again," she'd said after Boston was arrested for driving drunk, and had weed and meth in his possession.

I stared at the trailer as I walked up. It looked like no one was taking care of it even though we knew he lived there. There were cobwebs in the windows and the corners of the front door. The white dingy door matched the rest of the trailer. The grass around the building was burnt out. However, the weeds were bright green and high.

"Probably snakes all up and through here." Zelina lifted her legs high with each step as she stared at the ground. The image of her marching through the grass brought a smile to my lips. We cleared the grass, and I knocked on the door.

The sound of footsteps pounding against the floor toward the door was startling. I glanced at Zelina, who placed her hand on her holster. The door opened. My jaw tightened.

"What do you want?"

I held up my badge. "Who are you?" I knew who she was the second I saw her, but I still asked the question. I still waited for the answer.

"Why? I didn't do anything."

Tiffany stood in the doorway in an oversized t-shirt with no pants and fuzzy pink socks. My fist balled at my sides. We had been looking for her. People had been worried about her and there she was, just standing there with an uncaring look on her face. I burst through the doorway, past her and into the home. Zelina followed.

"You can't just walk in here. Don't you need a warrant or something?"

Boston stomped out of the bedroom still zipping up his pants. I held up my badge. "Hello again, Boston."

He glanced at Zelina and me. "What now?"

"You know that Tiffany here is underage, right?" I looked at Tiffany, who tried to pull her shirt down over her knees. "I guess you did know that. Well, now you are under arrest for statutory rape. And when you get down to the precinct, we will have a lot of questions on what you did to Jade."

"What do you mean?" Tiffany inched further into the room. "What happened to Jade?"

"She's dead," I said, maybe too bluntly. Tiffany's eyes went wide, and her bottom lip trembled.

"No, she's not. No, she's not!"

"She went missing the same day you did. And now she's dead." I glanced around the room. "Now everyone needs to get dressed because you're all going down to the station."

They both stumbled as they walked back into the bedroom. Zelina stayed by the door, watching them with her hand on her holster. While she focused on them, I eyed the room. It didn't look like Tiffany was being held hostage. The trailer had a small open kitchen next to the living room. it was neater than I expected judging by the outside. The smell of weed and something chemical hung in the air so thick it made it hard to breathe. We were both probably getting a contact high just being in the room. I walked over to the front door and opened it to allow some fresh air in. The living room had a dark brown sofa and a nice sized TV. There was a coffee table in the middle of the room with two mugs and a lighter near the remote. Tiffany was the first to stumble out of the bedroom, her sandals clutched to her chest. I watched her as she sat on the sofa and slipped on her shoes. She sighed when she was finished. I looked at Zelina, who shook her head.

It was clear they were both high. Her eyes were bloodshot, and she could barely keep her balance on her feet. Boston eased out of the room a moment later. With his sweats on and a shirt with a weed plant on it. I shook my head. We'd have to let them sit for a little while before we could talk to them.

"Come on." I held open the door as they walked past. I stood in the doorway while Zelina walked around. There were two bedrooms and one bathroom. She moved through each room and found nothing. Not a space where they could have kept Jade, but then why would they have had her? Something about that train of thought didn't sit right with me. They might not have taken her, but they had to know something. Jade and Tiffany were always together, and the one day she was not with Tiffany, she got kidnapped. It could have been a coincidence, but I didn't believe in coincidences, so there was something else going on.

Zelina emerged from the second bedroom and frowned. "There is nothing and no one in the other rooms. I didn't find any sign that Jade had ever even been here."

I had been expecting that. I didn't think they kept her here. We walked out and closed the door behind us. Tiffany and Boston stood by our car. If they had run, they wouldn't have gotten far. They were both too high to run; they were too high to walk, really. Boston leaned on the car. I opened the back doors, and they both slid in.

The scent of weed wafted off of them in waves, thick loud waves. As soon as we got in the car Zelina put the windows down. A smile pulled at my lips. We drove them back to the station and put them both in holding cells so they could sober up. They had to before we could talk to them. It was annoying because I really wanted to ask my questions, but I couldn't wait.

Zelina stayed to watch them and update their families while I went to the diner to get a late lunch. The second I walked in the cool air, the smell of onions and meat and something sweet hit me in the face. My mouth watered as I slid into a booth. I already knew what I wanted: a thick, juicy burger with bacon and fries. Maybe a fruit cup to go with it.

"Did it help?"

I glanced up just as someone slid into the booth across from me. Silence rippled through the diner. Hushed voices accompanied it. I stared at Logan for a long moment. He had been nicer to me lately. Or he had been pleasant, period. He talked, and there wasn't an edge to his voice anymore, and he'd actually been helpful on the case.

"It did, actually. We found her."

Logan visibly exhaled. "Was she okay?"

"Completely unharmed. Not exactly out of the woods legally, but she's been found. Her and the boyfriend."

"That's good, I think," he said.

"We'll see. Zelina's babysitting them while we get everything processed." I glanced around. "Where's your nurse?"

"She is having lunch with her mom."

"She didn't care for your company today?" A playful smirk danced on my lips.

He smiled. "Not today, I guess. Haven't been in the best of moods lately."

"Yeah, I noticed you dropped the jerk schtick this morning and were actually almost kind of pleasant to be around."

He blew out a laugh, but there was no humor in it.

I felt my smile disappear. "Everything okay?"

He shrugged. The waitress came and took our orders, and he still had a far-away look on his face..

"No, really, what's wrong?" I pressed.

He leaned back and sighed. "Just a lot of family stuff going on. My sister-in-law is not making things easy. But I think she will get over it eventually. Hopefully."

"I hope that works out the way you want it to."

"Yeah, me too." He took a slow sip of his water. "I keep thinking about it. What was the question you wanted to ask me the other day?" His lips curled into a smile as he pushed up the sleeves of his shirt, his tattoos on full display.

"You keep thinking about it? Really? As a doctor that's what occupies your mind?"

He grinned. "I like questions."

"Questions?"

The alarm on his phone dinged.

"You have somewhere to be?"

He shook his head as he fished his phone out of his pocket. "Nope. It's just a reminder to send someone a photo of a venereal disease."

I blinked. "I'm sorry; what now?"

He chuckled. He finished with his phone and slid it back into his pocket. "I know I bent the rules earlier, but I really can't tell you who the patient is. It's just something to get them thinking and... to do better."

I laughed. "You just told me who it was. And I stand by your decision wholeheartedly. Hopefully, that will make him change his ways."

A smile tugged at his lips, but he didn't say anything. I respected it. "How are you liking the town?"

I knew all too well that small towns were an adjustment for someone used to living in the city. Just like living in the city was an adjustment for someone used to living in a small town. I had wondered if he liked it from the moment I met him. Judging by his attitude, I thought he didn't.

When I moved back to Pine Brooke, it was a hard adjustment. It was so quiet here. It was a stark change from the bright lights and constant noise of the city. I missed it for a long time when I got back. A few months. I missed the noises at night. When I moved into my cabin, I would lie awake at night, waiting for the noises from outside. All I heard were crickets and the water from the lake. Eventually, it felt relaxing to hear nothing before I went to bed.

He shrugged. He did that a lot. "I don't know. The whole everyone knows everyone thing... I'm not sure how I feel about that."

"It can be annoying, but it can also be helpful. For example, last year, Molly Townsend, who works at the library, was always bright and happy. A ray of sunshine in the town until she wasn't. She stopped leaving her house and following her normal routine. In the city, no one might have noticed. She lives alone and isn't originally from here. Every morning she'd stop by and wave to her neighbors. But Mr. Brown and his wife noticed they hadn't seen her walking to work like always and stopped by to check on her. They saw her on the floor of her living room through the front window. Called 911."

"So, because they knew her routine and knew she lived alone, they knew something was wrong."

"Exactly."

He shrugged again. "What was wrong with her?"

"She hadn't been feeling good for a week; it turns out she had diabetes and didn't know it yet."

"Passed out because of low blood sugar."

"Sometimes it's good for people to know about your business. They'll have a feeling when something goes wrong."

"Point made." He bowed his head slightly.

"I hope so." I smiled.

"Just not used to it, I guess. Patients come in, and they ask me a million questions about me before I can ask them about their visit."

"Old ladies?"

He chuckled.

"Yeah. Now, some of them are just flat-out nosy. Like my mother, tell her nothing. Whatever you tell her, I will hear about it later," I said.

"Got it. Don't tell your mother anything I don't want you to know."

I nodded as I laughed. "Exactly." Our food was set on the table silently before the waitress walked away with a scowl.

"That girl really hates her job." Logan watched her walk away and shook his head.

"She failed a couple of classes, so she has to work here for the summer, and whenever school is on break. She's still a little pissed about it."

"Everyone really does know everyone here," he said.

"And soon enough, you will too," I told him.

A smirk danced across his lips. "I would have loved this kind of job when I was a teenager. Hanging around food all day. Perfect."

"So, you like to eat a lot."

He glanced down at my burger, back up at me, and grinned. My plate was stacked high with French fries. My burger overflowing with bacon.

I shoved two French fries into my mouth. "Point made."

CHAPTER TWENTY-FOUR

Logan Elwood

WE ATE OUR LUNCH, AND SHE TOLD ME ABOUT HER CASE. IT WAS fascinating to hear how they were running the investigation. I had never worked with the police before, so everything I knew about an investigation and how they worked was from *Law and Order*.

"That's insane! She doesn't watch the news?" I stole one of the fries off her plate and slipped it into my mouth. I had finished my grilled chicken salad a few minutes before and wanted something salty.

Riley glared at me, and I shrugged. She didn't like sharing her food, apparently. I'd bide my time and then steal another one.

"She's a teenager. What teenager do you know who actually watches the news?"

I paused for a moment. She made a good point. Teenagers were much like my brother; they were never interested in something unless it affected them directly. Some teenagers, anyway.

"It amazes me that she never tried to call her friend during all that time. What was she hiding out from?"

Riley slid a piece of bacon between her lips. "I don't know. Home doesn't seem to be a good place for her. There was something about that house... I wouldn't want to go back there if I didn't have to. Maybe she was staying there to get away from her parents. She didn't leave there because she didn't want it to get back to her parents where she was."

I nodded slowly and stole another French fry while she drank her soda. She shook her head, a playful smile on her lips. "Possible. But why didn't she call her friend unless she knew she wouldn't answer?" The case was strange but exciting. I had seen it on the news the past few nights. It was a welcome distraction from my life at home. I didn't want to think about Jamie or Dani or Marie right now. I just wanted to focus on what I was doing now in this conversation.

"Yeah, that's what I was thinking at first, but it still doesn't feel right."

I nodded slowly. I wondered what her process was when solving a case. I wondered what it felt like to put a bad guy away. I wondered if she had ever been shot. Her job was so dangerous. I wondered if she had any cold cases... I wondered if she was single...

I shook the last thought out of my mind. Shoved it into a box and locked it. It didn't matter. I wasn't ready for anything. and she didn't like me. I was an ass to her when I first met her and a few times after that. There was nothing there, but I enjoyed the conversation. The waitress, who hated her job and everyone in the diner who required her to actually do her job, brought a bag filled with food for her partner, Zelina. I paid the check, and she left. I wished her good luck. I was alone at the table for five whole minutes when my brother slid into the booth.

"Don't you have to work?"

"In an hour. What are you going to do about Jamie?" His voice was barely above a whisper; I had to lean forward to make out the words. He looked like he hadn't slept last night. His hair was a mess on his head, and his clothes were rumpled. He was taking it about as hard as I was.

I shrugged. I wasn't sure what I should do. Should I do anything or just let it die down? She couldn't take my daughter from me. No one could ever say she has more of a right to Dani than I. "What can I do? Sue her?"

Isaac frowned. "I know. We can run away with Dani. Start over somewhere new?" His eyebrows lifted slightly, hopeful.

A smile pulled at my lips. I had the same thought for a second. "She would hire a private eye to track us down. You know that."

Isaac shrugged. "Figured it was worth a shot."

I chuckled. "Yeah. It crossed my mind, but then I remembered something Marie had said." Marie talked about her sister a lot. She loved her, but she knew Jamie was a handful.

"Jamie gets what she wants. Always," she had said once, after a particularly stressful weekend with her sister. "Whenever she wants something, she doesn't stop until she gets it. She's always been like that. As far back as I can remember. Like a dog with a bone, she won't give it up."

If she wanted Dani, she would do whatever she could to get her. I just needed to make her understand that taking her away from me was not the best thing for anyone, least of all Dani. If she understood that, then maybe she would give up.

Isaac sighed as he leaned back. "I hate her. She really makes me sick. Why did she have to come all this way and ruin what we had?"

I felt my eyebrow raise. "*We* had? You just got here."

"So? I was here before her."

I had to laugh. He sounded like a five-year-old not getting their way. He was so serious; it was adorable. "I know. I know your concerns, but I feel like I should wait this out. Once she thinks about it and sees reason, she'll come to her senses."

"I hope you're right."

I hoped I was, too. I walked back to the office slower than usual. I had a patient coming in thirty minutes, but I just needed to stay outside for a little while longer. I needed the fresh air and space to think. To clear my head.

Who would believe she had more of a right to my daughter than me? How was that even possible? She wouldn't be able to get a judge or a lawyer to agree with her. She couldn't.

I finally reached the office and walked inside into the cool air. It was a relief. I enjoyed my walk, but the heat was fierce.

Nicole jumped to her feet. "There is a man in your office." Her voice was barely above a whisper. She moved closer to me. "He wouldn't say what he wanted, just that he needed to talk to you. He wouldn't leave until he did. "

My heart pounded in my chest. "Okay. Let's see what this is about." I walked into my office and saw a man leaning against the wall. He didn't look familiar. He was younger than me and had dark hair and gray eyes. He wore a short-sleeved light blue shirt and jeans. A backpack on his back. He straightened when I walked in.

"Logan Elwood?"

I nodded. "Who are you?"

"Doesn't matter." He removed a large envelope and handed it to me. "You've been served." He walked out without another word.

"Served with what?" I ripped open the envelope. "Are you serious?" I collapsed in my chair, my heart stammering in my chest. "I can't believe her!"

"What is it?" Nicole ran into the room.

"She's suing me for custody of Dani. She says that I'm an unfit parent and can't take care of her." Tears stung my eyes. How could she do this? What the hell was she thinking?

Nicole snatched the papers out of my hands. "She has no right to do that. You got to get a lawyer to help you sort this out."

"Yeah, I know one that might be able to help me. How could she do this? What gives her the right?"

How could she think she could give Dani a better life than me? What the hell is wrong with her? I slumped back in my chair. I would never let go of my daughter. Not for anything… not for anyone in the world.

Jamie would soon find that out.

CHAPTER TWENTY-FIVE

Riley Quinn

HE SEEMS SO LONELY. I WALKED BACK TO THE STATION WITH ZELINA'S food in my arms. Every time I saw Logan he seemed lonely, even if he was with his nurse or his brother. He seemed on his own a lot, and as my mother told me, often being on your own a lot was never a good thing. He just seemed like he had no one to talk to about whatever was going on with his family.

While I didn't like him before and I still wasn't sure how I felt about him now, his constant sadness bothered me. Made me feel sorry for him, and I hated that. My mother talked to his brother often, every time he came into her coffee shop. For her to tell it, he was nice and very personable. He was polite and always had a smile on his face. The direct opposite of his brother.

THE GIRLS IN PINE BROOKE

I walked into the station and let the cool air wrap around me. The days were getting hotter and hotter. I set the food bag on Z's desk. She smiled and grabbed at the bag with eager hands.

"They say anything yet?" I plopped into my chair.

"Mostly just 'let me out.' There's been some whispering back and forth though. Don't know if they're trying to figure out what's going on or trying to get their story straight." She slid a fry into her mouth and smiled. "Still hot and crispy."

"Yeah, I ordered after I ate so it would still be hot when I got here. Although with the sun out the way it is I could have ordered it earlier."

"I know... too hot. Way too hot. Finally got my air conditioner fixed though."

"Good. Maybe you'll stay home for a change instead of going out."

Z laughed before taking a bite out of her sandwich. She nodded as she chewed. "We can interrogate them after I'm done eating. I think Tiffany has sobered up a little more than him. She sounded genuinely worried about Jade, but if that were true, then why didn't she call her in two weeks?"

I nodded. "Something's not adding up."

Z finished eating while I took Tiffany into the interrogation room. She protested her innocence the whole way.

"I didn't do anything!"

I sat her in the chair on the far side of the table. Zelina walked in and closed the door.

"What did you two do with Jade?" I asked as I sat down. I wasn't in the mood to sugar coat anything. I had a million questions and I needed answers now.

"Nothing! We did nothing to her. I haven't seen her in two weeks. Haven't talked to her either. What is this about?" She leaned back in her chair, her hands in her lap. "I haven't done anything, and Jade didn't do anything either. She wouldn't."

I sighed. "You know we have been looking for you?"

She blinked. "Why?"

"A missing persons report was filed on you," I said. I tried to keep the edge in my voice dull but she was pissing me off. How could she be so oblivious to what was going on outside of the trailer?

She laughed. "It wasn't my parents. I know that."

"Jade's parents," said Zelina. "They filed the report."

"They don't even like me. Why would they care?"

"Because Jade was missing too," I said slowly.

She straightened into her chair. "What?" her eyes darted from me to Zelina in quick succession. "How could she be missing? She didn't go anywhere without me. Wherever she went, I went too."

"But you've been gone for two weeks."

She stared at me. "But if she was in trouble, she knew where I was. She always knew where I was. If I didn't tell anyone else, I would have told her."

"So she knew you were with Boston. Why wasn't she with you?" I asked.

She shrugged. "She doesn't really like Boston. She called him a loser. She was there with us for an hour or so after school, but she was ready to leave. I told her I was going to stay, and Boston's dad drove her home."

"He was there?" asked Zelina.

She nodded. "Yeah, he drops by sometimes to check on him and make sure he isn't doing anything stupid. Jade was ready to go, and he was on his way out and said he would take her home. He's really nice."

"Yeah, I know."

"Is Jade still missing?" She stared up at me, eyes glassy. Tears ready to fall at any moment.

I sighed. I had told her Jade was dead, but she was so high at the time she probably didn't remember it. Here we go again. "No. We found her body a few days ago."

A sob ripped through her. Her shoulders shook. Tears pricked my eyes.

"Who would hurt her? She never did anything to hurt anyone." She sobbed. Zelina moved her chair around the table and sat next to her. She wrapped her arms around her, and Tiffany sobbed into her shoulder. It was clear she didn't know anything about Jade's death. My fingers drummed against the table. None of this made sense.

I left them in the interrogation room and headed back to my desk, sitting down only for a moment before I jumped to my feet and headed back to the cells.

"You saw Tiffany the day she went missing, and your dad took Jade home."

Boston stared at me for a long time. He shrugged. "Yeah, he does that sometimes. She was ready to go home, so he took her home on his way to the store."

"Okay. Is he still in town?"

"Nah, he's back on the road. He should be back soon, I think. I don't think this was a long haul this time."

"Okay. Give me his number."

I handed him a sticky note and a pen. He wrote down his father's cellphone number, and I snatched the note from him and headed back to my desk. I dialed the number. It rang twice.

"Hello?"

"Mr. Craster, this is Detective Riley Quinn."

"Oh, yes! What did my son do now?"

A chuckle bubbled up my throat. "Nothing... well, that's not why I'm calling you. I heard that you gave Jade Bailey a ride home a couple weeks ago."

"Right... right. I did. I don't think she likes my son too much. Not that I blame her. She was there when I got to the house, and then I was getting ready to go to the store, and she asked if I could give her a ride. I said sure."

"Okay. That's what I heard."

"Yeah. I'm sorry I didn't call with that information. I've been on and off the road for a few weeks now. When I'm home, all I do is sleep. It slipped my mind, really."

"Did you see anything strange outside her house that night?"

He sighed. "Um... well, she didn't want me to drop her off in front of her house. She said her parents would be upset if she took a ride from some man. I dropped her off down the block. There was a red car down the street on the other side. I saw someone move inside the car, but I didn't think anything of it."

"I see. Did you get a license plate number?"

"Nope. It was pretty far away. But she didn't seem worried about anything. She walked down the street like nothing was wrong."

"Okay. Thank you for answering my questions."

"Sure. Anytime."

I hung up the phone and leaned back in my chair. Maybe someone was watching her house. "I'm curious..."

Zelina strode back into the room. "About?"

"I was just wondering if the Moore family were trying to get back at Tiffany and her family. Jade is her only friend. If anyone knew where Tiffany was, it would have been Jade."

"So, you think they attacked Jade to get back at Tiffany?" Judging by the sound of her voice, she didn't believe that theory, but I wasn't finished.

"No, not that. Maybe they couldn't find her just like we couldn't find her. But Jade would have known where she was. Boston's dad said there was a red car with someone in it down the block. Maybe they were waiting for her to come home and tried to get her to tell them where Tiffany was."

Her mouth made a perfect 'O' as she leaned back in her seat. "That might make sense… so they were looking for Tiffany. I mean, I guess that could happen. But why would they have it out for Tiffany? That's what I don't see."

She had a point. I didn't understand that part either. Why would the Moores have it in for the Cole family? Did they blame them for what Larry did to their family?

"I don't know. But something about this isn't sitting right with me. None of it. And I still want to speak with Noah Jameson. He knows something he doesn't want us to know. I can feel it." It was like a humming beneath my skin, beneath my bones. My body vibrated with it. My fingers drummed against my desk. I needed to talk to him.

Zelina looked down at her watch. "First thing in the morning. Let's get some sleep and look at this with a fresh set of eyes. I want to get some patrol officers to look at her neighbors and see if they have any surveillance cameras that might have caught the vehicle waiting on the street."

"Good idea. Both of them, really." Time both dragged and moved fast when we were working on a case. Slow when we had no evidence and no leads. Fast once everything started coming in. But we hadn't hit the fast stride just yet. Nothing was coming in. Nothing. And that was what I found so frustrating. Every lead had been a dry hole until now.

At least Tiffany was alive.

I drove home, made dinner, and crawled into bed with Luna snuggling against my feet. I was so tired I fell asleep as soon as my head hit the pillow.

I woke up a little after five. Earlier than usual. I couldn't sleep anymore after a long night of tossing and turning and flipping around like a fish out of water. I kicked off the sheets and sat up. Luna wasn't at my feet anymore. She had crawled into her bed tucked in the corner of the room, probably because of my tossing and turning. My phone was on the nightstand. I wanted to look at the screen, but I decided not to. Not right then.

I needed a second to decompress before I looked through my phone. My eyes felt like there was sand underneath my eyelids. I was so tired. I was tired of not being able to sleep. I was tired of not knowing what happened to Jade and why. And then there was Larry Cole.

Something about his case bothered me. I couldn't put my finger on it. It gnawed at me, unrelenting. Someone was hiding something.

I crawled out of bed and headed to the kitchen to grab a glass of water. I strolled outside. The cool morning air sent a shiver down my spine. The dark water of the lake seemed to sway in the breeze. Small waves moving back and forth. Fish dancing beneath the surface.

I sat on the porch for a long time. The sky lightened with streaks of purple and orange and then light blue. Birds and butterflies whirled around, and Luna poked her head out the door for a moment before running out to chase a bird. Her normal routine. I watched her for a long moment, running back and forth, following butterflies and birds. Trying to jump high enough to reach them.

I sighed as I pulled myself up to my feet. It was time to start my day. First, I had to get Luna's food ready, and then myself. My shower perked me up a little bit, and then coffee did the rest.

"You ready to get going?" I asked Zelina as soon as I walked in. I had been thinking about visiting Noah since he hung up on me. He had something to say, and I was desperate to hear it.

"Yes. Officers are already patrolling Jade's neighborhood and talking to the neighbors. So yeah, let's go."

Noah Jameson worked in Oceanway. His office was in a red brick building downtown. His name was on the door. Very fancy. Very official. And a little annoying. We walked in. A secretary, a blonde woman with curly hair and bright green eyes, sat at her desk and eyed us.

"Is Mr. Jameson in?" I asked as I held up my badge. She jumped to her feet.

"Um... sure... I mean, No." She looked at a door in the back of the room.

"Don't get up. We got it." I moved past her quickly, so she didn't have time to get to the door first. The doorknob was cold in my grasp. I turned hard and opened the door. The office was empty. The lights were off. It looked like he hadn't been there all morning. I spun around and looked at her.

"Like I said, he's not here. He hasn't come in yet."

"Is that unusual?" Zelina stepped closer to her desk. "Is he usually here by now?"

She nodded. "Usually. I've been calling, but there's no answer."

I glanced at Zelina, who nodded. We walked out of the office building and headed toward our car. I had gotten both his work and home addresses before we left the station.

The thought of him skipping town after I called crossed my mind a couple of times while we were on our way to his house. We turned the corner into his neighborhood. Zelina stopped short. Police cars and vans littered the street. My heart plummeted into my stomach. Bile coated the back of my throat. My fingers fumbled with my seatbelt for a long moment. Seconds ticked by slowly as I fought to unbuckle it. Finally, the seatbelt loosened, my fingers were on the door handle, and I was outside before Zelina could turn the car off.

I held up my badge and moved through the crowd quickly and wordlessly. Officers weaved in and out of the crowd. Pushing neighbors back, letting crime scene techs through. I reached the front door. Droplets of blood coated the door frame. I stepped through the doorway. Crime scene techs and officers moved around like flies, looking for somewhere to land. One tech moved past me and headed down the hall. I followed him.

The smell of death hung in the air, thick and hot. I followed the tech to a bedroom where officers started at the bed. I moved so I could get a better look at what they were looking at. Two bodies sprawled on the bed under the blood-stained covers. Blood spatter coated the wall and the headboard. I recognized Noah from his driver's license photo. It was him and a woman in bed next to him.

They were shot. It was difficult to see. Blood on the sheets and the front of their pajamas made it difficult to tell. They could have been stabbed to death. That would have been my first guess. However, according to the assistant medical examiner, they were shot in the chest point blank. Stippling on their clothes meant it was at close range. They didn't even have a chance to open their eyes, let alone roll over. I had assumed they were sleeping because of the body placement. The two, him and probably his wife, were under their bedsheet. She was on her side with her arms wrapped around his right arm. He slept on his back with his arms at his side. They looked like they had been tucked in. It could have been staged, or someone broke in and shot them in their sleep. *Just like the Moores*, I remembered.

"Who are you?"

Silence rippled through the room. I barely noticed it. My eyes were fixed on the bodies. Why now? Why kill him now? Opportunity, or was it something else?

"Excuse me?"

My eyes darted up and stared at the man who stood in the doorway. Judging by his clothes, he was an Oceanway detective. He stared at me expectantly. I held up my badge and inched toward the door.

"What is a Pine Brooke detective doing here?"

I shrugged. "I had some questions for Mr. Jameson. Went to his office, and he wasn't there. So, we came here."

"Well, you found him. Sorry, he can't answer your questions." He glanced at the bodies. "Now, I need you out of my crime scene, if you don't mind."

CHAPTER TWENTY-SIX

Riley Quinn

MY CHEEKS WERE HOT AS I INCHED OUT OF THE ROOM. A DOZEN eyes on me, watching me leave. I should have seen it coming. We had no business being at this crime scene, but I was curious. It was strange that the same day we started looking for him, he turned up dead.

I strolled through the house slowly, looking at the walls and the pictures he had lying around. Anything that would give me a clue as to who he was. I glanced behind me, and the detective still stood near the door frame, watching me leave. He was tall with bright blue eyes and a scar just below his right eye. He was clean-shaven with a mop of dark brown curls on his head.

I left the house and took a deep breath of fresh air as soon as I touched the driveway. Zelina stood at the end of the driveway, partially in the street, talking to an officer. She nodded slightly when she saw me. I kept walking to the car.

A few minutes later, she joined me. We got in, and she started driving.

"His neighbor across the street called it in. She reported she heard gunshots from this direction. Responding officer found a smear of blood on the doorframe at the back door. Called in for backup and entered the scene, but the perp was long gone. The bodies were still warm."

"So, this just happened."

"Yeah, Officer Parish said he'd let me know if they had any more details."

I shook my head. Zelina was good at pulling information from people. Especially men. She was pretty and a great listener and always knew the right questions to ask in order to garner information without the other person realizing that's what she was doing.

"What about the bodies?" she asked.

I told her what I saw. She shook her head.

"They must have been sleeping. I wonder what that was about, though. If he had any enemies."

"I'm curious about that too, but it's not our case. Detective told me to leave his crime scene, so I doubt he'd welcome us back." My phone vibrated in my pocket. "Hello? Okay. We'll be there."

I hung up and sighed. "Another body has been found where Jade was."

Zelina blinked. "Oh, I hate that."

Another body being found in the same spot as Jade could have meant a variety of things. It could have meant that Jade wasn't the only person killed that night. Maybe she was taken with another person, and they were both taken to the hill to be killed.

It could also mean that we might have a serial killer on our hands. It might seem like a large jump to reach that conclusion, but it was plausible. That part of the hill could have been his burial ground. If you knew the area, it would be easy to know when people were there and when they weren't.

I worried about the second one. How many bodies would we find if we started a search? The thought soured my stomach. We stopped next to the coroner's van. Officers were already taping off the area. I jumped out of the car less out of eagerness and more out of fear. What if they found someone else while we were on our way?

My heart sank into my stomach while I walked over to Keith, the medical examiner. He was bent down over the body, his gloved hands sifting through the dirt next to the body. The smell of rotting flesh became stronger and stronger the closer I got. Bile rose up my throat, and I swallowed hard, trying to push it back down. I wanted to puke so desperately, but I had to keep going. Didn't want to contaminate the crime scene. I would never hear the end of it. Not from Zelina or the medical examiners.

I stood over the body. The face almost not nonexistent. The flesh had disintegrated. Leaving nothing but bone behind. It was an ugly sight. Zelina gasped when she walked up. Judging by the clothes and some of the flesh that was left behind, the body was female. Her long pink nails shone through the dirt. Still looked fresh.

"Wow," I said.

Keith looked up for the first time since we got there. He blinked at me like he just noticed I was there.

"Yeah," he said quietly. "It's a lot. The flesh on her neck is still present for the most part, and there are ligature marks on the flesh. Deep too. Someone wrapped something around her neck and pulled so hard the markings are still there. I would say that was the cause of death, but we will know more once we get her on the table."

A crime scene tech was near the victim's legs, brushing dirt away from the body. "We are doing this slowly to make sure we don't miss anything or disturb anything. We want to make sure we keep her intact as much as possible," she said.

"Can you tell how long she's been buried here?" asked Zelina.

"Long before Jade. A couple of weeks before Jade was found here. We will figure out more once we get her out of the dirt. I will say this: she is very skinny. I mean, before she was found here. Before she was killed, before her body decomposed, she was nothing but skin and bones. And look here." She lifted the woman's arm. "See those ligature marks. She was tied up for a long time."

"Just like Jade," I said. "Who found her?"

Keith pointed at a group of two young-ish guys who were giving their statement to the responding officers. "Those guys were camping and smelled the body. I guess it got exposed in the storm."

I nodded to Z and she went over to talk to the campers.

"I'm starting to wonder if we have more bodies up here. It might be possible," I said, pinching the bridge of my nose with a sigh. "I'll try to get an order to dig this area up. I mean, with two bodies being found here, it would make sense that there might be others."

The tech shook her head. "Yeah, that would make sense. But just because we think it makes sense doesn't mean they will."

I knew what she meant, and so did Keith. Without having to say it, we all understood. While working on cases, we got up close and personal with the victims and their families. We understand how our cases are going and what should come next. Sometimes, I can see where a case is headed before I start working on it. But just because I can see that doesn't mean the captain and the other higher-ups can. If I can't prove that something is required, that there is probable cause to search a house or dig up a forest, then they won't let me. It would take too many resources that the office doesn't have. That's usually the answer.

Another body being found here; it made sense that there would be more. But before we could dig up the area, we would have to show that the two murders were connected. From where I stood, it looked like they were related. Both victims had ligature marks around their wrists, showing that they were tied up for a long period of time. Jade wasn't strangled, but that might have been because she ran away from her captor and fell off the cliff before he could kill her.

But everything else was the same. Jade had lost a considerable amount of weight when she was kidnapped. She was starved, too. There was a link. I knew it. I felt it. The longer I stared at her body, the heavier the realization settled on me. It was connected, but how? Why? Was it random? Were they both just picked up one night and taken?

Or was it a planned abduction? Was someone watching them? Waiting for them? With another body being found in the same area as Jade, it made me believe that the murder might not have been tied to Tiffany and her family. It was something else.

I sighed. "Okay. We will need a prelim as soon as possible. We need to figure out who she is, so we know where to start."

Keith nodded. "Her fingers are pretty much intact. I'll see if I can get fingerprints. We might be able to do dental records, but we would need something to match them against."

"Right. Do what you can."

I followed Zelina as she scanned the area on the way back to the car. There was nothing there. Most of our evidence had washed away during the thunderstorm. I glanced back at the scene before I got in the car. Zelina started the car.

"What are you thinking?"

I shrugged. I was trying not to think about anything. I didn't want to think about the other bodies that might be buried next to the victim. I didn't want to think of the victim they were slowly uncovering. How old was she? Who she was? What happened to her, and how long she was kept captive before she was killed?

We went back to the station and immediately started combing through the missing persons' reports, looking for only females. I wasn't sure her age, so I looked for any female with dark brown hair. There were a lot of them, not just from our small town but also from the surrounding towns. It was a large stack.

Tiffany was still in holding with her boyfriend. I could have let her out, but I didn't feel like it, not yet. I definitely wasn't letting him out. He was on the hook for statutory rape. Tiffany wasn't even seventeen. A thought flashed in my mind, and I jumped to my feet. I rushed back to the holding cells. Tiffany sat on a bench with her arms wrapped around her body.

I knocked on the bar, and she looked up, her eyes red and her cheeks wet. She had been crying over her friend. Her only friend. Wherever she went, Jade went too. And now that was no more.

"Have you noticed anyone at your school that just stopped showing up?" I leaned against the bars.

She straightened. "What do you mean stopped coming? People move."

"No, not move. I mean, like students who just stopped coming. Any rumors of some girl being missing with dark brown hair?"

She sat quietly on the bench for a long moment. I watched her as she stared off into space. Her face twisted into a frown. "I don't know. I'm not really into school like that. I don't pay attention to that shit. Who goes or who doesn't? Jade would have known, though. She noticed everything. I mean, teachers change their hair or stomachs start bulging, and they might be pregnant. She knew everything. Always did."

"I get that. Anyone come to mind, though?" I looked at Boston in the cell next to hers, and he was watching us. "What about you? Anyone come to mind for you?"

He shrugged. "No. I'm not in school anymore." He laid on the bench and stared up at the ceiling.

"Right."

"Amara... something. She had dark brown hair. She used to come to school every day, and then she just stopped. I noticed because she was in my chemistry class. Everyone thought it was strange. I know I did, and so did Jade. She was the smartest kid in class, so why would she just stop coming to school? Jade was suspicious. But I just thought she might have moved. Or maybe because she was so smart, she might have been sent to a magnet school or something. No one knew, though."

"Okay. Thank you for the info." I ran back to my desk and searched through the reports that I'd set there. Then I looked through Zelina's and found what I was looking for. "Amara Cordova," I said. Her parents had filed a missing persons report on her four months ago. "She's been missing for four months." I studied the picture. It could have been the body we found, but I wasn't so sure. Amara was fourteen with long brown hair. She was a pretty girl. I wasn't sure what to do with that information.

Did we go to the family and ask for a DNA sample? Do we give them hope or break their hearts? We didn't know anything just yet. We didn't know anything about the body. "Maybe we should wait to inform them we might have their daughter in the morgue until we know more about the body. Age and all that." I looked up at Zelina; her lips pressed into a thin line as she nodded.

"Yeah. I don't want to scare them or... I don't want to say anything until we have the prelim. Definitely need that before we say anything."

"Yeah. Agreed." I slumped into my chair. I was tired already, and the day just started. It wasn't even ten yet, and we had found two... no, three dead bodies already. Two we couldn't investigate. I wanted to, though. I fought the urge to turn on my computer and start typing. *It isn't my case. It isn't my case*, I had to keep reminding myself. If I did start the investigation on Noah and the woman he was found with, it would cause all kinds of problems between our departments, especially if I did it without permission.

"You still thinking about Noah?"

I looked up. Zelina stared at me, a smile on the edge of her lips. She always knew what I was thinking. It was mildly annoying. I nodded slowly. "I can't get the image out of my head. I can't understand why now. Why kill him now?"

"You don't know that it's connected to Larry's case. You don't know. It might not be. He was a defense lawyer. He had to piss a few people off."

She made a good point. So many people could have hated him. But again, it wasn't my case. I had to let it go so I could focus on Jade and the other victim. "We need the prelim. I really want to know who she was."

Zelina nodded. "Me too. But what can we do until then?"

I jumped to my feet and headed toward the captain's office. The door was usually open, so I knocked on the doorframe. He looked up from behind his desk. "Can we talk?"

He sighed. "What happened now?"

A smile pulled at my lips. Zelina followed in behind me and closed the door behind us. "We wanted to inform you that another body was found where Jade Bailey was found."

He straightened in his chair. "I see. And you think there is a connection?"

"I think there might be. It would be great if we could dig up the area and see—"

He waved his hand dismissively. "No can do. We can't pay for that. The department is pretty tapped right now. If you want the order, then you need to find a link between the two victims as soon as possible. Until then, we can't do it."

My shoulders dropped. I knew before I asked that he would say no, but I was still hopeful. There was a link, but we just needed to prove it.

We left the station in silence and headed back to the school. My sole purpose of being there was to ask the principal about Amara.

Claudia sat at her desk when we walked in. She frowned when she saw us. "Is there something else wrong with one of my students?"

I glanced at Zelina and took a deep breath. "We don't know. We came to ask about Amara Cordova."

She leaned back in her chair and slowly exhaled. "Yes. Amara was a great student. One of our best and brightest. I had high hopes for her."

"What happened?" Zelina leaned against the door.

"She was there one moment and then gone the next. She just disappeared. Her parents came here looking for her and talking to her friends, but no one knew anything."

"Do you think she ran away?"

She looked at me. "No. I don't think so. She was a good kid. A great girl. I can't believe she would run away. She just didn't seem like the type."

"Right."

"Did you find her?"

I shrugged. "We don't know."

Claudia pulled out a notepad and started writing. "Here are some of her friends. They were really close and distraught when she went missing. Her parents asked them a lot of questions. Mrs. Cordova even blamed one of the girls. Said it was her fault. She claimed that the girls were always together. How could they not know where she was? She was very upset." She handed me the piece of paper. I stared at it for a long moment.

"Are they here?"

She nodded. "I think so. If so, I'll have them sent to the counselor's office. I know she talked to the girls in the aftermath of Amara's disappearance."

CHAPTER TWENTY-SEVEN

Riley Quinn

W E WALKED TO THE COUNSELOR'S OFFICE AND WAITED FOR HER to return with the students. She seemed surprised to see us. As soon as I walked in, she jumped to her feet.

"What happened now?" She stared at Claudia. "What is this about?"

The principal explained that we were looking to talk to the students who were friends with Amara Cordova. She nodded slowly. She wasn't expecting it, but she went along without explanation. We would explain it better once we talked to the girls and got a better understanding of Amara.

Almost ten minutes later, she returned with the students and closed the door behind her. She introduced them as Brianna Compton and Lindsey Navarro. I held up my badge, too, and smiled at the girls who looked uneasy.

"We just want to ask you about your friend Amara and her disappearance. We are looking into it and have a few questions."

"It's about time." Brianna, a taller girl with long dark hair and beautiful light brown eyes folded her arms across her chest. "We've been saying she didn't run away for months, and no one believed us."

"I know. And I understand how frustrating that can be. But we believe you. And we want to know more about your friend. Everything you can tell us, including the last time you saw her, would be helpful."

She sighed, and her shoulders dropped away from her ears. "The last time I saw her, it was at the park. We go there sometimes after school just to decompress after class, you know. Not in a rush to go home and deal with the parents. We talk and just hang out. One day we hung out, and then I went home, and so did Linds. We went in opposite directions, as always. When we left, Amara was still in the park, and she said she would see us the next day."

"And that was the last time you saw her?" asked Zelina.

She nodded. "Right. When she wasn't in first period, I thought maybe she had woken up late. And then, when she wasn't here for lunch, I called, and then I texted her, and nothing. I thought she might have gotten in trouble with her parents. You know, because she didn't go straight home after school."

"Was she supposed to?" I asked.

She rolled her eyes. "Her parents were always riding her about studying. She studied so hard, and it was never enough. She had perfect grades, but she got a B once, and they went off on her and said she would never amount to anything."

"Horrible thing to tell a child," I said.

"Right. But her parents kept pushing and pushing her. They wanted her to be perfect, and she tried, but no one is perfect. No one."

"You think she could have run away to get away from her parents?" It was my first thought. If her mother was constantly pushing her, maybe she would have had enough. Maybe she just wanted to be free from them.

Brianna shrugged. "I mean, maybe. It's possible, but I doubt it. She never wanted to disappoint her family. Especially her father. She wanted to please him. She... she wouldn't just run away from them. And that day at the park, she didn't have anything with her other than her chemistry book. That was it. No backpack, nothing. If she were going to run away, she would have taken something with her, right?"

It made sense. Hard to run away and stay away if you don't take anything you might need. Either she had other plans, or she didn't run away. "That is a good point. What do you think happened to her?"

The girls exchanged nervous glances, seeming to pass some unspoken communication to each other. Lindsey took a deep breath and finally spoke up in a small voice. "I don't think she would just run away. I think someone took her. Just like Cynthia."

"Cynthia who?" I glanced at the counselor.

"Cynthia Harmon. She was a student here last year. She left, though. Her family was moving."

Brianna shook her head. "Nope. Her family was not moving. That wasn't what I heard. Her parents were still here long after she went missing. They were looking for her. Until Mr. Harmon killed himself, and then his mother moved away."

"He killed himself?" Zelina looked at the counselor. "Seriously?"

The counselor nodded. "That was what I heard. Can't say why he did, though."

"Because no one was looking for his daughter, and he was distraught," Brianna insisted.

Lindsey sat there in silence. She wasn't like her friend—talkative and full of opinions. She was obviously much more nervous and withdrawn about this whole situation.

"What about you? What do you think?" I turned toward her and waited for an answer.

"Amara didn't run away. She loved her parents, but she hated them too. She wanted to prove them wrong. Her dad told her she wasn't worth anything. He said that she would never amount to anything in this life, and she wanted to show her parents that she would, and the only way to do that is to stay here and show them."

"Understood. Did you see anything strange that evening while you walked home?"

The girls exchanged a look for a moment. "I didn't."

Lindsey shoved her hands into her pocket. "I saw a red car. It stood out because it was this pretty wine color, and I had seen it three or four times just in that day. I didn't pay too much attention to it. There was someone in the car, though, and I saw movement. But that was it. Nothing else happened. I never noticed anyone following us or trying to talk to us or anything weird happening."

"Yeah, me either. Is this connected to what happened to Jade?"

I looked at her for a moment, trying to figure out what to say. I didn't want to lie to her. But I felt one coming. If we told her yes, it would get around town rather quickly. "We don't know."

"So that's a yes."

"No, that's a *we don't know*. Until we know for certain, we can't say for sure. I would like to know more about Cynthia Harmon, though."

"She was in my math class. She was nice," said Lindsey. "Smart. Not real popular, though."

"Right." I glanced back at Zelina, who shook her head. This was so strange. I wondered for a moment how many young girls had gone missing from this school alone and why no one had put it together before now. That was infuriating. If people had been paying attention, then maybe this would have stopped long before now. But now, here we were.

"Okay. Thank you for your time." I followed Zelina out of the room. We walked to the car slowly. "Did you see Cynthia Harmon in the stack of reports?"

"I wasn't really paying attention to other names. I was just looking for young women who matched the body in the ground. We should go back and look through them, though. The mother moved away, but maybe we could still find her."

"Hopefully we can." The ride back to the station was quiet. Filled with many words left unspoken. A million things ran through my mind, and I processed my thoughts better when everything was quiet.

I kept thinking about Larry Cole, and his lawyer Noah. It didn't feel right, but I couldn't do anything about it. Jade and Amara slipped into my mind as well. We didn't know that the body was Amara just yet, but I still felt like it was likely. It could have been her, and if she had been there, then maybe Cynthia would have been too. There had to be more bodies in that area.

I was curious about Mr. Harmon and his reason for suicide. Did he do something to their daughter? Or was he so distraught about her being missing that he couldn't get past his grief? Either was possible. I wondered if his wife would answer my questions. It was a tough thing to ask of any mother who lost her family. But I needed to know.

Zelina sorted through the missing person's reports while I looked up Mrs. Harmon's phone number. It took me a while to find it. I did several searches. She left a month after her husband killed himself. She didn't stay long to figure out why or to learn about her daughter. She left, but she didn't sell the house, and I found that curious. If she was leaving town, why would she keep the house unless she planned on coming back? Maybe she thought Cynthia would eventually find her way back, and she wanted the house to be there for her just in case. A familiar place. It made sense.

I took a deep breath and dialed her number. The phone rang several times before someone answered.

"Hello?"

"Is this Camille Harmon?"

There was a sharp intake of breath and then silence. "I... yes. Who is this?"

"Detective Riley Quinn. I have some questions about your daughter if you don't mind answering them."

"Did you find her?"

"Not yet. But I need you to answer some questions about the last time you saw your daughter."

"The last day I saw her, she was headed to school, as always. She walked there, and she walked home. She never made it home that day. I waited for a few hours. I thought she might have been hanging out with her friends after school, but when I walked out of the house to look for her, her best friend was walking home. I asked her about Cyn, and she said she hadn't seen her since PE."

"And that was strange for her? To skip her classes?"

"She never did that kind of thing. She loved school. She loved her teachers and her classes. She hated missing a day. I looked for her along the path she usually walked—"

"Did you see anything strange along that path?"

She sighed. "Umm. It was pretty empty. The students had walked home already. When I neared the school, I saw a red car driving away. I only remember it because it was the second time I had seen it that day."

"When was the first?"

"That morning, when I was leaving for work. I saw it down the block. I figured it was someone new to town."

"Right. Can I ask about your husband?"

She drew in a shaky breath. "I should have seen it coming. He was so broken when she disappeared. I mean, he blamed himself. He felt like he should have been able to find her. He should have noticed something was wrong; he should have protected her. I came home from work, and he had hung himself in her room."

"Wow. He blamed himself."

"Yes. He didn't believe she was still alive. I held out hope as long as I could, but he knew she was gone as soon as the police couldn't find her.

He knew it. He kept trying to tell me that she was gone and wasn't coming back, that someone took her. But I just couldn't believe it. I believe him now."

"I see. Did he leave a note?"

"He did. It basically just said that he couldn't go on, knowing that he wasn't able to protect his daughter. The paper he wrote it on was wet from his tears."

"I'm sorry. If I hear or find anything, I will call you and let you know."

"I imagine that you will need DNA at some point. If you go to the house, her stuff is still there. Kept her room just the way she left it. I think a hairbrush and a toothbrush are still there. You are welcome to it."

"Thank you. If it comes down to it, I will let you know." I hung up the phone and stared at my computer screen for a few minutes. Her voice still rang in my ears. She sounded so calm. No, not calm, defeated. Deflated. Her voice was soft, without a trace of emotion. Like she was all cried out, she had lost everyone in her family, and now she was just a shell of a person. Tears stung my eyes. It was a hard thing to hear. To witness.

"Rough call?" asked Zelina.

I leaned back in my chair and blew out a heavy sigh. "She is a sad, sad woman. You can hear it in her voice. She's heartbroken and believes that her daughter is dead."

"I can't even imagine what she must be feeling. Oh, I found Cynthia's missing persons report."

"Any new info there?" I asked.

"Nothing we don't already know. She went missing after school, I'm sure the mom told you the rest of the story."

"Get this. Her mother said while she was looking for Cynthia and neared the school, she saw a red car. It was the second time she had seen it that day. The first time was in the morning when she was leaving for work."

"He was following Cynthia. Watching her and her family." She leaned back in her chair and took a deep breath. "Wow, so if that was the same car that was waiting down the street on Jade's block…"

"Right. And the red car that was near where Amara went missing. You think it is just a coincidence?"

She shook her head. "No, not this many times." Her phone buzzed on her desk. "They want us to come down to the morgue."

"I wonder what they found."

The chilly air in the morgue was a nice, welcomed treat to the heat outside. I sighed as soon as I walked in. Relieved.

Keith waved as we came in. "You two got here fast."

"Eager to hear your findings," I said. I was. Very eager. I wanted to know everything he knew.

"Okay. These are just my findings. Prelim only. We still need to run a few more tests, but I knew you two were waiting. I haven't done a full workup yet, but this is what I have."

"Ready whenever you are."

"Well, for starters, this girl was abused for a long period of time. After you left, we were able to uncover her feet, and there were ligature marks around her ankles. She was tied up for a long time. The rope wore through her skin, down to her bone. Oddly, three of her teeth were pulled out. This is consistent with Jade's body, which also had three teeth missing."

I nodded. "I remember from the file. At first, we thought maybe she had them pulled for some reason. But with both victims missing three teeth and only three teeth, it doesn't seem like a coincidence."

Zelina shook her head. "He kept three teeth as a souvenir."

"She had two fractured ribs at the time of her death. A broken wrist, fractured jaw, and a broken nose. They beat the crap out of her before they killed her. I would say sexual assault, but it's hard to say at this point. The parts of her body shielded by her clothes were protected from decomposition. I don't know if we will find anything other than some scarring. I still did a swab, so we will see."

"Can you tell us anything about her last meal or anything about where she was held before she was buried?"

"No. There... so far, there is nothing that I can see that would tell us where she was held before. It's strange. Her stomach was still intact, but it was empty. Looks like it had been for a long time."

"She was starved."

He nodded. "Very little muscle mass. It's like a coma victim or someone who has been immobile for a long time. They kept her tied up and immobile for a long time."

"Okay." Zelina handed him Amara's report. "Could this be her?"

He quickly scanned the piece of paper, then looked over to examine the skull and then the hair of the body. "Maybe. The hair looks the same. Here, it says that she has a birthmark on her thigh." Keith handed the paper back to Zelina. "Give me a minute."

He pushed up the white sheet that covered the body. "Yup. Red birthmark on her right thigh." He held up the sheet so we could see. There it was... the birthmark. "It also says that she broke her left arm when she was younger." With a gloved hand, Keith lifted the half-bone, half-loose flesh arm. He pushed some of the flesh back. It wasn't difficult. Her skin was barely hanging on. It was loose around her bones and already starting to fall off.

"Yeah. I see a remodeled break here." Keith sighed as he covered the body back up. "I'd need to do a DNA test, but I think this is your girl."

I sighed. "Now, we need to inform the family."

Zelina took a deep breath. It was the part of the job we hated the most. But it had to be done.

CHAPTER TWENTY-EIGHT

Riley Quinn

Mr. and Mrs. Cordova sat in their living room in perfect silence. Their eyes fixed on us. It was a nice house. One story with a large living room, a built-in bookcase, and a large sofa. I watched them while they watched us. Seconds ticked by in complete silence.

Finally, after a few more minutes, Zelina said something. "We aren't sure the body is hers. Not completely. We need DNA to confirm it."

A sob bubbled up Mrs. Cordova's throat. She squeezed her lips together to stop the sound from tearing through the room. Her husband wrapped his arm around her and pulled her close.

"I understand. We thought this would happen... her being found this way."

He couldn't bear to say she was dead. He was talking around it. "Um... we still have her hairbrushes and her toothbrush and her clothes.

Everything. We have everything she left behind." He pointed down the hall. "Second door on your left."

I stood up and wandered down the hallway. Family photos littered the walls along the hallway. They looked so happy together. Smiling big in every photo. Laughing and hugging each other. I found the room and walked in. The walls were yellow with white trim. Her bed was near the window, next to a nightstand which housed a lamp and an alarm clock. Her hairbrush was on a dresser. I grabbed it and slipped it into an evidence bag.

Her room was clean. Nothing out of place. It made me think of Tiffany's room. Her room was clean in a sea of chaos. But unlike the stark emptiness of Tiffany's room, this was the room of a girl who took a lot of pride in her surroundings and wanted them to look and feel nice. I walked out of the room, slowly inching down the hallway.

"Um... so the last time you saw your daughter, what was she like? Was she upset about anything?"

I stepped into the living room just as Mrs. Cordova shook her head. "She looked fine. She seemed fine. She wasn't stressed or anything like that. She was trying to study for her exams, but that was it. There was nothing else going on in her life at this point."

"No boyfriend or crush or anything?"

Mrs. Cordova looked offended by the question. Her mouth twisted into a scowl. "Of course not. She didn't have the time for a boyfriend or a crush. Amara was going to go to Harvard. She had to stay focused. Anything that took her focus away from her schoolwork had to be removed."

I glanced at Mr. Cordova. He sat still and didn't open his mouth, his eyes glued to the floor. His wife was the one in charge, especially when it came to Amara. Amara must have felt so alone living in this household. Like there was no one that she could turn to. Her father probably went along with everything her mother said regardless of what Amara had to say or how she felt.

"Thank you for your time and if we learn anything, we will let you know," I said.

Zelina jumped to her feet. "If you have any questions or any new information comes to light, please contact us."

I led her out of the house, waiting until we got into the car before I said anything. "That mother," said Zelina as soon as she stuck the key into the ignition. "She is a piece of work."

"I gathered that from the tail end of the conversation. She was very strict with her daughter and the father was no help. He just seemed to go along with everything."

"I doubt she gave him much of a choice. While you were back there, I asked a few questions and she and *only* she answered them. She was the only one who had something to say. He opened his mouth to answer one and she cut him off."

"She put a lot of pressure on that girl. Didn't even let her enjoy her teen years. It's not all about studying, you know. It's upsetting… I wonder if Amara hadn't wanted to go home… if she stayed a bit too long at that park the day she was taken."

"I was thinking the same thing."

We drove the brush to the lab so it could be tested. While they processed it, we went back to the station. Zelina looked into the database for a red car. None of the witnesses could describe the car except for the color. That made it harder to pinpoint who owned the car. It might be a while before we could narrow it down.

While she did that, I searched through the database looking for missing girls from the school Jade and Tiffany went to. It seemed unusual that so far three girls had gone missing within the last year or so, and no one had picked up on it until now. But then again, we just figured it out ourselves.

We both had our assignments. I searched through our database and found three more missing girls going back as far as six years. I stared at the screen for a moment. The young girls all kind of favored each other. Pretty but not overly beautiful. Plain janes. Not popular in the least. Nice girls who did well in school, but who generally had problems with one or both parents. Our killer had a type. He tried to take girls no one would miss. He was both right and wrong, I guess.

They were missed, but their disappearance did not elicit a large-scale reaction. If Jade hadn't stumbled off the cliff, we wouldn't have noticed ourselves. It was a sad thing to think but that was the truth. We were only on the track because of her. Because she tried to get away.

"Hey, Riley! Call for you. I tried to take a message, but he wouldn't talk to anyone else, and he wouldn't hang up until he spoke with you." A new patrol officer named Olivia Bennett stopped at my desk. "He seemed shaky. Stressed about something."

"Got it. I wonder who this is." I picked up the phone as she walked away. "Detective Riley Quinn speaking."

"You were the detective that came to my house the other day." It wasn't a question. The shaky voice was raspy and familiar. "You were nice. The doctor was too."

"I glad you thought so, Mr. Gil. Is there something I can do for you?"

"Yeah, I need you to come to my house so I can show you something. And bring that nice doctor you brought last time. I need him to look at something."

The dial tone was loud and startling in my ear. I pulled the receiver away. That was fast. I guess that was all he had to say. I hung up the phone. "Mr. Gil wants to see me and Doctor Elwood."

Zelina looked up. "Oh... well, I guess he likes you."

I rolled my eyes. "I was just nice to him, that's all."

"He might be looking for wife number two."

"Shut up." Most people in town were not nice to Mr. Gil. He was an ornery old man who didn't like people and did not hide it. So many of the high school kids trashed his property but he never reported them. He never made a big deal about it, he just ignored it. Kept moving. I respected his restraint. *Wouldn't be me, though.*

I slid behind the wheel of my car and called Logan, hoping he wasn't in the middle of yet another emergency.

"We're graduating to phone calls now?" he asked, instead of saying anything normal like 'hello'.

I blinked. "What?"

"Usually you just text me."

"Well, usually I'm not behind the wheel of a car. I don't text and drive."

"Good. I'm always telling people that's one of the worst things you can do. You don't want to know how many injuries I've treated from texting-related collisions."

"And you don't want to know how many tickets I've given out for it," I countered. He laughed. "But anyway, I'm sorry to bother you so late like this, but I need your help."

"Again?"

"Again."

"If I didn't know any better, I'd think you were just making excuses to hang out with me."

I blushed. "Hey, *you* came up to *me* at lunch the other day. And anyway, Mr. Gil said he has something to show me, and he wants you to come with me."

"Why?"

"Not really sure. He says he needs you to take a look at something."

THE GIRLS IN PINE BROOKE

"That sounds ominous. Um. Sure, I guess."

"I'm already on my way to your house. Have your bag or whatever packed up, I'll be there in a few."

When I pulled into the driveway, Logan was already waiting out front, sitting on his porch step with his medical bag in his lap. I rolled down the window and waved as he approached.

"I am both curious and concerned at the same time," he said as he slid into the passenger seat. "I hope he didn't hurt himself."

I backed out of the driveway and headed toward Gil's house. "It's possible. He's all alone up there, and no one's checking on him. He could have hurt himself on anything up there. Sorry to bother you, though."

"No, it's okay. Whatever I can do to help. It's kind of my job."

A smile pulled at my lips.

"I'm surprised you're still working though. It's late," he added.

I sighed. "He called just when I was getting back in the office. Said he wanted us to come over and then hung up. No room for conversation or rescheduling."

"Not a patient man... got it."

"It didn't sound like an emergency, though," I said. "Hopefully."

"Hopefully," Logan echoed.

We made small talk as we drove further into the woods, but the closer we got, the quieter the drive became., curiosity making my blood buzz beneath my skin. *What could he possibly have to show me? Why didn't he think of it the last time I saw him? Why did he need Dr. Elwood here?*

Gil was leaning against the door frame with the door open when I pulled up. "Got here fast."

"Sounded important."

He shrugged, his bony shoulders rising slightly. "Might be. I'm not sure what you can do with it. I'm only showing it to you because you have a good head on your shoulders. You seem to take your job seriously. Reminds me of my father a little." Nearly a century ago, Gil's father had been the county sheriff before he had a massive heart attack at a crime scene and died. By all accounts he was a good man. A fair man. "Hey there, doc."

Logan smiled. "Heard there was something you wanted to show me. Everything alright?"

"Just a bit of a bruise, I think. Best to be sure, though." He looked from me to Logan. "Well, you two had better come in so we can get this done."

I eased onto the porch and into the house. Logan followed close behind. It was dimly lit, the smell of dust and musky furniture filling the air. The windows probably hadn't been opened in a long time. "Okay. So what do you have to tell me?"

"I got security footage for you."

"You have cameras?" I asked.

He smiled. "All around my property," he said, pointing to a few corners. "Here, and here. You can't tell anyone I have this. I want to be left alone."

"I got the picture," I said.

But he was still muttering. "Kids always coming up here and throwing things at my door. Riding around my property and ruining my flowers. But I let it go. I had hoped that if I ignored it, they would stop. I ignore it, and they get tired and go away. But every generation, here they come."

I followed him through the living room, into the kitchen and then into a back bedroom, noticing he was walking pretty slowly. The house was filled with stuff, but it wasn't cluttered. I wasn't falling over stuff as I followed him. It was neat, but he could still stand to clear out some of it. In the room was a desk and a very old computer. Ancient. Well, not that old—at least it could fit in the room.

He slowly lowered himself into the chair and turned the computer on. "You can't tell anyone I have these," he repeated. "They'll just see them as something else to destroy, and I can't afford to replace them every time that happens." His eyes darted to Logan. "You either, doc."

Logan held his hands up. "Understood."

Gil chuckled and looked at both of us. "You two are so cute. Nice to know this town is being taken care of by a good-looking couple like you."

My back straightened immediately. Logan stopped leaning on the door frame. We exchanged a nervous, confused glance.

"Um. We aren't together, Mr. Gil," I said. "Just… acquaintances."

"Friends," Logan said at the same time.

I looked back at him. "Yeah. Friends," I added quickly.

Logan gave me a look, a *we are going to talk about this later* kind of look. I fired back with a *can we not do this right now in front of a stranger* kind of look.

Thankfully, Gil didn't seem to notice the awkwardness in the room. He chuckled and shook his head. "Shame. I'm always right about these things."

"Um… maybe I should sit in the living room." Logan glanced back toward the front door, itching to get out of the room.

"No, it's fine. It'll just be a minute," said Gil.

The screen flickered to life and he pulled up a video file. "I just saw it this morning. I don't check them often because it's the same every time. And no one ever does anything about the damn kids coming up here and destroying things, so I don't see the point in involving the police."

He pressed play. For a few seconds, the video only showed the empty forest—and then a young girl fell into view. She looked back for a moment before jumping to her feet and running. She stumbled again. When she looked behind her, I got a clear view of her face. It was Jade running for her life.

My breath caught in my throat. She was there, running for her life. I waited for the killer to come into view. Jade ran out of view, and a few seconds later, a man stepped into view. I waited for him to look around so I could see his face.

"That girl looks like the one I saw in the paper. That's why I called you."

Logan stayed in the doorway, leaning against the frame. He didn't say anything, nor did he crane his neck to look at the screen.

"Thank you for calling me." The man stood in the same spot for a long moment. He wasn't chasing Jade, he knew he could catch her. His mouth was moving, maybe he was calling her name or trying to get her to come back. His frame looked familiar. like I had seen him before. He turned his head. all the air evaporated from my lungs. My heart plunged into my stomach.

"Hey, I know him," said Mr. Gil.

"Yeah, me too."

CHAPTER TWENTY-NINE

Logan Elwood

"Now, what do you need me to take a look at, Mr. Gil?" I straightened in the doorway. The two of them were staring at the screen, and Riley made a copy of the video. I wanted to know what it was, but I knew it was none of my business.

I was curious, but it was probably police business, and I didn't want to get involved. Riley slipped the drive into her pocket. Mr. Gil having evidence of a crime was strange to me, but his reasoning made sense. I would probably have secret video cameras placed around my property too if I had to deal with people constantly trespassing and bothering me.

Gil sighed, then looked from Riley to me. "It's in a sensitive area."

"I'll leave you two alone now," Riley announced. She walked past me into the living room.

"Well?" I asked. *A sensitive area?* I gulped at the thought of what that might mean as he limped over to me and lifted up the back of his shirt.

"I've been having a tough time with my lower back lately," he explained. "Right here, just above my... well, my ass."

I let out a breath. At least it was above that region. "Alright, let me take a look."

I did a quick examination, checking his range of motion, his reflexes, listening for his breathing, and feeling for the spot that hurt. Gil winced as I ran my hand across the muscle.

Gil gasped as I ran my hand across his spine. "Right there," he groaned in pain.

"You know, I was beginning to think you didn't really need me out here," I said. "You seemed pretty alright earlier."

"Pain's not usually so bad. But it's getting worse."

"I see. Have you been doing a lot of hiking lately? Any strenuous physical activity?"

He grumbled. "I don't really leave the house like that, doc. Was trying to clean up the place a bit when I tweaked it real bad."

"Well, that would do it. I think you have a herniated disk. Not a big deal though."

Gil looked up at me with worry on his face, but I gave him my best reassuring smile. "We'll need to get you in the clinic for some further tests and treatment options. I promise that with some mild painkillers, maybe some light physical therapy, you'll be right as rain in no time."

He hesitated. I could tell the man was nervous to leave his house, surrounded by his things. But he had asked me to come for a reason. I couldn't just let him suffer.

"I can come by tomorrow to pick you up," I offered.

"That would be good," he finally said. "Thanks, doc."

"Anytime. It's like you said—we gotta take care of this town. And that includes you."

He laughed and ushered me out into the living room, where Riley was waiting on the couch. I glanced around the room. While everything was neatly stacked, it was still a lot of stuff in such a small space. No wonder he'd hurt himself cleaning up.

"Now take it easy for a few days," I told him. "No more strenuous activity until at least we get you in. And I promise, I'll come by tomorrow afternoon to get you in for some tests. Can you behave until then?"

Mr. Gil laughed. "I can behave, young man."

Riley smiled. "And if someone comes here trying to mess with your property, give me a call. If someone is bothering you, give me a call, and my partner and I will get them to stop. I have an idea of what can be done about it. And that goes for everything else around here too."

He followed her gaze around the room. "I know it's a lot of stuff. I keep meaning to clean it up, and then when I get around to it, I throw out my damn back."

Riley laughed. "Ain't that the worst? Tell you what—I'll see if we can come back and help you out one of these days, alright?"

A smile tugged at his lips. He nodded slowly. "Thank you."

"No, thank you for this." She held up the USB drive and smiled.

"Goodnight, doc. Goodnight, detective. I really appreciate you guys coming out so late."

"Really, don't mention it," I said. "Have a good night."

We waved goodbye and headed out. The night air was cool against my skin, a welcome change from the sticky heat of the day and the thick, dusty staleness of the house. Riley leaned against her driver's side door on her phone. I shoved my medical bag in the backseat.

"Yeah, Z. I'll head back to the station as soon as I can. Just let me take the doctor home."

"I guess what he showed you was pertinent to your investigation," I said as we got in and buckled our seatbelts.

"Yes, it was. Nice word," she said, a smile on the edge of her words. "Is he okay?"

"Yeah, he's okay. Herniated disk. Nothing too serious, but I'll follow up with him about it." I stared out the window. "Weird, him thinking we were a couple, though."

"Not so weird. I'm quite the catch."

I stared at her for a long moment. Was she serious, or was this a joke? A few seconds later, she cracked a smile, and her laughter bubbled through the car. I shook my head.

"I am a catch, though. And you are the hot doctor."

"Oh, is that what you think?"

"That's what people call you. Not necessarily me."

I laughed. "I guess I'm a catch, too."

"Older people think every young person they know should hook up with the *other* young person they know. Purely based on proximity."

"Probably just 'cause they're *freak-ayy*," I said, setting off another round of laughter as we drove back toward town.

"So, Doctor Elwood, how are you liking it here in Pine Brooke?"

I shrugged, not sure what to say. "Seems like a nice town. But the police department does seem too busy for my liking."

Her chuckle rippled through the air. "Funny. And we are not that busy. Busier in the city."

"I'll give you that, I guess. But you do seem busy."

"Comes with the job. I mean, you're one to talk. You're a doctor. That must be crazy."

I leaned my head back against the headrest. "Not really. This is nothing compared to when I was an ER doctor. That was nonstop."

"I didn't know that. An ER doctor? That's gotta be exhausting. Judging by what I see on TV, at least."

"Well, being a detective doesn't seem so great on TV either," I countered.

"Point taken."

Riley glanced over at me as if to say something else, but then cut those bright blue eyes back to the road. She did it two more times before I finally called her out on it.

"What?"

She cleared her throat. "Did you make the change, because… um… ever since…"

The death of my wife?

I guess I was glad she didn't say the words out loud. Even though she was right. I don't know exactly how she knew, but it was true what she said about small towns: everyone knew everyone, eventually. Tears stung my eyes. I turned my head toward the window so she wouldn't see.

"For my daughter?" I asked.

She took a minute, then nodded.

My hand gripped the edge of my seat. I hadn't really talked about Marie to anyone outside my circle. My very small circle. It was difficult to know where to start. I took a deep breath and looked out the windshield.

"Yeah. It's just Dani and me now. I needed a slower pace, something to get my mind off things. I couldn't really deal with the fast pace of life anymore. Especially not with a young kid. So I found this opening out here."

Riley was silent for a long time. "I see," she finally said.

"I do like it here. It's quiet. Relaxing. I think it's a great place for Dani to grow up. And I get to spend a lot of time with her."

"I'm so sorry for your loss. It must be so hard doing all of this on your own."

"Well, I have a nanny, and she's amazing. And lately Isaac's been staying with us, and Dani loves him. So he's there too. A small circle, but it's all we need right now." *And Jamie,* I thought, but I didn't count her. She would never be part of my circle. "Dani seems happy."

"Well, that's what's important. Her happiness. And yours."

I grunted wordlessly. I hadn't thought about my own happiness in a long while. It just wasn't important anymore. My focus was Dani. If Dani was happy, I was happy. It was all that mattered.

"You should think about your own happiness, you know," she said, that smile returning. "A little anyway. Dani can't be happy if you're miserable. Trust me, children pick up on that."

I sighed. That was something I knew all too well. My mother went through six different moods in an hour. Deciphering each mood and looking for the signs was my job as a child. I could tell when she was miserable, happy, worried, and angry, and it completely colored my childhood. I didn't want Dani to have to grow up that way.

"I know. Right now, I think I'm in a pretty good place. About as good as can be expected, probably. I just want peace. That's all."

"Well, that's good."

I twisted in my seat to face her. "What about you? You grow up here and move away or something?"

She nodded. "For college. All I wanted was to get out of this tiny-ass town. I dreamed of getting out of here. Of going to LA. Seeing the big city lights. And I did. And I was happy. But now… here I am, right back where I started." Her voice trailed off.

"What made you come back?"

She inhaled sharply. "A friend died… she was killed during a mugging. Died in my arms."

I stiffened in my seat. I never would have guessed that was the answer. "I'm so sorry. So you moved back because your friend died? Were you an officer already?"

Her chuckle had a nervous tone to it. "Nope. Never even thought about it. But when she was killed, I just…"

"Needed to do something that mattered," I finished.

"Yeah," she said weakly.

"Save people because you couldn't save her."

"It's like you were there."

I chuckled bitterly. "I was, in a way. Marie was killed in a car accident. I was driving. I… couldn't save her. And I live with that every day."

"Like a wound that refuses to heal. Better yet, it heals, little by little, and then something presses on it. A smell, a memory, a special date, and then it bursts open."

"Yeah, something like that. Exactly like that, actually."

Her hands gripped the steering wheel. "I miss her every day. If I just hadn't wanted to go out that night, she would still be here."

"You don't know that," I said. "Something else could have happened. You are not the reason she got mugged. Don't blame yourself."

She pulled into my driveway. "You blame yourself for your wife?"

I opened the car door. "Every day. It's easier said than done, but it's still true."

She smiled sadly. "I'll work on it if you do."

"I've been working on it. But yeah, we can work on it together."

A long moment passed between us. I stood there, my bag in my hand, in front of the open door, while she sat there with her hands still on the wheel.

"Good night, Doctor," she finally said.

A smile tugged at my lips. "Good night, Detective. Good luck on your case. You going home?"

"Not yet. We have a few more leads. It's already taken too long to get these young women justice. I don't want them to have to wait any longer. Might be an all-nighter."

"You think of your friend?"

"Kind of. She didn't have the best childhood. Mother ran off, father was abusive. But she made something of herself because someone gave her a chance. These girls deserved a chance, too."

"Well, you can't give them that. But you can get them justice, and I wish you luck with that. I know you can do it."

"Lot of faith in me, Doctor."

"I wouldn't say it if it wasn't true."

Riley cleared her throat. "Thank you, again, for your help. Seriously."

"Yeah, of course. Anytime."

"Well. I guess I'll be seeing you."

"Later."

She backed out of my driveway and turned out onto the street. I stayed out there watching her for a long time, until I could no longer see the flash of her taillights, until I could no longer hear the roar of her engine.

CHAPTER THIRTY

Riley Quinn

I BLINKED AWAY THE TEARS AND THE EMOTIONS OF MY CONVERSAtion with Logan. I couldn't afford to dwell on my personal problems, or his, when I had a job to do.

I would have plenty of time to cry later.

"There you are," said Z as I walked into the station. "We've got a team already out to the scene digging up the skeletal remains. It's pretty close to where we found Amara's body. And get this—Keith said the body has been there for a long time. Maybe a year."

"Seriously?" I was both surprised and not surprised at the same time. I had a feeling there were even more bodies in that area. "So are they going to dig up that area, now?"

"Yeah, they're getting started now."

"Who found the body?"

THE GIRLS IN PINE BROOKE

"A dog got friendly with the dirt. Started digging and sniffing at the grass and came up with a bone. They said that the thunderstorm might have washed a lot of the dirt away and that's why the dog might have smelled the bone."

"I guess it was good that storm was so bad. But now I've got something to show you. Let me use your computer." She rolled back out of the way. I plugged the USB drive into her computer and pulled up the video. "Tell me what you see here." I pressed play.

I stood back out of the way and let her watch it without a sound from me. I wanted to make sure I wasn't going crazy. I wanted to make sure that I wasn't the only one seeing what I thought I saw. Who I thought I saw.

While she watched the video I strolled over to my desk and sat down. My pulse was racing, my heart pounding in my chest.

"Oh, that's Jade!" A minute later Zelina took her mouse and paused the tape. "Wait a minute, that can't be." She moved closer to the screen until her face was only inches away. "I can't believe it."

I nodded slowly. "Tell me who you see, and I'll tell you who I see."

"Tory Craster."

"Exactly." I had been worried for a second that my mind was playing tricks on me. That's because I had just seen Boston and perhaps that was why the man looked familiar. But that wasn't it. It was Tory Craster. The helpful, lovable Tory Craster. The man that everyone loved and viewed as the kindest person in town. The man that helped my mother when her car broke down.

I leaned back in my chair and Zelina did the same, her mouth still open in shock. She stared at the screen.

"How is it going?" The captain stood next to our desk, his eyes darting from Zelina to me and back again. He frowned. "What's wrong?"

Zelina rewound the tape and then pressed play. He moved behind her and watched. "Well there's your victim." A minute later he paused the video. "I don't believe it. Where did you get this?"

"An anonymous witness. He doesn't want anyone to know there are cameras outside his home."

They both looked at me like they already knew who I was talking about. "I told him I would keep him out of it."

"You might be able to do that now, but if it goes to trial it will come out," he said. "I'm not saying he did it. There has to be some kind of explanation. There has to be a legitimate reason." He stared at the video. "There has to be." I saw it in his eyes. He didn't want to believe Tory had something to do with this. I understood that. I didn't either. Everyone in town would have found it difficult to believe. He was known throughout the town as a good guy. The kind of guy you could call on if you needed help. He was a nice guy and seemed so sincere.

"I don't know how," Zelina turned off the screen. "He saw her that night. It's been all over the news that she was dead, so why didn't he come forward… if he wasn't involved?"

She had a good point. "And he drove her home the night she went missing. She was with Tiffany at Boston's and wanted to go home so he drove her home. He was the last one to see her alive, if she never made it home that night."

Captain Williams sighed, as his hand slid through his hair. "I understand all that. But tread lightly. Tory Craster is a hero to the people in this town. So many people depend on him. So many people aren't going to believe this even if you show them all the evidence in the world. I'm not saying don't pursue it… I'm just saying make sure you have all your ducks in a row."

"Got it."

Zelina pulled her hair into a loose bun. "Understood."

"Okay. Keep me updated." He walked away.

"So now that we've been told to tread lightly, what do we do?"

I looked toward the cells in the back. "I want to talk to Boston about his father.

Lucky for us, we still had him in custody. Boston was taken to an interrogation room. He looked around the room.

"Listen, I didn't do anything."

"Well, right now, we have you on statutory rape."

He exhaled loudly. "I didn't rape her. She wanted me."

I shook my head. "She is still a minor. That's not how this works. But that's not what I want to talk to you about. I want to talk about your father."

"My dad? What did he do?"

"That's what I'm trying to figure out. Has your father been acting unusual in the last few months?"

He shrugged. "I don't know. I don't spend that much time with him if I can help it."

"Why don't you like your father? Is it because he doesn't like you doing drugs or messing with young girls?"

Boston laughed. The sound rippled through the room. It was a loud, hearty laugh. "Seriously? He doesn't care about me. He never has. He just cares about himself and his reputation with the town. He thinks I'm ruining his reputation. He doesn't want people in the town to look at him differently because of me."

"I get that. His reputation was important to him. But why don't you like him?"

Boston smiled. "He's a fake. He likes for people to think that he's this great guy. But he's not. He never was. He's a brute."

"Your father is abusive?" I couldn't picture Tory having anything bad to say to anyone, let alone beating someone. But then, I'd seen him on that video with Jade.

"He was to my mom. Beat her so bad she ran away and left me behind. I heard them one night arguing and she said she was going to leave and take me with her. He was so angry, said if she tried to take me, he'd have her arrested for kidnapping and the police would find drugs on her."

"Social services wouldn't have let her have you after that."

"Exactly."

"I thought your mother died." I thought that was the news around town. She passed away from some illness. That was what my mother told me.

He laughed. "That's just what he told people. He didn't want it to reflect badly on him. If the town knew that my mother ran off because she was tired of my father beating on her, what would the town think?"

"That would have definitely ruined his reputation."

"Exactly. I was never allowed to talk about her. I've tried looking for her, but I don't know where she is or where to start looking. I don't even know if she's still alive or not. He would never tell me. Can't even bring it up when it's just us. He hates hearing her name."

I leaned forward resting my elbows on the desk. "Do you know where your father is now?"

He shrugged. "He might be on his way home... I think he might have gotten home yesterday, his wife would know."

I blinked. "Your father got remarried?"

A ghost of a smile kissed his lips. "No one knows, but yeah, he's been married for a while. A few years."

"Why is it a secret?"

"I don't know. She doesn't leave the house much... or at all. think I've only seen her a handful of times. My dad says she's shy, but I think he's keeping her captive."

Boston had no loyalty toward his father. He would have talked about him for hours, especially if he thought he was going to get him in trouble.

"Does your father have a red car?"

"No. My stepmother does though. Like a dark red, but like I said she doesn't leave the house much. My dad drives it sometimes. What do you think he did?"

"I think he might have hurt Jade."

He laughed, though there was no humor in the tone. "Yeah, I could see that. He likes women, girls. I wouldn't put it past him, I know that."

"Okay. Thank you for talking to me. What's your mother's name?"

"Lydia Craster. Her maiden name is Dennis."

"Okay. "I'll see what I can do about finding her."

He took a deep breath. "Thanks."

I walked out of the room and closed the door behind me. I felt bad for Boston in a way. His father worked hard to make him seem like the bad guy, but maybe Tory had something to do with his behavior. It wasn't all his father's fault, but he held some of the blame. And it didn't exactly get him off the hook for everything else he'd done—especially in whatever the hell he was up to with Tiffany Cole.

Zelina stood next to her desk waiting. "He tell you anything?"

"Did you know Tory had remarried?"

Her jaw twitched. "No, really? Where is she?"

"She lives at his house. Apparently, she doesn't come out much or at all. He's not sure if it's her choice or if it's because she isn't allowed to leave the house."

"Really?" She sat on the edge of her desk. "I can't believe that."

"Boston told me a lot about his father. Tory said he is more concerned about what people think of him than he is about being a father. He beat his first wife so much she left him. He forced her to leave Boston behind."

Her mouth fell open. "It's so hard to believe. I can't picture him raising his voice let alone hurting anyone."

"Like they say, you never really know anybody anymore. I'm thinking that's why he always bails Boston out. He knows things about his father that we don't. Doesn't want it getting out, and I think Boston would tell everything if he was given the chance. He seems to hate him because of what he's done to his mother. He also said his father likes women… and girls."

She exhaled a shaky breath. "Does he know where he is?"

I shook my head. "But the wife might know."

She jumped to her feet. "I want to see what she looks like."

"Yeah, me too. And she has a red car," I said as I followed her out of the station.

"And if she doesn't really go anywhere, then he's the one driving it."

"What I don't understand is why did Tory talk about the red car when I called him. Why did he mention it? That red car is our link between the crime scenes, so if it's him, why bring it up?"

Zelina stuck the key into the ignition. "Maybe he was trying to throw us off the scent. He doesn't know that there were witnesses at the other kidnappings. Maybe he mentioned the car because he didn't think anyone could link it to him or to the kidnappings."

"That's what he gets for thinking."

We drove to Tory's house. The red car wasn't in the driveway. Either he wasn't home, or she wasn't home. I got out of the car. Movement in the window caught my eye. The front curtain moved slightly. Someone was home. I looked at Zelina, who stared at the window. I placed my hand on my holster as I walked toward the door. The door opened before I could knock. A woman with long black hair stood in the doorway in her robe. She pulled it closed.

"Can I help you?"

I held up my badge. "We are looking for Tory Craster. Is he home?"

She shook her head. "No, he left a while ago. Should I call him?"

"No, you don't have to do that. Just tell us where he is, and we'll go see him."

"Come in." She opened the door wider and stepped away.

I eased into the home carefully. It was clean and homey looking. Lived in and taken care of. We waited for her in the foyer. I glanced around and noticed something strange. There were no family pictures. I peered into the living room and saw a sofa, two cream-colored chairs, a coffee table and a bookcase. There was no television. No pictures. No family photos.

There was nothing personal about the house. It felt less like a home and more like it was being staged to be sold. The woman emerged from the kitchen with a slip of paper.

"And what is your name?" I asked as I took the paper from her and handed it to Zelina.

"Lydia Craster."

"Are you guys moving?" I pointed to the vacant walls.

"Oh, no. Tory doesn't like stuff on the walls. He likes everything neat and tidy. Pictures on the walls make a room look cluttered."

"I see. Well thank you for your time. I'll call Tory and let him know we are on our way."

She nodded slowly. "Okay. I *won't* call him and let him know you're coming."

"Thanks," I said slowly. There was something about the way she said it that gave me pause. Like she knew why we were there and was trying to help us. We walked out and she softly closed the door behind us.

"There's something about her," said Zelina when we got back in the car. "She seems broken."

"Yeah, I noticed that too. Where are we going?"

She looked at the slip of paper before handing it to me. "Apparently, he has a cabin. I wonder if that's where he took the girls. Where he kept them."

"Probably. It's out of the way, not a lot of people around. No one to hear them scream. Makes sense."

The ride to the cabin was forty-five minutes. The cabin stood in the middle of a wooded area. So many tall trees surrounded the place almost hiding the cabin from prying eyes.

The sun was setting by the time we got there. A red car sat in the driveway. I took a picture of it and sent it to the captain. I walked to the door with Zelina following close behind. I knocked softly. The sound of heavy footsteps nearing the door made my heart race. The door opened a moment later.

"Hello, Tory."

A smile eased across his lips. "Hey! What are you doing here? Looking for me?"

I sighed. "Yeah, I'm sorry about this, but we need to talk to you about your son."

He drew in a long, slow breath. "Come on in."

CHAPTER THIRTY-ONE

Riley Quinn

"Thanks. I hate to do this to you, but we needed to get some information from you, and we need to inform you about what happened."

He shook his head. "I knew he had to have done something. I've been calling him, and he didn't answer. He was too quiet so I should have known." He gestured to the brown leather sofa. "Please have a seat. I'm sorry he's so much trouble. I don't know where I went wrong."

"My mother says raising kids is like flipping a coin. Sometimes they turn out great and sometimes they don't."

"She's right. I felt like I did everything right with him. Gave him attention when he needed it. Gave him love and affection, but was still firm with him. I guess that wasn't enough." He leaned back in his chair. "So what has he done now?"

I glanced at Zelina. "He's been arrested on statutory rape charges."

Tory's jaw twitched. For a moment, his kind smile faltered. He quickly pulled it back and smiled. "Really? I wasn't expecting that. I guess I thought it would be drugs again."

"Yeah, me too. But that wasn't what it was. We found him with Tiffany Cole, and they were both half naked."

He sighed. "He told me they were just friends. I shouldn't have believed it but I did. I didn't think she would be interested in someone like him, but I guess I was wrong. She seemed like a smart girl."

"Smart girls love bad boys," said Zelina.

A smile tugged at his lips. "Fair point. Is he still in jail?"

"He is. Her parents might want to press charges against him."

"I understand that." He ran a hand through his dark hair. "He has to finally start paying the consequences for his actions. I can't bail him out every time he does something—that's why he is the way he is. If they want to press charges, then he has to deal with it. Might do him some good spending a while in jail."

"It might be what's best for him and Tiffany. Give them a break from each other," I agreed.

"Right. Thank you for letting me know."

There was a soft knocking sound down the hallway. I glanced in that direction. So did he.

"That's just the dog. I put him in the back room when I heard someone drive up. He doesn't like people too much."

I pasted on a smile. "I get that. My dog Luna is the opposite. She likes people a little too much. Anyone comes over, I have to put her in the room or outside before she jumps on them."

He chuckled. "He might bite you before he jumps on you."

I laughed. "Yeah, keep him in the room for a little longer, if you don't mind."

He smiled. "Have you figured out who took Jade, yet?" He looked at Zelina. "I'm sorry, you probably can't say anything yet. Ongoing investigation and all that."

There was another muffled noise from the back. It didn't sound like a dog. There was no barking.

"You're right about that. We can't say too much. We might have a lead, but we still aren't sure how it will pan out."

He nodded. "You know what I was thinking... the killer might have been looking for Tiffany. You know people still blame her and her family for what her brother did. I never understood why anyone thought the family was in on it, but some people need to put the blame and their anger on someone."

"I've heard that. But I've also heard people say that Larry and his cousin didn't do it... and the families that were killed had some kind of beef with each other."

He opened his mouth for a moment and then stopped. "Hmm... I'm not sure about that. I know they had some issues with each other about one of them running for governor."

"Governor?" asked Zelina.

"Yeah, I think one of them wanted to run. Well you know that the Moores had a history of holding office, not just in this town but the state. Governor, decades ago. Mayor years ago. I think Winston Moore wanted to follow in his grandfather's footsteps and run for either Mayor or Governor, I can't remember which one, but so did Elias Hayes. He wanted to run for office and thought he was the better man for the job. I heard it caused a lot of arguments between them. They used to be friends."

"That's quite interesting. I had heard they were friends, but had a falling out. No one said why."

There was another muffled sound that sounded like something was hitting the wall. I looked at him, and his eyes were fixed on me.

"Why don't you take him outside? I'm sure he would like to run around and get some fresh air," Zelina said, as she stared down the hallway.

"He'll be okay." He waved his hand dismissively.

She jumped to her feet. "I'll get him and take him out. I'll watch him too, while you two talk." She was halfway down the hallway when Tory jumped to his feet.

"No! He's fine. He's probably just hungry. I'll let him out once you all leave so he can be comfortable." Something on his left side glinted in the light. I drew my weapon.

"Drop it!" I pointed my gun at him as he turned his head toward me. The knife in his hand came into view. There was another muffled noise, and Zelina looked down the hall.

"Can't help but notice that your dog is making all that noise without barking," I said.

He shrugged. "He's not a barker. He's pretty quiet."

"Right. Or maybe it's not a dog at all. Maybe it's a teenage girl you have locked in there like Jade and Amara and Cynthia."

A smile slid across his wet lips. "I don't know anything about Cynthia." The look on his face sent a shiver down my spine. He looked like a creep; the kind face and warm smile vanished. A broken mask disintegrating at our feet.

Before I could say a retort, he lunged at Zelina, knife raised high in the air. My heart stuttered in my chest. I squeezed the trigger. Three loud pops echoed through the room, followed by a scream.

And then nothing.

Silence settled over us as blood snaked down the carpet.

CHAPTER THIRTY-TWO

Riley Quinn

"Like I said, it was a good shoot. He lunged at my partner with a Ka-bar. What was I supposed to do?"

Two detectives sat across from me, frowning. Their eyebrows pulled together as they stared at me. Asking me the same questions over and over. In the days since the shooting, I had gotten so many dirty looks from everyone, not just officers. No one could believe what Tory had done. No one wanted to believe it. Hell, I didn't want to believe it either. It was hard to wrap my brain around, but once I saw him in his cabin, the muffled sounds from the back room, and that knife in his hand, I knew. I knew what he was and what he had done.

"Can I go now? You've asked the same questions a million times, and my answers have not changed. What more do you want from me?"

The taller and older IAB agent leaned forward. "Just having a hard time picturing the scene. We've interviewed several people who knew the victim, and they have nothing but great things to say about him."

"And when you say you interviewed people that knew him, do you mean his son, his wife, and the young girl he held captive in his cabin?"

The agent bristled at my comment. "We haven't gotten to them just yet."

"I see. So you're only interrogating me. Did you ask him what happened?"

"He's still not fit to talk. That's what the doctors say. I don't know if or when he will regain consciousness."

"What a shame. Can I go?" I glanced toward the door. I was so ready to be out of that room. To be beyond these walls and away from these two assholes.

"Yeah, you can go. We know where to find you when we have more questions for you."

"Answers won't change." I jumped to my feet and hurried toward the door. I rushed outside, breezing past my desk, past Zelina, and out the front door. The hot air seared my lungs. My skin missed the air conditioning inside the station, but my mind needed space to breathe. I had been in and out of the interrogation room for days since the shooting. The agents just couldn't wrap their heads around the fact that I shot a guilty man. To them, Tory had to be innocent. We accused an innocent, well-loved man of a horrible crime and then shot him and got a girl to act like he held her captive.

Tory had everyone snowed. But not us. Not me. Not anymore. When I shot him, he fell to the floor. Zelina handcuffed him while I looked for where that noise came from. In the last bedroom, there was a young woman tied to the bed.

"Hello. I'm Detective Riley Quinn, and I'm here to help you." She was blindfolded with a scarf tied tight around her eyes. "I'm just here to help. I'm going to remove the blindfold, okay? Do you understand me?"

She nodded slowly. Her face was wet as I lifted the blindfold off her head. I removed the hand towel stuffed in her mouth.

"He—"

"Shhh. I know. I'm going to untie you now."

Zelina stormed into the room and immediately started untying her legs. I started with her wrist. The cord was tied tight around her wrist, already starting to dig into her skin. I pulled it off gingerly. When we had freed her, she sat up. A sob rippled through her. Zelina wrapped her arms around her while I called for backup.

After that, everything happened so fast. The crime scene unit swept in, the medics got the victims out, and the instant we got the scene covered and cleared, I was whisked off into an IAB interrogation room. Zelina was at least allowed to stay with the girl that we had rescued. I hadn't really seen her after that. The IAB agents wanted to keep us separated so that we couldn't get our stories together.

"You okay?" Zelina's voice made me jump.

I spun around. "Hey. Yeah, I'm okay. Just had to get out of there."

"Are they done questioning you?"

I shrugged. "I don't think they would tell me if they were. They just keep asking the same questions over and over. My answers don't change, and yet they keep asking."

"Yeah, they asked me a shit ton of questions too. I think they are just having a hard time believing he did it. But the evidence is all there."

"We need to search that house and the cabin and that whole area where Amara's body was found."

Zelina and I agreed that we just needed to get everyone else on board. A minute later, the captain walked out.

"You've been cleared of all wrongdoing. I still don't think they believe Tory did anything wrong, but without any concrete evidence proving differently, they are going to take your word for it."

"We need to search that cabin."

Zelina nodded in agreement.

"Have at it," he said. "But I want you to know some people in town have voiced their unhappiness that you shot him. Tread carefully." He walked back inside without another word.

"I'm hungry," I said.

"Yeah, let's go to the diner, and I can tell you everything that's happened since we last were allowed to talk to each other."

I walked into the cool diner; silence echoed through the room. I walked to an empty booth and slid in. Zelina followed suit. Hushed voices trailed behind us. I looked at Zelina, who shrugged. I guess he was right; people in the town were upset. It took twenty minutes for the waitress to come to our table and take our order.

"Probably shouldn't eat what we ordered," I said when she walked away.

"Think she spit in it?" A chuckle bubbled up her throat. But she agreed with me because she didn't touch her sandwich when it was on the table. I only drank my soda because I watched her pour it.

"Now, what happened while I was being interrogated?" I leaned forward, resting my elbow on the table. "I am all ears."

"Well, I spoke to the victim before in the hospital. She was scared and kept asking for her mom while she was being examined. She said that she was walking home when she saw Tory. She knew him. He told her that he would give her a ride because it was supposed to rain. She agreed. She trusted him. He knew her parents and had been to her house a couple of times."

"I think that's how he sucks them in. They know him, or they've heard about him. They trust him. He uses that to his advantage."

"Exactly. There were signs of rape, and they did a rape kit. After that, I haven't been able to speak to her. We need to do a search of his cabin, I'm sure he was hiding something, like the teeth."

I nodded. The victims we found had three missing teeth. We assumed he had kept them as souvenirs. We finished our drinks, paid for the food we didn't eat and left. The silence evaporated as soon as I closed the door behind us. I could hear the voices through the door. I shook my head. I would not be made to feel bad for saving a victim from a serial rapist and killer. They would see it eventually.

We called for crime scene techs on our way to the cabin. They arrived minutes after we did. The cabin was still cordoned off as an active crime scene. There was a musty smell inside so heavy it felt like I was suffocating. The place had been dusted for prints; there was powder on almost every surface.

"Okay. I don't know what we are looking for, but let's start looking." Searching the house was like trying to find a needle in a haystack when you didn't know what a needle looked like. I searched the main bedroom. There was a king-sized bed, a dresser, and a large leather chair in the corner next to the window. There was something that I noticed and found strange. His wife said he didn't like putting pictures on the walls because it made a space look cluttered. But in his cabin, there were pictures on the walls.

But they weren't of his son or his new wife—rather they were of his first wife. Pictures of Boston's mother were all over the walls. *Why?*

"Hey Z, come look at this!"

Zelina came rushing into the room and I nodded to the walls.

"There are pictures in the other room too," Zelina remarked. "All of her. I wonder why."

"Boston said his father hated his mother. If he hated her so much because she left him, why would he keep her pictures?" I moved closer to the pictures on the wall while Zelina left the room to retrieve the pictures she saw in the other room. I took one of them down. Gold frame with hearts carved into the corners. Mrs. Craster was lying down on a bed staring up at the...

"Wait a minute." I lifted the frame closer to my face to get a better look. "Is she?" I took another picture off the wall and stared at it. It was her lying on her back but at a different angle.

"These are the ones that I found."

I held up the pictures. "She's dead."

Zelina rocked back on her feet. She turned her pictures over and stared at them for a second. She turned them over and held them up. "Yeah, I think she is dead."

My heart sank. Boston believed his mother was still alive. He was even trying to look for her, but he couldn't find her. He didn't know where to look. I glanced around the room. "We need to search the area around this cabin. I wonder if he buried her here."

"Why put these up?" Zelina stared at the pictures.

"Control, I think." I set the pictures on the dresser. "She was trying to leave him, and he wanted to make sure she would never leave him again. And when he was here, he could stare at them..." I stared at one of the pictures still on the wall. She was alive in this one. Boston had her eyes. She was smiling at the camera. "Does she look familiar to you?"

Zelina stared at the photo.

"She looks like Jade. The same eye color, hair color. Jade could be her as a teenager."

"All the victims resemble each other."

"Maybe that's it." I took the picture off the wall. "She tried to leave him, so he killed her. Now he takes teenage girls that look like her and recreates what he did to her when he killed her. I think that's what this is about. He's still angry at her, and he's taking it out on these girls. And he keeps her pictures up there so she can watch. So she can see that it is all her fault."

"That's insane."

"How am I going to tell Boston? I told him I would help him look for his mother."

"Well, we still need to find her. You're still helping him look."

I sighed. "I want this place and his house torn apart. Lift up the floorboards, search the walls and the ground. Crack the foundation if they have to. There is something here, I know it."

"Okay. And I'll send techs to the hill and see what else we can find there."

The search was slow, agonizingly slow. At first, we found nothing. Tory Craster was a master at hiding his secret life. After all, he had been doing it for years. Hiding his true self. Constantly wearing a mask in town to hide the monster he was. But then a tech found something underneath the floorboards. A metal box that required a key to open. We busted the lock.

"I figured as much," I said as I scoped out the contents. In the box were teeth. So many teeth.

"Like a demented version of the Tooth Fairy."

"The Tooth Fairy *is* a demented version of the Tooth Fairy. She creeps into your room in the middle of the night, takes your discarded teeth, and leaves you money. How is that not demented?"

"She leaves you money," said Zelina.

"That doesn't make it okay."

"Found something else," said the tech. He reached under the floorboards and pulled up another metal box. "There's another one under there. Let me see if I can get it."

We popped the lock on the box while he tried to get the other one. Inside the black metal box were pictures. I thought it was more pictures of Mrs. Craster. All the young women looked alike. I flip through the pictures and find Jade and then Amara. He took pictures of the young girls in various positions. All of them naked.

My stomach soured. I stuffed the pictures back in the box and shut the lid. No one should have to look at those pictures. I never wanted to see them again. He pulled up another box. I knew what was in it before we opened it. More pictures. Someone would have to go through them and group them together, but it wouldn't be me.

"Okay, so this is the evidence we needed to make the charges stick. No one can deny these photos. No one." After a thorough search of the house inside, dogs, officers, and more techs arrived at the house to search the ground. Zelina and I could have gone home or gone back to the station and waited for the news, but we refused to leave. We waited by our car and watched them work. Dogs sniffed the area, starting close to the house and then inching out. An hour ticked by, and then another.

"We are going to need more dogs," said one of the officers as he walked over. He was young with short blonde hair and light brown eyes with a deep dimple in his right cheek. "We brought three dogs, and they've all sat down in different spots. There are definitely bodies here."

I exhaled slowly. I knew it. I knew he had killed them here. I knew there would be more bodies. Zelina's phone rang and she stepped away. I looked at her… wondering who was calling at that hour.

"Okay. Get what you need and start digging."

He nodded and walked away just as Zelina walked back over. "They found two more bodies at the hill."

"They've found three here." On the other side of the cabin the three dogs sat with their trainers waiting. They were spread out. I leaned against the car, wondering how many bodies they would find in both locations. With that thought an even darker one snuck in.

How many other spots in town were his own personal graveyard?

CHAPTER THIRTY-THREE

Riley Quinn

Over a dozen bodies. So far. Four around his cabin and eight on the hill. He had buried them deep, but with the thunderstorm washing away so much of the dirt it made it easier to find them. Tory regained consciousness eventually, and was arrested. He maintained his innocence.

"I don't know why these women have a vendetta against me but I'm telling you, I didn't do anything. they are framing me," he said to his lawyer as well as our captain. His lips were pressed into a thin line but there was a smile in his eyes. I walked out of the room, so I didn't have to look at him. He was smug and thought he could rely on his reputation to beat the charges.

Some people in town, those he helped, still believed him. Even with all the evidence against him, they believed he was innocent. That the department had framed him.

My mother didn't believe that though. "If you say he did it, I believe you. End of story." It was great to hear.

"Thanks Mom."

She wasn't the only one who believed us. His son did, and so did his future ex-wife. Five bodies were found around the cabin. A fifth body found at the cabin site was an older white female according to the anthropologist.

"We think we have found your mom, but we are going to need DNA to match to the remains." I looked at Boston, evaluating his reaction.

He leaned back and stared up at the ceiling. "You believe she's dead?"

I took a deep breath while I searched for the right words to use. I didn't want to give him too many details. He didn't need to hear everything. "We found some evidence that points us in that direction. But we need DNA to be sure."

"And he's not going to admit to nothing. That's not his style." His fingers tapped against the table. "I don't have anything of hers to match it to. I wasn't allowed to keep any of her stuff. What she... he threw it all away in front of me."

"Your DNA," I said slowly. "We can match it to your DNA, because you are half hers."

Tears streamed down his cheeks. he looked up again, blinking rapidly. "Sure." His voice wavered slightly. "Whatever you need, you can have."

"Okay. Thank you." I took out the DNA kit and removed the swab from the tube. "Just need to swab the inside of your cheek." He opened his mouth, and I did it the way the coroner showed me, then I slipped the swab back into the container. "Okay. When I know something, I will let you know."

"Thank you for trying to find her for me."

"I'm sorry I don't have better news for you."

His shoulders rose slightly. "I feel like I always knew, just didn't want to admit it to myself. I knew what kind of guy he was. I shouldn't be surprised. I just hope you found her. One of them has to be her."

"I'll let you know." I walked out of the room before I started crying. Before the test results even came back, I knew that we had found her, and when Keith ran the results, it was confirmed. Boston's mom had been one of the skeletal remains closest to the house. Right next to the front porch step. I pictured him sitting on the porch drinking coffee looking down at the ground, knowing she was there.

It made me sick to my stomach. He just had to keep control over her. In the weeks after finding the bodies, we were able to match most of the bodies to a name. Three were left unclaimed. And of those three, none of them were Cynthia. He had said he didn't know her, maybe he was telling the truth. The courts would have to sort it out.

I walked into the coffee shop and let the cool air caress my body. It was getting hotter outside and walking from the car to the building was like trekking through the desert. The smell of coffee beans was intoxicating. I ordered a cup and decided to drink it in a booth instead of going outside.

"Hey, long time no see."

I looked up. Logan stood next to the booth with a cup in his hand. "Yeah, been pretty busy."

"I heard." He slid into the booth and the girl behind him came into view. They faintly resembled each other. She slid in after him. "This is my daughter Dani. Dani, this is Detective Riley Quinn."

I grinned. "The famous Dani, nice to finally meet you."

She turned her face away nervously, but smiled. "I'm not famous."

"Your father talks of no one else."

She laughed. "You're a detective?"

I nodded and slid my badge across the table. She took it eagerly in her hands. "Can I hold your gun?"

I laughed. Logan shook his head. "No," we said in unison.

Her shoulders dropped. "It was worth the ask."

"I admire your confidence," I said with a smile. "What are you two up to today?"

"Daddy-daughter day. We hang out."

"Sounds like fun."

"Yeah, it's been a fun day. Papa, can I go get a pastry?"

Logan slid some money into her hand, and she took off back toward the register. "How is everything going?"

I shrugged. "Brought down the town hero, people are still pissed about it." I rolled my eyes.

"Can't ignore all of that evidence. You just can't. No one can frame you by burying a bunch of people on your property and under your house without you knowing. I mean... I don't get it."

"Me either. But it is what it is."

"Yeah."

"Nice to see you getting out more."

He rolled his eyes. "I'm a work in progress."

"Well, since you are doing things outside of your house and your job, you should come to town movie night in a couple of weeks. There's a projector, and we have a picnic and watch movies."

"That sounds cool!" Dani's voice caught him off guard. He nearly jumped out of his skin when he saw her. "Can we go? And we can bring Uncle Isaac and Miss Bonnie."

"It's a lot of fun. You guys can even sit with my family. My mother would love it."

Logan chewed on his bottom lip. "I'll think about it."

"Think hard." I slid out of the booth. "I have some loose ends that I need to tie up. I'll see you later."

EPILOGUE

Riley Quinn

The case was finished, the paperwork was done, and Tory Craster was under lock and key awaiting trial. But even after his arrest and the search of his property, I had a feeling we still didn't fully understand just how depraved he was.

"There has to be more victims. I refuse to believe that there were no more bodies." Zelina stretched on her lounge chair. Her bare feet skimmed the sand.

I looked around. On most Saturdays, the ones where the weather was nice and not too hot, most of the town was found at the beach. Our town was weird and special, with the lake on one end and the sea on the other. Houses near the beach were expensive and far out of my price range. Living by the lake was a great consolation prize, as far as I was concerned.

"I know. I don't care what he says; he's killed more young women."

THE GIRLS IN PINE BROOKE

Zelina bolted upright. "What if the bodies aren't here? He was a truck driver. There could be some anywhere now."

I sank into my chair. She had a point. If it were true, that would make finding more victims much more challenging. Even if we followed his routes, I doubted he buried them on the side of the road.

"Alright! You two promised no shop talk today. Enjoy the sun and hush!" My mother, in her bright orange floppy hat and matching one-piece, stood at the edge of the water, glaring at us. We didn't say no shop talk; she did. Zelina chuckled next to me. I could have used a break, but it was so difficult to turn my brain off. This case was solved, and yet it wasn't because so many bodies still hadn't been found, and he wasn't talking. Tory was just trying to be annoying. Milk his thirty seconds of fame.

But I really should have been trying to disconnect. I was lying out on the beach on a gorgeous summer day with a fruity drink in hand, my best friend by my side, and the mouthwatering smell of hot dogs on the grill just a few feet to my right, where my brother was hard at work. In fact, it was a perfect day. The only thing that could have made it better was if I ran into…

"Surprised you're not working."

"Logan?"

My eyes burst open as I bolted upright. "Hey." I fought the urge to shield my two-piece bikini from his glinting eyes. *He's seen naked women before; he has a daughter already.* "What are you doing here?"

"Dani got good grades in school. We're celebrating." He pointed to a little girl with her teal swimsuit and matching hat who was stomping happily through the shallows. She giggled as the water lapped at her feet.

I smiled. "She looks happy."

"Yeah. She loves the beach. What are you up to? Surprised they don't have you doing paperwork or whatever." Logan stretched out his towel next to my chair and sat down.

I shrugged. "Officially, the case is closed, so there's not much else to do."

Logan shook his head. "At least you get a break."

"I'd be happier to have my questions answered." I glanced out at the water. Dani walked over to my mother, who had just picked up a large shell. They gushed over the shell.

"I get that. But you did your job. You did what you set out to do, and that has to count for something. You got those girls justice."

"Yeah. Maybe. I just wish I could stop thinking about it."

"That bad?"

231

I leaned back in my chair. His knee brushed against my fingers. Heat rose to my cheeks.

I turned my head away from him, toward Zelina, who grinned. "Oh, don't get her started. She's like a dog with a bone. She works a case, she has to know everything. All the whys."

"You can never really know all the whys in medicine," he said. "Like, yeah, you can always point to specific viruses, or specific reasons for certain symptoms. But sometimes the why is something completely unexpected. Sometimes diseases just clear up on their own. The human body just kind of does whatever it wants."

"Well, that's comforting," I said. "Anyway, how is everything?"

He shrugged. "Just a bunch of stuff I'm trying not to think about. Figured I could use some time out of the house."

I grinned. "Getting out of the house is always good."

"Papa, Mrs. Quinn gave me a shell." Dani ran over and held the shell in his face.

He laughed. "I see. It's really pretty."

"I'm going to look for some more." She rushed back over to my mother and started following her, laughing and giggling as they picked up shells of all sorts of shapes and colors. Collecting shells was something my mother did every time she came to the beach. Most of the time with my father, but he wasn't feeling well.

Logan looked around us. "Where's your dad?"

"He's not feeling well. Blood pressure was a little high this morning."

He frowned. "Tell him to come see me Monday morning. We'll see what's causing that."

"Tell my mom. She'll make sure he gets there."

Logan laughed. "That works, too."

He smiled at me, and for the first time since I had met him, he looked relaxed. His shoulders were relaxed, a bright grin on his face and piercing green eyes. He didn't look mean or uptight. His smile made me smile instantly.

"You should stay over here. We've got snacks. Hot dogs. I think there's a few beers in the cooler over there."

"Always open to a free meal."

I laughed. "Who said anything about free? A conversation comes with that food, and you will get the brunt of it."

He grinned. "I see."

"We appreciate your sacrifice," I said just as my mother started to walk over. "Smile and nod, Logan. Just smile and nod."

It really was a perfect day.

AUTHOR'S NOTE

My dear reader,

Thank you for diving into *The Girls in Pine Brooke!* I've been planning this story for what feels like forever, and finally sharing it with you is like letting you in on a secret I've been bursting to tell. It's been a while since I introduced a whole new cast of characters, and diving back into creating a new town felt like coming home again—only with a few more murders! Spending time with Riley Quinn, our small-town detective with a big heart and a fierce determination—was an absolute joy. She's a lovable mix of strength, fearlessness, and quirky humor, and I had a blast exploring Pine Brooke through her eyes. I hope you were captivated seeing her in action! There are still so many mysteries to unravel, secrets to uncover, and stories to tell, all with Riley leading the charge. And the *best* part? The next chapter of her story is just around the corner.

Murder in the Pines is almost ready and will be in your hands soon. I can't wait for you to join Riley on another tangled mystery that's sure to keep you guessing! This time, Riley finds herself wrapped up in a missing person case when a young woman named Delilah Preston disappears after a baby shower. The plot thickens when a body matching Delilah's description is found—but it's not her. Pine Brooke is about to wake up to a shock, with a truth more twisted than anyone could have imagined. And with secrets from Riley's own past starting to resurface, things are about to get even more complicated…

Your support truly means the world to me. As an indie author, getting to live my dream of writing these stories is possible because of wonderful readers like you cheering me on. If you enjoyed this installment, I would be so grateful if you could share your thoughts in a review or tell your friends who love a good mystery. Word of mouth and your feedback are my lifelines, helping me continue writing Riley's story and sharing it with more readers. Even just a few lines about what you enjoyed can make a huge difference!

With endless gratitude and excitement for all the mysteries still to come, I'm so glad to have you along for the ride. See you in the next book!

Yours,
A.J. Rivers

P.S. If for some reason you didn't like this book or found typos or other errors, please let me know personally. I do my best to read and respond to every email at mailto:aj@riversthrillers.com

P.P.S. If you would like to stay up-to-date with me and my latest releases I invite you to visit my Linktree page at *www.linktr.ee/a.j.rivers* to subscribe to my newsletter and receive a free copy of my book, Edge of the Woods. You can also follow me on my social media accounts for behind-the-scenes glimpses and sneak peeks of my upcoming projects, or even sign up for text notifications. I can't wait to connect with you!

ALSO BY
A.J. RIVERS

Emma Griffin FBI Mysteries
Season One
Book One—The Girl in Cabin 13*
Book Two—The Girl Who Vanished*
Book Three—The Girl in the Manor*
Book Four—The Girl Next Door*
Book Five—The Girl and the Deadly Express*
Book Six—The Girl and the Hunt*
Book Seven—The Girl and the Deadly End*

Season Two
Book Eight—The Girl in Dangerous Waters*
Book Nine—The Girl and Secret Society*
Book Ten—The Girl and the Field of Bones*
Book Eleven—The Girl and the Black Christmas*
Book Twelve—The Girl and the Cursed Lake*
Book Thirteen—The Girl and The Unlucky 13*
Book Fourteen—The Girl and the Dragon's Island*

Season Three
Book Fifteen—The Girl in the Woods*
Book Sixteen—The Girl and the Midnight Murder*
Book Seventeen—The Girl and the Silent Night*
Book Eighteen—The Girl and the Last Sleepover*
Book Nineteen—The Girl and the 7 Deadly Sins*
Book Twenty—The Girl in Apartment 9*
Book Twenty-One—The Girl and the Twisted End*

Emma Griffin FBI Mysteries Retro - Limited Series
(Read as standalone or before Emma Griffin book 22)

*Book One— The Girl in the Mist**
*Book Two— The Girl on Hallow's Eve**
*Book Three— The Girl and the Christmas Past**
*Book Four— The Girl and the Winter Bones**
*Book Five— The Girl on the Retreat**

Season Four

*Book Twenty-Two — The Girl and the Deadly Secrets**
*Book Twenty-Three — The Girl on the Road**
*Book Twenty-Four — The Girl and the Unexpected Gifts**
*Book Twenty-Five — The Girl and the Secret Passage**
*Book Twenty-Six — The Girl and the Bride**
*Book Twenty-Seven — The Girl in Her Cabin**
*Book Twenty-Eight — The Girl Who Remembers**

Season Five

*Book Twenty-Nine — The Girl in the Dark**
Book Thirty — The Girl and the Lies

Ava James FBI Mysteries

*Book One—The Woman at the Masked Gala**
*Book Two—Ava James and the Forgotten Bones**
*Book Three —The Couple Next Door**
*Book Four — The Cabin on Willow Lake**
*Book Five — The Lake House**
*Book Six — The Ghost of Christmas**
*Book Seven — The Rescue**
*Book Eight — Murder in the Moonlight**
*Book Nine — Behind the Mask**
*Book Ten — The Invitation**
*Book Eleven — The Girl in Hawaii**
*Book Twelve — The Woman in the Window**
*Book Thirteen — The Good Doctor**
Book Fourteen — The Housewife Killer
Book Fifteen — The Librarian

Dean Steele FBI Mysteries
Book One—The Woman in the Woods*
Book Two — The Last Survivors
Book Three — No Escape
Book Four — The Garden of Secrets
Book Five — The Killer Among Us
Book Six — The Convict
Book Seven — The Last Promise
Book Eight — Death by Midnight
Book Nine — The Woman in the Attic
Book Ten — Playing with Fire

A Detective Riley Quinn Pine Brooke Mystery
Book One —The Girls in Pine Brooke
Book Two — Murder in the Pines

ALSO BY
A.J. RIVERS & THOMAS YORK

Bella Walker FBI Mystery Series
Book One—The Girl in Paradise*
Book Two—Murder on the Sea*
Book Three—The Last Aloha*

Other Standalone Novels
Gone Woman
* Also available in audio

Made in the USA
Monee, IL
23 December 2024